THE BIRD BOYS

A DELPHA WADE AND TOM PHELAN MYSTERY

Praise for
The Do-Right

The first
Delpha Wade and Tom Phelan Mystery

WINNER
The Dashiell Hammett Prize, 2015
The Shamus Award, 2016

BEST OF LISTS
Kirkus Reviews Best Books 2015
Kirkus Reviews Best Mysteries and Thrillers 2015
Kirkus Reviews Best Debut

REVIEWS
This book is flat out excellent…I heartily recommend it.
—Sheryl Cotleur, Copperfield's Books

Delpha Wade is conscientiously following her parole
officer's rules for finding a place to live and a job: act as polite
as possible and ask for what she needs. …Sandlin blends
pathos, humor, and poetic prose in a strong debut.
—*Kirkus*, STARRED REVIEW

Sandlin's clipped prose style is pleasingly eccentric, and
can become downright Chandleresque ("The nose had a curve
a school bus'd run off of.")
—*Publishers Weekly*, STARRED REVIEW

When a critic praises a writer's original voice, what does that really mean? In the case of Texas native Lisa Sandlin, it means dog-earing page after page in her novel *The Do-Right* to reread particularly terrific passages or, even better,
share them aloud…
—*Dallas Morning News*

Sandlin makes fantastic use of familiar, archetypal characters—the neophyte sleuth, the woman with the troubled past, etcetera, etcetera—and brings new life into them by crafting narrative that, past the surface of an exciting detective story, seems to search for a sense of grace or forgiveness…This novel has it all—murder, mystery, abuse, corporate espionage. Take your pick. The prose reads like movie stills from an old detective flick. —*Killer Nashville*

THE BIRD BOYS

A DELPHA WADE AND TOM PHELAN MYSTERY

LISA SANDLIN

Cinco Puntos Press
EL PASO, TEXAS

FIRST EDITION
10 9 8 7 6 5 4 3 2 1

Library of Congress Cataloging-in-Publication Data

Names: Sandlin, Lisa, author.
Title: *The bird boys : a Delpha Wade and Tom Phelan mystery* / Lisa Sandlin.
Description: First edition. | El Paso, Texas : Cinco Puntos Press, [2019]
Identifiers: LCCN 2018049003 | ISBN 978-1-947627-13-0 (pbk. : alk. paper)
| ISBN 978-1-947627-14-7 (e-book)
Subjects: | GSAFD: Mystery fiction.
Classification: LCC PS3569.A5168 B57 2019 | DDC 813/.54—dc23
LC record available at https://lccn.loc.gov/2018049003

The cover photo is called "Nevermore," and was taken by the amazing photographer KEITH CARTER in 1985 and used with his permission. Like Lisa Sandlin, Keith is a native of Beaumont, Texas.

Book and cover design by ANNE M. GIANGIULIO
Cooking with Crisco!

Dedicated to librarians everywhere

Freedom is what you do with what's been done to you.
JEAN-PAUL SARTRE

I

SOON AS THE office was cleared for business, Phelan trashed the yellow crime tape and hired industrial cleaning guys to blast the blood from the wood floor, patch up the stain. He'd paid them extra to work on the weekend. Still smelled funky though. Bleachy—and underneath, a whiff of something live, gone over. He pushed up the windows and let Beaumont's August heat K.O. his stuttering AC unit.

The radio hijacked his attention: the Senate had, for once, done a day's work, slapping Kissinger and Nixon away from Cambodia. Mitts off the bomb money, boys. The news segued into War's song *Why Can't We Be Friends*? Was KJET's DJ feeling cynical? Wistful? Both?

Phelan, dressed in ragged jeans and an undershirt, squatted down and pried up the paint can's lid with a screwdriver. He popped it open to a round of Apollo White, a creamy ivory. Poured some into a tray and let the fuzzy roller drink it up.

One swipe across his slug-green office wall and he stepped back, mouth drifting open. Look at that. Like a wash of spotlight.

The office must have been shabby all along. Dingy. Had Miss Wade noticed that? Boy, he hadn't. To Phelan, this two-room office suite, home of his new business, had appeared vacated by angels.

He dipped into the paint tray again, more white swathes,

wasn't sure he liked it. Kind of glaring. But the least he could do was make the place look different from the office where Deeterman had tried to kill her.

The phone rang. He rubbed his right hand with a rag, tossed back the drop cloth from the metal desk—and *Aw, man* still hand-printed its black receiver white when he clutched it.

"Phelan Investigations."

"Would I be speakin' to Mr. Phelan himself?"

An older voice, deep, slow, borderline courtly.

You be, Phelan thought and replied, "Yes, sir. What can I do for you?" He was facing the wall most needing paint: the one behind his desk, with the spray and the spots and the rusty line bleeding down.

"My name is Xavier Bell. I b'lieve I spoke with your secretary, Miss Delpha Wade. She informed me about your fees. I would like a personal consultation next month. I thought it best to book an appointment well in advance."

"That's wise, sir, considering our schedule. Tell me when you'd like to come in, and I'll check the book." Which meant: look straight down onto the blank desk calendar.

"Allow me to deliberate a minute, Mr. Phelan."

"Sure thing." There was some muffled exchange, like Mr. Bell had a deliberation partner. Man could deliberate with the U.N., as far as Phelan was concerned.

He was already waving in the delivery of a new-used couch for the secretary's office. Phelan had bought two fattish pillow-chairs that, shoved together, made a short couch. Pretty aquamarine color, like water before ships got in it. He'd got a deal because the couch was originally what L&B Pre-Owned Furniture described as a "sectional," a bunch of pieces that stuck together, and Lester, the furniture-entrepreneur, was missing an end piece. Wanted to rest your elbow on a nice solid couch arm, you were out of luck.

Lester waited by the door as two L&B employees seized the old plaid sofa and began hauling it off. As it passed, he pointed at the plaid and pinched his nose. Phelan, muting the receiver, blew him a raspberry. Lester himself rolled in a gently used client chair, lined it up with the pillow chairs. He raised his eyebrows and escorted out the blood-stained leather one that hydrogen peroxide and leather-cleaner had failed to rehabilitate. Stuck his head back in the door, rubbed thumb and forefinger together. Phelan flexed his fingers: five, he'd be over to pay around then. Lester hoisted his thumb and thumped down the stairs.

Mr. Bell cleared a phlegmy throat. He had decided on Friday, September 7 at ten o'clock in the morning, if that was good.

"Good," Phelan said. "Would you be the gentleman who was concerned about...being located?" Miss Wade had reported they'd had a caller who wanted to be invisible. To someone.

"I want you to find my brother, Mr. Phelan. I suppose you'd say that he is the one...concerned about being located." As for more details, Mr. Bell would prefer to wait until they could speak confidentially.

All righty. Appointment recorded on the 7 square in September. Phelan hung up the phone, picked up the roller soaked in Apollo White and vanished smudges and patches of spackle. His spirits were rising from around his ankles where they'd been puddled.

He finished painting the wall with the window that faced the New Rosemont Hotel, running the roller up to the cut-in portions. My god, this place was looking different already. He moved on to the wall with the connecting door in it. That one went quick. He set up the paint tray behind his desk, near the wall screaming for coverage—a starburst spray of reddish brown drops and drips like a frozen firework—squatted and bounced to loosen up, rolled his shoulders. The phone trilled.

Again? He made a fist, raised it straight up. Phelan Investigations was booking work. He picked up the receiver with a rag and answered cordially.

His face hardened as he listened. "Yeah, I'm Tom Phelan. 'Scuse me, say again—who are you? OK, OK, Doctor, got it. Now, they took her where?"

Phelan slammed down the receiver, forced the rotary dial around as fast as his index finger could shove it. He blasted his way past the law office secretary on the other end by barking the word *URGENT!* When Miles Blankenship Esq., attorney at law, took the line, Phelan rattled out what he wanted: he had a friend in police custody who not only needed counsel, she must NOT set foot in a cell.

He laid out the situation: had Miles read the *Enterprise's* headlines about those murdered kids? The man who'd murdered them had been killed down on Orleans Street—Miles read that? OK. Well, it was Phelan's office he'd been killed in— and Phelan's secretary who'd taken him out. Pure self-defense. The man attacked her, stabbed her. But there was some crucial history Miles had to know. She was on parole after fourteen years in Gatesville. The charge back then had been voluntary manslaughter: she'd killed a man who had been raping her.

"So this is the second guy—"

"Only been out five months. Don't want her going back in a cell."

"You're clear on that point, Tom. Tell me, was she also armed?"

"No. Unarmed. Broke a liquor bottle. Used that."

Phelan overrode all objections. Didn't give a flying fuck if Miles Blankenship's field was divorce. Miles had passed the Texas bar, he was the single lawyer Phelan knew, and Miles had to hit it, please, for the police station now—in Watergate terms, *at this point in time*. Phelan would see him there.

Down at the curb, he unlocked his trunk, grabbed out the spare shirt and pants he kept in his P.I. kit. Stripped and dressed on Orleans Street, ignoring a wolf whistle from two guys in a Chevy C-10.

He double-timed the concrete steps.

His route: shoot past the Formica front desk and its likely guard, venerable Sergeant Fontenot with the wire-brush eyebrows. Swerve left into the squad room past bulletin boards tacked with mimeographs, past the cops shooting the breeze in school desks, others jabbing typewriters, a thief or two in the folding chairs. Jog straight to the back past a holding cell and bust into E.E.'s office, where he would persuade his uncle, the chief of police, to take Delpha Wade's statement without first arresting her, printing her, locking her in a cell.

This fantasy was forbidden by station policy. Also by the Policemen's Etiquette Guide and the Nephew's Codebook. Moves like the one Phelan was entertaining were why the Suck-It-Up manual existed. Nevertheless, he nodded to the desk sergeant and kept on walking.

"Whoa dere! Where you passin' yourself by to, Tom Phelan?"

Couple of uniforms off to the side gabbing. He stared them down and leaned over the scarred Formica to the sergeant. Instead of saying he was here because he'd been the first on the scene—his own office—or that he was Delpha Wade's employer, which around the station was generally known, Phelan muttered, "You told me they wouldn't charge her."

Two riotous gray thatches thrust down over Sergeant Fontenot's small, blue, troubled eyes. He had said that very thing, and now, appearing irritated by his own turmoil, he stalled. "Who you talking 'bout?"

Phelan's lips pulled to one side. "Delpha Wade. Doctor just called me, said police are down at the hospital hustling her in."

"Hustlin'? Naw, naw, Abels and Tucker, they left here like a herd of turtles. We just bringing her in aks her some questions."

"Lemme ask you one, Sergeant Fontenot. How many boys you dug up down at Deeterman's house? What's the tally?"

Now the uniforms angled toward Phelan.

"Six. So far. They off lookin' in some other places now."

"After he did what he did to those kids, you tell me offing that guy wasn't a bona fide public service."

"Fucking A," put in one of the uniforms, a white kid with scrappy hair and a large red ear angled toward the front desk.

"Shut up, Wilson," Fontenot said wearily. He lowered his chin and challenged Phelan. "Ain't nobody don' know that."

"Then why y'all bringing her in?"

"Cause your uncle, he say so. He's the chief of police, you don' notice. You don' tole him what to do. Pardon your ass, cher, you a private bird dog hadn't did six months' worth a business yet."

"Got me there, Sergeant. But…allow me to remind you what you said to me after my secretary had to fight for her life. You said, 'Nobody's touching that girl.'"

"Not makin' an argue wit you. But 'low me to mind you that anybody get dead, we got forms to fill out. Set your behind in a chair, you."

Fontenot waited until Phelan's back was turned then grumbled into the intercom. To E.E., Phelan knew, because the old snitch was grumbling in French.

Edouard Etienne Guidry, hometown: New Orleans, Louisiana; appearance: short, dark, and handsome; sartorial taste: radiant, was married to Phelan's aunt Maryann, his mother's younger sister. He was a man Phelan took stock in, and there weren't so many of those.

Chief Guidry rounded the corner and strode past the desk area, raking thick fingers through his silvered hair. Shirtsleeves, the knot in a kaleidoscope tie wrenched half-way down his broad chest. He rolled his eyes when Phelan started to rise and made a mashing motion at his nephew. Phelan sat back down.

E.E. stood there, hands on his hips, two pinkie sparklers and a wide gold band. "*Tete dure*, you. Who warn you about hirin' a ex-con?"

Phelan's hard head lowered. "She served it. As you know—went in in '59 and got out in this year of our Lord 1973. She started over. Going back to jail, that's the worst thing that could happen to her."

E.E. continued to glare.

"All right, OK, I'm an asshole messing in police business. You got my sincere apology. But I gotta be here."

"*Mais*, there it is. This about you."

"Some is, OK? She was just sitting in my office, putting letters in envelopes, and I shoulda been there, shoulda taken that knife. But most of it's about her. About what's right. And that is—it was the clearest self-defense there is."

"That girl's been around law enforcement almost as many years as your right hand's been around your dick. She knows the drill."

"Doesn't mean she can't use a body on her side."

His uncle's eyes slitted. "This here the body you talkin' 'bout?"

Phelan turned to see attorney Miles Blankenship entering the double doors, slipping off his aviators to display a neutral expression. At least, Phelan was pretty sure that was who that was. He'd spoken to him on the phone, but hadn't actually laid eyes on Miles in ten years, and the last time he had, Miles was wearing a long black robe and a mortarboard hat. The elegant man walking through the door wore wide-lapelled navy pinstripe, nipped at the waist, modest bell to the creased trousers. His black calfskin briefcase might have been rubbed with twenties to give it the mellow sheen.

"You know, Tom," E.E. was squinting toward Miles, "I seen you be lost, be steady, be stupid in the head and a brave little son of a bitch. This the first time you ak like Judas Iscariot."

"C'mon, E.E. No disrespect. That's a friend from high school, and he was what I thought of to help Delpha out."

"You payin' his fee?"

Phelan nodded.

"Cause you overflowin' with cash. The private eye business that hot. You a man of means."

He let E.E.'s words curl, topple, and break against his forehead. He held his peace as his old friend from high school joined the conversation.

"Miles Blankenship, Chief. Firm of Griffin and Kretchmer. Honor to meet you. I'll be representing—"

"I got it." E.E. shook Miles' hand, dropping it when the door opened again.

Detective Fred Abels, 'burns and 'stache and houndstooth jacket, had hold of her elbow. Must be Detective Tucker bringing up the rear, a husky pug-nose in a park-bench green leisure suit with his collar fashionably wide-spread. Phelan felt a flash of gratitude toward E.E. for the lack of cuffs on her, flash of *Blessed Jesus* when he examined a pale Delpha Wade braced between the two detectives. A glance around—at E.E., Fontenot, Miles—assured Phelan she had gripped the general attention.

Shirt from a slaughter yard.

Heat crept the back of Phelan's neck.

He knew what had gone down in his office because he'd arrived not too many minutes after the fight was over. Cops would ask her who started that fight, the man who walked in—or Delpha? And being as how hospitals do have access to various types of clean clothes—yeah, they do—her wardrobe today must mean she wanted the police to get the picture.

The hole in the crumpled white blouse drew the eye, rusty rosette formed around it, broad rust-stripe trailing down. The brown patches and gout and spray around the collar would not be hers, Phelan guessed, but they sure enhanced the grisly effect. The navy blue skirt was blackened at the waist. There was a spoiled, iron smell in the air. She seemed to be walking with an effort.

Delpha's head turned, stopped at Phelan. The light-brown hair an inch above her shoulders had felt some wind, and she had not combed it into place. No powder or rouge on the high cheekbones. Just lipstick the color of lips. She looked at him for a long second before her gaze retracted.

E.E. introduced himself to Delpha and told her they'd like to ask her some questions, get everything squared away, standard stuff in this situation. Miles was next. Told her he was here to act as her attorney, if that was agreeable to her. Delpha's head nodded slightly. She took a small side-step, almost a dip, and the lawyer cupped her elbow. Had the detectives read her her Miranda rights?

"She's not under arrest, counselor," E.E. said. "We just fixin' to take a statement. Determine what's what." He hooked his head at Abels. "Y'all go on."

Miles, ex-drum major, valedictorian, high-dollar divorce lawyer, was not on his own ground. Still, he emitted serene, tailored, carnivorous readiness: man was capital-B Billable. Phelan took scrupulous note. He knew something about masculine presentation, but he hadn't honed it like this.

Delpha looked at Phelan again. "You call him for me?" Faint light in the blue-gray flatness of her eyes, and she said it private, like only he could hear her.

Phelan lifted his chin.

The detectives shepherded her past him. Miles shot Phelan a glance and went with them. All squad room activity—breeze-shooting, questioning, report-writing, filing, phone-talking, candy bar-eating, and cigarette-smoking—everything buzzing back there would pretty much freeze, Phelan bet, while they watched the woman wearing the bloodbath pass by.

E.E. tapped Phelan's chest. "We got your statement the boys took at the scene. Don't need you, Tommy." He wheeled and followed them.

Phelan went to the restroom and scrubbed his paint-crusted knuckles and nails, stump of his left middle finger, wrists. Came back. Sat in the chairs lined up beneath a long window that despite central air and Venetian blinds still beat with sun. The wall clock's hands puttered around, stuck a while, went backward and scooped up some minutes forgot, trudged onward. He sat and smoked and sweated.

From time to time, Fontenot disappeared from the desk and then returned and busied himself answering the phone and doodling on a clipboard. Addressed himself extra-conscientiously to visitors. Trimmed his gaze so it did not reach the border of Phelan's outlands.

II

THE HITCH FROM the wound's incision made her feel like she had a hook in her, from belly button to backbone. Her stomach was tight, sore.

But at the sight of Miles Blankenship's magazine suit and easy carriage, Delpha Wade's knees unlocked. Her head went feverishly light. Had not had a lawyer who'd walked like that—like wherever he went, the street beneath his feet welcomed him. Wearing a suit that looked like somebody'd sewed it only for him. Spoke naturally, courteous, to the police chief, and she could tell he never *once* wondered would he get spoken back to or how. Miles Blankenship was equipped for *How*, he belonged here, in the station, belonged behind the nice oak desk he was sure to have, in a restaurant with velvet curtains, in a forward pew. And here he was, on her side. Speaking for her, god-almighty, throwing the protection of the law over her like a coat and not a net. Here was the difference between fourteen years and walking around free. She widened her stance to keep steady, in case gold sequins broke out before her eyes.

Detectives Abels and Tucker took hold of the chairs across from where she and the lawyer were standing. The wall to her right was being held up by Joe Ford, Delpha's parole officer, six foot five and glum as a buzzard. One of Joe Ford's many instructions during their first meeting: *The parolee must not own any knife with a blade longer than two inches, except for a kitchen knife, and only if their parole agent says so.*

Joe caught her eye, his gaze flickering. He probably didn't favor being called to this room over a parolee of his, with police chief and lawyer, maybe any minute the D.A., men far above his pay grade. *Mr. Ford, I didn't have a two-inch knife. Or a ten-inch one. Just a whiskey bottle resting in a bottom drawer. Doesn't signify, not a plug nickel, because it come down to me or him.*

Pug-nosed Tucker took the first chair, head drifting back, eyes squeezing shut, and produced a misty sneeze. He patted his pockets, fished out a handkerchief. Mr. Blankenship pulled out the chair across from Tucker for Delpha, inclined his head at it. She sat. Unexpectedly, he ushered the chair—with her suddenly unbalanced in it—to the table. He took his place next to her. Abels, the detective with the mustache and sideburns, slid off his hounds-tooth jacket and hung it on the back of his chair. He plopped down a white tablet and sat heavily. Scraped the chair forward, uncapped a pen.

"OK, Delpha. On the afternoon of August 15, 1973, where were you?" A bulldog wearing a drill sergeant's hat glowered from his forearm.

"Office of Phelan Investigations, downtown on Orleans Street."

"Was anyone with you?"

"No."

"Where was your employer?"

"Out on a case."

"When the…deceased came to the door, you invited him in?"

"He walked in."

"Door wasn't locked?"

"No."

"What did you say to him?"

"Asked how I could help him."

"OK. What did he say?"

"Said a girl said she left a book for him outside the door, but it wasn't there."

Abels waited for her to continue and when she didn't, said, "What did you say?"

"Told him I brought it in and I'd get it for him and he could go."

"You were in a hurry to get rid of him?"

"Yes, sir."

"Why was that?"

"He wanted to know if my boss was gone. Looking around to make sure I was by myself."

"Maybe he was just looking at his surroundings," Abels said, maintaining the neutral-cop tone.

Delpha's eyes flicked to Tucker's then settled back on Abels'. She answered nothing.

"You believed he intended to harm you?"

"Yes, sir."

"Without him making any kind of threat?"

She nodded.

"How'd you come to think that?"

"Front of his pants was standin' up."

And so on, slow and methodical, through the moment her attacker had pulled a knife, and the events that followed. Then, a detailed recapitulation of those events. It was eighty-nine minutes before Abels switched gears and the lawyer sitting next to her meaningfully shifted his posture forward.

"OK, Delpha. In April of this year, you were released from Gatesville Women's Prison?"

"I was."

"You were incarcerated for what charge?"

"Voluntary manslaughter."

"Your victim was—"

Miles Blankenship finished the sentence. "A rapist,

Detective. That's enough of those questions. They're irrelevant to the matter at hand. We all know Miss Wade happens to be on parole. And we all know that what we have here is justified self-defense. An individual with more than a reasonable belief that the use of force was necessary, defending her life against a depraved and aggressive predator. As any man in this room would have done without a second thought. Let me emphasize that. Without a second thought. Any man." He scanned the faces in the room, skipping Delpha's.

"There is no crime here, gentlemen. Miss Wade was carrying no weapon, so there is not even a parole violation. Not even that. This interview is a formality, the necessity of which we all understand. But let's get this formality over with. Keep in mind that you've removed my client from a hospital bed."

Whereas the cops gazed flat-faced at Miles, Delpha noticed that her parole officer Joe Ford straightened up against the wall. He had unfolded the long arms he had barricaded in front of his chest and slipped his hands in his pockets. No violations, no way he could be faulted.

Abels, brow raised, cut his eyes toward the Chief, who hiked his chin a quarter inch.

The detective's gaze sank back to hers. He jerked his neck to the side and back, getting his head on tighter. "All right, say again for the record, you were alone when the deceased came to the office?"

"Yeah."

"You invited him in?"

"He walked in."

"OK. Did you talk with him?"

Their verbal exchange was repeated for a third time. Delpha told the same story, reiterated that No, she had not met the man prior to this time nor seen him. Yes, she had heard of him from her boss, Mr. Phelan.

"And what was it your boss told you?"

"That he was preying on boys."

"You knew that for a true fact?"

"Know for a fact Mr. Phelan believed that."

Abels' mouth screwed to the side. Irritation sparked in his eyes. For only a second—then his tone traded its dogged neutrality for a mild, false curiosity. "Why'nt you just run, Delpha?"

"'Cause he was hopin' I would."

Without unfolding his arms, Chief Guidry spoke up. "You read his mind?"

"Read the way he waved the knife."

"What waving technique was that?" Fake confusion from Abels.

"Invitin' me to make a break for it."

Tucker sawed at his nose with a horizontal finger. "You coulda hollered for help."

She nodded agreeably. "He woulda liked that."

"How would you know? Explain that for us." Tucker sniffed.

"No, sir. You hadn't been in a knife fight, I cain't tell you. Ruther you asked me a specific question."

The eraser of the lawyer's pencil bounced on the yellow legal pad he was smiling down on.

Abels balefully resumed the lead. "So you had no hesitation before you killed him?"

"Not after he stabbed me."

Pause in the interrogation as, possibly, Abels regrouped and the other men measured themselves against this answer.

"All right, then. Delpha. Just for a minute setting aside what we know now, that your assailant is also the chief suspect in six murders...on the afternoon in question, you didn't know that—"

Her lips parted. She stared straight-on at Abels and his coarse mustache with a few gray hairs in it. He would've been on that site, she knew it. At his rank. Case like this. Abels'd have pictures in his head of whatever was left of those young bodies in dirty plastic, he'd have putrefaction fresh in his nose.

"Nobody sets six dead boys off to the side," she said. "You don't."

Abels' head twitched like there was a bone inside he had to pop straight. There was silence. Breathing. Then, "I do not. No, ma'am."

Ma'am. Purely a figure of speech, but there it was. First shred of respect.

As though a buzzer had sounded, Miles Blankenship checked his silver watch and glided to his feet. "I believe we're finished here, officers," he said pleasantly.

He turned his head and addressed the chief. "If there are further questions, sir, please direct them to me. Miss Wade, I'll be at your disposal."

He tilted toward her and began to ease back her chair.

Delpha grabbed the sides of the seat.

She craned back at Mr. Blankenship, who smiled kindly, murmuring *Allow me*. She then let go of the chair, let it be guided back from the table, but feeling embattled still, rose and scanned each in turn: met the weighing eyes of the chief, angled toward Joe Ford's familiar bony face, then the two detectives facing her. Abels blew out a short sigh, coughed to cover it. Either Tucker winked at her, or he was afflicted by an allergic tic.

Out in the hall, some uniforms were gathered, spilling out toward the squad room. Some of them had surely seen the bodies dug up. A couple of them nodded deliberately as if in support of the woman in the bloody shirt, others gawked as at a spectacle. Delpha passed by the badged chests into the open squad room, beginning to feel a sharp pain between her shoulder blades from holding herself upright. Feeling, in a rush, her exhaustion, the twanging ache of her incision, the barb in the middle of herself, as she neared the station's waiting room. Behind her, low conversations were commencing.

"Fuckin' A right," she heard, along with *steak knife*, *motherfucker*, and *bite-size pieces*. Somebody sniggered.

Keys jingled. Joe Ford mumbled, "See you," and excused himself by.

Yeah, she'd see him in the parole office. Wouldn't that be a session.

Around three p.m., Fontenot slid behind the desk again, blue eyes snapping.

"Tole you," he sang, and Phelan knew they were cutting her loose.

His friend Joe Ford appeared first, passing Phelan with a widening of the eyes and a simultaneous twist of the jaw. Then Miles. They weren't charging her. Likely result: finding of self-defense to be forwarded to the D.A. Miles couldn't stick around. He was off to mediate between a feuding couple, bone of contention: an aged beagle named Betty.

"Send me your bill," Phelan said.

"Have to, Tom. I'm on the partners' clock." Miles smiled wryly. "She'd've done OK without me. Good to finally lay eyes on you again, buddy." He shook Phelan's hand and strode out.

"Give you a ride," Phelan said to Delpha when she and Abels walked out past Fontenot's front desk. "Back to the hospital? Or home?"

"Home."

Once in the car, Phelan asked her if she wanted a clean shirt. "Yeah, thanks," she said, "ruther not scandalize the

Rosemont." He stopped at Gus Meyer, pulled a woman's white shirt off a rack. In the car she put it on, leaving him with an image of a tender-looking red track across a rib, a rust-spotted cotton bra, and the curve of her breasts.

He escorted her back into the New Rosemont, through the wide lobby furnished in sheenless blue velour, floral-print chintz, fringed lamps, scratched-up side tables with aluminum ashtrays. Couches and chairs grouped for cozy conversation were at that moment occupied by elderly clientele imitating arthritic marble statues. At the foot of the stairs, they stopped. Her boss looked at her a little while, like he wanted to say a thing, or say several things, his face pained. Finally just said, "Get well, hear?"

Delpha whispered *thanks* and went up. She found she needed to hold to the rail.

A night nurse who'd woken her to measure temperature and blood pressure had mentioned Mr. Phelan. *That your husband or your boyfriend?* she'd wanted to know. *He's not wearing a ring. I like the ones with no belly fat. You let me know if he's not your boyfriend.*

He'd come to see her those days after the surgery, even during the week-long haze when she was mostly sleeping off an infection. He sat by the bed during the after-work hour, not saying much. The August sunlight through the window had picked out auburn glints in his dark hair. Getting long. His blue shirt usually looked like a chicken had ironed it. He'd been noncommittal about any new jobs, and she'd guessed there were none. She was afraid she'd ruined his business. Mr. Thomas Phelan, ex-roughneck, Worker's Comp recipient for a lost finger, new private investigator. Employer of Delpha Wade when not another soul in Beaumont, Texas, would accept that title.

III

THE NEW ROSEMONT Retirement Hotel's residents had picked through the *Beaumont Journal's* front-page columns or watched Channel 4's Evening Report—and spread the big story to others who hadn't. Miss Delpha Wade, up in Room 221 at the top of the stairs, had killed a man in self-defense, and according to an astonishing paragraph farther down in the article, not her first. Why, when she'd walked into their lobby last spring, she had been fresh out of Gatesville Women's Prison! There were dire looks and looks askance, clucking and jaws sagging below coffee-stained dentures.

Delpha had avoided putting any of them on the spot. For the last ten days, if it wasn't raining, she'd carried her coffee outside in the mornings and sat in the open air watching the downtown pass by. Last two of those days, she'd worn a skirt and blouse suitable for office work.

Now her coffee was churning in her stomach, a mouthful gurgling back up into her throat, and again, she was dressed. The sky was lowering by the minute, a wood-handled black umbrella leaning against her hip.

Droplets splashed her hair. Delpha cast an upward glance at the big, running clouds, purple along their bottom edges, then she stood and forced the umbrella to open its black vault.

Phelan stared out the window at the rain, then at legs under an umbrella, crossing the street with less speed than might seem natural for such ugly weather. Walking deliberately in black flats. Wet black flats.

Tropical Storm Celia was now whamming into Freemont for the second time, having hit land two days ago, sucked herself back out over the Gulf to do a *HaHa U-Turn* and then gathered her waters and her winds to boil into the same coastline. Beaumont was picking up the overflow wind and rain.

When Phelan heard the steps on the stairs, not fast, not slow, he sat down in the boss chair. Then he stood up again. Ran a hand through his getting-long hair.

Miss Wade came through the door of Phelan Investigations and stopped mid-stride. Her head swiveled as she surveyed the Apollo White walls.

His neck warming up, Phelan surveyed her.

The crease at the left side of her lips seemed etched a cut deeper. Her weight had fallen off some. Less than the 120 lbs. on her discharge paper from Gatesville Prison. Still five foot six. Still the gray-blue eyes, but something farther in their gaze. Not tough to figure. Jailhouse tan, long gone: there was sun on her cheekbones and in strands of her ash-brown hair. Miss Wade had been taking in the parade of downtown life from the New Rosemont Retirement Hotel's outside chairs. He'd studied her from his window, being as the Rosemont was just across the street, wondered what was healing or not in her mind and in her body. Wondered did Phelan Investigations or its proprietor figure in anywhere.

There was more than sun on her cheekbones now—there was deep pink embarrassment. She closed the door behind her, saying, "I shoulda called, but I decided to speak up face to face, so whatever way this went, I could tell you in person that I am grateful that you hired me and sorry you and your new business got pulled into such a dirty mess."

Phelan felt like he'd swallowed a bowl of concrete chili. The heat from his neck was lapping at his ears.

She wasn't coming back.

"I got you into the mess, or Phelan Investigations did, and that's the same thing. You know that's the truth."

"Neither one of us to blame for that man, Mr. Phelan." This judgment sounded settled.

Phelan cleared his throat and went for it. "You well enough to come back to work?"

They looked past each other, him to her mid-section, where a pale blue blouse tucked into a swirly skirt he'd seen on many days. She was glancing sideward toward the new furnishings. The pink on her cheeks spread down to her jaw.

"*Is* there any work, Mr. Phelan?"

"Matter of fact. We got a ten o'clock today." He'd said that with a shitload of relief. Shoulda just sounded businesslike. And...*we*, he'd said *we*. "The gentleman who called you up before...well, before."

"The one wanted to be invisible? Yeah. I 'member." She turned directly to the two-piece sectional and broke out a finer smile than people usually give to used furniture. "Where'd the plaid couch go? What'd you do to the urp-green walls with the scratched and chipped-off patches?"

Phelan shrugged self-consciously. "Spiffing up our business image."

"I see that."

"Tax deductible, right?"

"Right." Her chin lowered. She scrutinized the fat-pillow couch. "That blue's a nice color. But, you know, it could be two chairs, you pushed it apart. People might not want to sit right smack next to each other. And if we put a coffee table—"

We. He exhaled.

She looked down, shifted one black flat to the other.

Hooked her hair behind an ear. "Guess we could start using first names now, Mr. Phelan, if you want. Being as there's water under the bridge. Being as you're keeping me on after what happened. Lotta people wouldn't—"

"If I'd a been down here like I should've been…" Phelan shoved his hands in his pockets, addressed his gaze to the floor. "…that good deed you did wouldn't have fallen to you."

"That's not how those people work, Mr. Phelan. Tom. You were here, he wouldna tried nothing. Still be out there." A shudder crawled through her shoulders. Delpha turned and placed her umbrella in the coat closet. She went over and sat down at her desk. There she repositioned the Selectric an inch, pulled out the tray drawer and stirred the pencils. She opened her middle side-drawer and set a new manila file folder onto her desk, hovered a pen over its tab.

"What's the ten o'clock appointment's name?"

IV

DELPHA RELIEVED XAVIER Bell of a dripping umbrella, set it in a corner of her office to dry. She showed him into one of the mismatched client chairs. As she turned, she had a strange sense of wind changing against her face. Unlikely, because the air in the office came from a flaky AC unit. She squinted at it.

"Wait a minute." Phelan stopped her before she got out his door. "Why don't you bring in a pad and take down the details of this meeting shorthand? Like we do on all cases this important."

Her gaze examined his. Phelan's eyes roamed downward. To date, zero case-notes had been recorded in shorthand, a language Miss Wade had learned in Mr. Wally's business class at Gatesville Women's Prison. She went into her office, opened and closed desk drawers, and returned with a new steno pad and a ballpoint. Peeking out beneath, Phelan could see a folder that she used to hold their standard contract form. A sheet of carbon paper would be clipped to it. Discreetly, she pushed the second client's chair away from Mr. Bell, all the way to the side of the room, where she sat and poised the pen.

"This is my secretary, Delpha Wade. She'll make sure we record every detail of your case accurately."

"Yes, I spoke to Miss Wade on the phone." Mr. Bell's spine stretched a mite before he dipped his head in her direction. "Well, look at you. Miss Wade, would you do me the favor of turning your head to the side?"

Delpha lifted her gaze from the steno pad. She looked directly at the client, and again, for a second, her eyes narrowed. Then she turned her head in the direction of the wall that had most needed repainting.

"I am right. You've got the profile of Madeleine Carroll. Not the hair of course, hers was wavy. And blond. But, really, the nose, the chin, a dead ringer for—"

"'Fraid I don't know who that is." Delpha returned her attention to the pad.

"You're too young. She was the star of, no, Robert Donat was the star, of course, but she was the lead actress in 'The Thirty-Nine Steps.' Alfred Hitchcock, 1935. You've seen it?"

No, at Gatesville, movie-time was Doris Day and Elvis Presley. Delpha placed her chin a fraction higher in the air and a slight smile on her lips, to act out interest.

"I'm a film buff. I realize it's not everyone's passion, but for me, well…" The client's gaze turned to rope in Phelan. "Let me remind you that I'd like my identity to remain confidential."

The sunglasses had told Phelan that.

The man's nose—straight-bridged in profile but red-veined and lumpy from the front—suggested that he liked the bottle. The gray tinge of its tip, that he was an ardent smoker, and the vertical folds in his cheeks, that he had some decades on him. But he didn't have an elderly hump or a spindly frame. He was built thick like a wrestler or boxer who gravity had weighed down. And he was turned out—wore a navy blazer over a blue plaid shirt, the snap-brim fedora with neat brown hair around its edges. The hair and the mustache, sort of a briefcase brown, looked less than natural. That he kept his hat on—a man of his age, indoors and in the presence of a woman—said he was hiding what was or wasn't under it. Vanity? Probably. But sunglasses in the rain, well, that said eye problem, ugly, or disguise.

"Yes, sir. We got that part. I assure you confidentiality is one of our principles. What is it you want us to do for you?"

"I...I'm all by myself now."

The client halted, lips still open. "Excuse me. It's startling to say that." A gust hit the window, and the glass rattled. One of his hands moved to hug the other. "I want you to find my brother. I have reason to believe he's recently purchased a house in Beaumont. We went our separate ways long ago. One of those family matters." Bell looked away. "My health...well, I'm not young, as you can see. I'd like to see him once more. Clear the air, as it were."

"And he's not in the telephone book?" Phelan's head angled toward a corner, where they had twenty-seven or eight phone books piled up because sometimes phone books were useful.

"I don't even know what name he'd be using."

Phelan's head inclined. "Why would your brother use an alias?"

"He's...Rodney's got this cloak and dagger mania. He's always had it. As kids, we'd play hide and seek, and Rodney would just run. He'd never come in, even when we called 'Ally-ally-in-come-free.' Our mother had to call him. Then he'd come in." Mr. Bell's brows squeezed.

"Rodney got your goat."

Bell looked at Phelan, angled, and threw a glance toward Delpha. "He knew he did. That's why he did it." After a moment he took a breath, and his head sank. "Ridiculous, I know. Here we are at the end of our lives, and Rodney is still running." He drew a tobacco pouch and small packet from his jacket pocket. "Do you mind?"

Phelan pushed over an ashtray, eyebrows lifted. Bell was using Patriotic rolling papers, the C-note pattern.

The man nimbly fashioned a cigarette, saying, "Things

happened in our family. Like any family. I told myself the sky was still blue without Rodney. But now I've changed my mind. I want to see my brother."

"Whatever family things happened—they didn't bother Rodney?"

"Ohhhh." Pondering. "They did. But we have to be realistic. Neither of us can take it back."

"Take what back?"

"My word! The past, of course." He leaned back, homemade clamped between his lips, drew a small coin from the breast pocket of his blazer. Phelan took it: gold, worn out of round, foreign words bracketing the head etched in the middle. Which, as near as Phelan could tell, was two Siamese twins with fat lips, joined together at the back of the skull.

He glanced over at Bell.

"Roman. The god Janus, who faces both the past and the future. Nice to look at, isn't it? To remind yourself that the past is gone." Bell plucked back the coin and stowed it again in the blazer's pocket, gave it a pat. "Or that, in the future, something can be done to make up for it."

"OK, you want to talk to your brother, maybe make up. You're retired, Mr. Bell?"

"Yes. I'm retired. And I want to see Rodney again, just one more time."

Phelan damned the sunglasses. He'd have liked to have studied the old fellow's eyes.

"Then I'll go home. Go to the movies, tavern, gymnasium, attend Classical Club meetings until, well, until I can't do those things anymore. You have a great many years before you'll know what I mean, Mr. Phelan." He bent his head toward Phelan in what maybe was meant to be a fatherly nod, but his bottom lip bowed upward.

"Classical Club?"

An expression of pleasure lifted the man's heavy face. "A group of professors. I taught an occasional night class at Loyola, just an elective, a history of early film. Paid practically nothing. But the credential allowed me discounted entry to some events. My favorite is The International Film Festival in Houston, I always drive over. Maybe you've gone?" Bell threw a glance at Phelan and turned inquiringly to Delpha.

"I missed that," Phelan said, so that Delpha didn't have to find a reply. What Phelan did not miss, some years back, was movie night at a base camp in Kon Tum province—"The Alamo" projected onto an outdoor screen with holes in it. Him and Jyp Casey still wired from the night before, hauling a guy around downed and blasted trees, Zion Washington striding beside, both hands on his M-16.

"Too bad. Film's my passion, but my livelihood…it was drearier. I took over my father's business. While my brother Rodney was off gallivanting here and there, I was selling coins, like the Roman one I showed you. Sabres and pistols, assorted antiques. I added movie memorabilia, autographs to our stock. I kept the shop going. Cooped up inside the same four walls every day. Same noisy little streets, my god, the racket tourists make, the local fools. Yowlin' like cats."

"Where was that?"

Coy smile. "Confidentiality, remember? Let's just say, a city."

Having connected Loyola, the client's accent, noisy little streets and yowling tourists to New Orleans, Phelan was annoyed by the lack of verification. He injected the atmosphere with a friendly smile. "Born and bred in New Orleans, Mr. Bell? Sell a lotta sabres down there?"

With the nicotine-stained fingers of his right hand, Bell doffed the black glasses and set them on Phelan's desk. His eyes were darkest brown and hooded, the lax skin of his upper lids balanced on pale lashes. "I suppose it's not that difficult to guess. Born and bred. Yes, we sold sabres. Daggers, dirks, fancy pistols. Weapons, you know, of war."

"Was your brother Rodney a part of your business?"

"A long time ago. He kept the books. When he moved away, he simply got an allowance for doing nothing."

"And that chapped you."

"Oh, not really. They thought…they thought that was better for everyone."

"They?"

"Our parents."

Had his bottom lip quivered? His voice sounded hollow. His clean-shaven jaw had slipped sideways. Bell had, for a moment, become unhinged.

"Happy family?"

"Like any other."

"Uh huh. Do you have more siblings?"

Xavier Bell took a last deep draw, spit-extinguished the homemade, and dropped the butt into the ashtray. Exhaled the smoke. "No."

"How old are you?"

"Seventy-five."

"And Rodney?"

"Seventy-three."

"Is he married?"

"Not that I know of. He never seemed inclined toward marriage." Bell's face was bland.

As was Phelan's, while he batted around questions he decided could wait. "OK, got it. We find your brother, you spend some time, say goodbye and godspeed. Correct?"

"That's close enough."

"You mentioned an alias. Is Rodney your brother's real name?"

"No. He uses different names."

"Really," Phelan said, adjusting to this information. "How do you know that?"

"Because in the early days, I'd call, but then I stopped being able to find him. During this last decade of our... estrangement, I happened on the name he was using. Rodney Harris. I followed up. But then he moved again." Xavier Bell resettled his shoulders in the blazer.

Phelan noted again that they were not frail or humped shoulders. "That how you found Rodney was here in Beaumont? Somebody happen to tip you?"

"Within this last year, financial conditions changed. Some aged relatives passed away. A portion of the estate was deposited into a bank here."

"I see," Phelan said. "Large estate?"

"That's hardly relevant. Or your business, Phelan. But I will say that the apple of our mother's eye was real estate, and she never sold a property. The sweet old miser."

That description rang for a beat.

"How long ago was it you found your brother? And where, sir?" Delpha's tone had taken on heavy-cream, she managed to pump the question full of courtesy and concern.

Bell angled toward her. "He was around Jacksonville, Florida. About four years ago. 1969, that would make it."

"Four years ago. That's the last time you saw him," Phelan said. "You saw him in person then?"

"Briefly."

Delpha offered a sympathetic smile. "Y'all couldn't fix things up?"

The old man's hands opened and stretched. "I'm afraid not. My brother is a coarse man...coarser than he once was. We took different paths in life, I suppose. I told him I forgave him—"

"For what, Mr. Bell?"

"Everything! Forgiveness…is an attribute of the strong, they say. But I fixed nothing. As much as I tried to."

"What was it that you hoped would happen?" Now Delpha's softened voice was a balm directed to Mr. Bell's ear alone, and Bell oriented his whole body toward her.

Phelan's forehead wrinkled. How was she doing this?

"Just…just…just to be his big brother again, for a little while. When he was small, he thought I hung the moon. To feel how that felt again, well, that…that was worth a great deal, and I'm a man who knows what things are worth."

After some seconds of silence, Bell glanced at Delpha and then passed his hand over his eyes. "I've embarrassed myself again, haven't I?"

Phelan changed the subject, asked, in a matter-of-fact tone, for Rodney's description, a picture of him if there was one, list of habits or pastimes Bell knew about. Like, was Rodney a bowler? Or a Baptist, so they'd know where to look for him.

Bell drew from the navy blazer a yellowed black and white photo. "That's Rodney and me."

Phelan studied the photo: two men of different heights standing on a street corner, a broad door behind them. Part of a street sign above their heads read "Orle." Their faces were alike: same black brows, straight nose, and slightly upturned lips. The men wore identical clothes: lightish suits, double-breasted unlike the blazer Bell wore today, but tacked in at the waist, two-toned shoes buffed to a sheen. Straw boaters. The taller man had an arm extended to the shorter one's shoulder, the hand blurred as though he'd reached out at the last minute. These two could have been any youngish, well-enough-off white men in the United States in, say, 1930, '32, '34—sometime in there. Which told Phelan about the brothers' conditions, being as how a fair number of Americans in the 1930s could not have produced a shiny pair of cap-toed, two-toned shoes without the aid of a fairy godmother.

"Which is you?"

Bell touched the photo. The taller one.

"And this is the most recent you have? How old were you?"

"Thirty."

Great, a forty-five-year-old picture. Phelan mentally rolled his eyes.

"As for habits. We were Catholics, but I don't know that my brother has kept up attendance. Rodney likes birds. Always did. Birds. Nature." That was why he'd been in Jacksonville because that's where a lot of birds nested or flew over or some such. And now Beaumont. There were wetlands all around the area.

"Birds. All right. That's helpful."

"That's really all I have to give you. Oh, then there's this." Xavier Bell reached into his inside jacket-pocket, pinched bills from a wallet, and counted out a dozen real hundreds onto the metal desk. "Your fee for three weeks. I'm willing to pay a bonus if you find him by, say, September 30. Five hundred dollars. If you find him in a week, I'll expect an immediate per diem refund. And of course I want a receipt."

Phelan kept his voice even. "Thank you, sir. Miss Wade will need your signature on our contract. That will also serve as a receipt for your retainer."

As soon as Delpha had added the financial details, she rose from the client chair. Contract and ballpoint appeared on Phelan's desk, squared into place by her hands, for the client. "Please add your telephone number, sir. Below your name there."

"Certainly. But…I'm quite often at a film. I might call you," he said, gaze darting to her. "Progress reports."

"That'd be fine. And, 'scuse me," she said gently, "but…"

"Yes?"

"Is Rodney dangerous?"

The client pulled back. "I didn't—I never said the first word about dangerous. Why would you ask that?"

As if teasing, Delpha said, "No special reason, Mr. Bell." Her uneasy expression transformed into a smile of mild sweetness. Phelan noticed that the smile stopped short of her eyes but didn't think Bell would.

Bell still stared at her, but when her smile broadened, he relaxed again in his chair.

Phelan shut down his own amusement—see, having her in here was a primo idea—lit a cigarette, and sat back in his swivel chair. "Routine question." He gestured vaguely. "Miss Wade is being thorough. In this business, we have to know what we're getting into. What's the answer, Mr. Bell?"

The dark eyes gazed at the left side of Phelan's desk, skimmed across it and fixed on the right side. "Rodney… caused dangerous things to happen."

"How did he do that?"

"He…" Bell's pinkish nose reddened. "Was not a loyal brother. Took what wasn't his."

"Say Rodney's a thief?"

"Oh yes."

"What did he steal?"

The client, apparently conducting some inward dialogue, did not reply.

Finally, Phelan cut off the silence with, "All right, then, your retainer will buy you around, as you said, three weeks from Phelan Investigations. Full weeks but spread out over whatever time period is required, including nights and weekends if we're obliged to work then."

Bell seemed to stuff his preoccupations back into himself and attend to the office around him. "Surely that's long enough?"

"Can't say. Depends on how deep your brother's buried

himself. But you should know that we do work several cases at a time." Phelan spread his palms. "Busy schedule. Now. Yours is a heavy research case. Any reason you're in a hurry?"

Bell stroked his mustache with a knuckle. "Not really, I suppose. Having someone working for me already helps." He nodded, almost bashful. "It's, well, it's been such a long time since I've had...allies."

"Got allies now, sir. Phelan Investigations will do our best."

The flash in Xavier Bell's dark eyes was that of a yearning six-year-old who knows better than to ask for anything, but dogs you anyway. It passed. But the tremulous smile combined with the mossy old nose activated Phelan's sympathy gland.

Phelan scooped up the hundreds and set them in his desk drawer on top of a bank deposit booklet. He came out from behind the metal desk and walked their client to the door, making a detour for the client's still-wet umbrella.

Behind them, he heard Delpha say quietly, "Mr. Bell."

Xavier Bell did not turn toward her. Instead, he offered his hand to Phelan and a speech that he seemed to be cranking out from memory. "I will be relying on you—"

"Mr. Bell." Delpha, a shade louder this time.

Phelan glanced back at his secretary, saw the client's sunglasses dangling from her hand, returned to Bell, who, reciting *confidential discretion results*, either didn't hear her or didn't want to lose his place in the speech.

"...and I do appreciate your best effort. Thank you." The old fellow exhaled.

With a flip of his hand, Phelan directed his attention to Delpha. Bell twisted himself back toward her and exclaimed, "My word, I just walked right off without those!"

Delpha presented the glasses to him as if they were General Eisenhower's binoculars, smiled.

Her smile imprinted on his face. He fit on the sunglasses

and wagged his finger at her. "Madeleine Carroll." They heard him descend the stairs carefully.

Phelan went back and nabbed his camera from his desk. He was thinking that Bell was a nice enough old guy. A mixed bag. Delpha could melt him with sweet talk, but Phelan had the feeling he wasn't always meltable. A tiny bit of unstandard about Xavier Bell.

Hearing the outside door shut, Phelan trotted down to the dentist's office on the first floor. Jogged across the waiting room with a nod to the receptionist, who trailed a hand at him. He dodged into a room where a girl reclined on a chair with her mouth gaping and her eyelids squeezed shut, the dentist bent toward her with a silver hook.

"Beg your pardon, Milton, this'll just take a second." Phelan leaned toward the window and took hurried photos of Xavier Bell. The rain had let up some, but the man had unfurled his umbrella, looked left, right, then crossed the street.

Here was something different: a brisk gait, unlike the deliberate steps on the stairs. Old age was afflicting Bell, but it had not yet unsteadied his legs. On the corner he paused, leaning out from the umbrella—perfect profile snap—to speak to a guy with a hat sitting in a dark car. For a second, he turned full face and looked toward Phelan's eyes. Phelan snapped the button and pulled back.

"Tom, I'm gonna charge you rent for my window. It's not sanitary."

Phelan straightened. "Borrowing your window is helping me make your rent, Dr. Building Owner. Very sorry for the intrusion, Miss."

Phelan exited the treatment room, raised a hand to salute the receptionist behind the desk, and was rewarded by a paper airplane to the jaw.

V

HE WAITED WHILE Miss Wade, no, Delpha, deciphered the shorthand and typed up the case notes in English complete with a carbon copy, installed them into a manila file folder, labeled the folder 'Bell,' and delivered it to his desk. The woman kept to her order of things, and she liked those folders.

She was sort of standing over him now, so Phelan read out, in crisp Courier, their missing person Rodney Bell's given name, former name and places of residence, age, hobby; and Xavier Bell's name, his age, former profession and pastime, city, his pouch of tobacco. She didn't know the name of the rolling papers—hadn't ever seen such before—but she'd described them: looked like the man was burning hundred dollar bills.

"Hadn't seen those? Patriotics. Writing on the bills says something like...like..." Phelan grinned. "'A free country rolling in money is the greatest government.' If I remember right. Wait, no. Is the *highest* government. Hippie dippie joke."

"Have yet to meet a hippie, Mr. Phelan."

He looked up at her. "Not too late. Plenty still around. Listen, let's don't go backward. I'm Tom, and you're Delpha, and I didn't say yet—welcome back. I'm glad...I'm...glad."

Well, that sounded stupid.

"Thank you. I mean it, I do. Been stuck in my room or watching a little TV in the Rosemont lobby. Watergate hearings hitting a lull, I got so bored I helped Oscar in the kitchen couple days. Can that man cook! But it's funny. In the lobby, Oscar's pretty regular, but once he crosses the kitchen threshold, he turns into this…Egyptian pharaoh. Says I've got a heavy hand on the cinnamon."

"No such thing as too much spice."

That just about did it for the small talk.

"OK," Phelan said, "we got an odd duck for a client here. As it were. Please don't make me ask you to sit down. Pull over the chair." He didn't look up. "So we search out Rodney's new house. Which'd probably be bought under another name. But not his real name. And, I'm wondering…if you were seventy-three, would you blow a lot of money on a house? Why not rent? I mean, have a landlord mow the yard and all. No taxes, no upkeep."

"You could wanna leave it to somebody. Maybe Rodney's got a life Mr. Bell doesn't know about."

They looked at each other, agreeing. Delpha pushed over the client chair and sat down.

It was one of the two original chairs, identical to the one she'd sat in that day Phelan had found her in the office. Shoulda spent the extra fifteen bucks and replaced both of them. That day flashed in on him, the day he knelt at her knee, listening as she talked about the book, the diary of victims Deeterman had come to get. That she was holding in her bloody hand.

He backhanded that picture right out of range. There was a lot to be said for not thinking about what you didn't want to think about.

"Listen, when you said 'Mr. Bell' twice, were you doing what I think you were doing? That wasn't just about handing over the sunglasses."

"Kinda a test. Name's not really your name, you might could forget it. Then again, you're seventy-five, you might not hear right. I don't know, Tom. Had this feeling when he came in he brought something with him. Silly, I guess."

"Brought what?"

Delpha's shoulders lifted, fell.

Troubled, Phelan got up and strolled over to the window to find out how the rain was doing. It was on the job again. Spearing down and splatting on the street, joining its brothers and sisters in the gutter and rolling industriously along. Rain was independent as hell.

However, it was conceivable that Thomas Phelan was not as solid-state, 24-carat Independent as he had once believed. Could that be? Could he need help with this business? The random thought beaned him. Like his brain was a pitcher brushing him off. He turned and faced Phelan Investigations' sole employee.

She met his gaze. Her eyes inquired and then battened down.

He had no idea what would issue from his mouth.

What did: "Where'd you learn that way to talk to him? Thawed him out every time."

She considered telling. Then said, "You fix cars, Tom?"

"Change the oil, tune-ups, tinker a little, like that."

"Got different wrenches for different-sized jobs?"

"Sure."

"Well, there you go," she said.

VI

HOW'D SHE KNOW how to talk like that? Zulma Barker.
Zulma was serving the last weeks of a forty-one month
stretch—she'd driven getaway for a toy boyfriend who'd
robbed a pharmacy at gunpoint. Maybe because the young
man, a would-be model, scurried out with a gym bag of
dexedrine, the judge didn't buy Zulma's story, that she'd just
been idling in her own car while her lover filled a weight-loss
prescription for his mother. The prosecution also noted, in her
act of aiding and abetting, the use of an alias as a cover up.

Previous to her bad-decision day, Zulma Barker'd been the
popular and respectable receptionist for the Beatrice Adcock
Agency in Dallas. She got the job once she agreed to use the
pseudonym Cynthia, Beatrice nixing "Zulma" as glamorless.
The Agency handled a lot of high-strung people. Zulma
learned to supply blandishments to pretty and not-pretty-
enough girls panting to be models and to fend off their bitchy
mothers. She developed the tone and patter to charm pricey
designers and the proper worshipful timbre for photographers.
This skill had never been any ambition of Zulma's. She'd just
discovered that her day went easier if she turned her voice into
Karo syrup. In time, she discovered a disconcerting side-effect:
the secret of feeling like she sounded.

Delpha was working a stint in the kitchen then, winter,
around the time President Eisenhower left and John Kennedy
moved in. Sometimes she had a cut or a burn to nurse, not

to mention the blaze in her heart and belly. She lay on the top bunk after the count and lights-out, tolerating Zulma's farewell tutorial, which, more or less, went like this: You start with a base of welcome. Use their name if they give it to you, but not a lot because that's phony. They want to explain, you listen. Listen, listen, listen. Agree, like *mmm, uh-huhm, I'll be.* Save your breath, don't over-talk. Apologize when you're turning them down. Remember, they're feeling sorry for themselves—so have your sympathy ready to spool out like scotch tape.

"This is phone work," Zulma said. "But in person, you got all kinds of advantage, hear?"

Delpha said nothing. Zulma knew she was hearing her.

"You got eye contact, however you want to use it. You can touch 'em. Their hand. Their elbow, you know, nothing too friendly. You be careful about that." Zulma had been. Until the would-be model. Profile like James Dean, only his nose was chunkier. But his ears were better. James Dean'd had ears like an elf. "Hey, wanna hear her?"

"Hear who?"

"Cynthia."

"Thought I was hearing her."

"Not full force."

Delpha hung her head down over the bunk. She held on, her light-brown hair swinging upside down, while Zulma sat up crosslegged, said pleasantly, "Good evening, Beatrice Adcock Agency." She said, "Well, hello, Delpha" as to a friend, went on from there with a whole make-believe conversation: complimenting Delpha's photos but putting her off until the right shoot came up, saying Delpha didn't have to do a thing, they'd call her. It was all polite. But Zulma's contralto carried a startling current of connection, like maybe the girl-caller on the phone had a sister somewhere she didn't know about, and this was her. Smiling, making eye contact, Zulma reached toward the upper bunk. She squeezed Delpha's fingers, briefly, gently, leaving Delpha with the sensation she'd been promised something nice. A goosepimple or two tingled her arms.

Zulma hadn't looked like her usual, pinched, forty-six year-old self. Must have been Cynthia's smile that had, for a moment, lit up the bottom bunk like a fugitive moonbeam.

It was three or four years before Delpha really understood why Zulma-Cynthia's method worked. Wasn't the pitch of her voice. It was the need of the person she was talking to.

VII

RECORDS. THEY WERE going to search various records
to root out Rodney, and they agreed on this: their first order
of business was his house purchase. A phone call to Golden
Triangle Realty informed Delpha that each real estate
company kept only an account of their own sold listings.
Not other companies'. "No county-wide list, no city-wide.
Inefficient, you ask me."

"Shit." Phelan's head chopped downward. "They gonna
make us run around to every damn one. How many realtors
are there?"

Delpha's finger pecked through the yellow pages.
"Twenty-two agencies. Gimme a little bit."

After a while she entered Phelan's office waving a legal
pad. "Here's the realtors to call. I'll do that, no problem, but,
you know, it might be harder to brush off Mr. Tom Phelan
in person, you go in there with your pretty smile. A lotta
realtors are women. Lotta secretaries, too." Her eyes were
questioning, but the corners of her lips moved up.

She thought his smile was pretty. He'd save that for thinking
about later. He liked being out and about on the job, but twenty-
two chatty realtors meant he was sure to get trapped, and more
than once. Tom Phelan scrutinized his secretary.

"You know how to drive?"

"Got groceries for the Rosemont. Drove my landlady's old
Ford, Miss Blanchard's car."

"Legally?"

Delpha shook her head no.

"Well, get a license soon's you can. It'll be helpful for the business."

Faintly, she said, "OK."

The first time she'd driven a car after prison, Delpha had slipped into the driver's seat tingling-excited. Soon thereafter—terrified. Each and every car was a four-wheeled rocket-ship blasting along. Cars lunged out of alleyways. Cars gunned around her and swerved back in her lane, cutting her off. Cars honked past her. Slunk through stop signs, burned rubber at lights. Most folks would have considered the '55 Ford she was piloting a brawny automobile, but to her it felt mashable as a tuna can. Used to the lumbering of a heavy old bus loaded down with women, Delpha had forgotten the true speed, recklessness, and chance of motorized transportation. She had to pull over on the gravel shoulder and steady her head on the steering wheel between her gripped hands. Gave herself a talk. *Doesn't matter you're scared to death, it is only you in this car. Only you. Drive.* She'd put it in gear again.

Phelan signaled her, and they went downstairs together. Outside steam was masquerading as air, and the small parking lot to the side of the building was an archipelago of blacktop islands amid a rainwater-sea filling its ruts and dips.

"Guess this is it."

He paused by a dented, side-scraped '68 Dodge Dart, green or black depending on which side you were standing. Besides being Delpha's parole officer, Joe Ford was an old high school friend of Phelan's. He'd told Phelan he'd be dropping off a car this morning. Keys'd be under the seat. The Dodge belonged to Joe's wife's father, and it was supposedly in a garage for repair. In the last year, by the father-in-law's own grudging confessions, he'd hit several Godzilla potholes, sideswiped a couple parked cars, and rear-ended a cement mixer. Had the bruises and a concussion to prove it. The father-in-law had staggered into the Texas Department of Public Safety, where they'd extended his driver's license for four more years. Joe had swiped the keys, and instead of taking the Dart to a body shop, he'd left it for Phelan to hide for a while.

Phelan dropped the keys in Delpha's palm. "All right, I've got some phone business we can talk about later, and I'm gonna go eat. You take your lunch, too, and then—the realtors are all yours."

As he strode away, Delpha admired the back of his head, that thick hair, barely curling at the ends, and the long lines of his body, thinking how graceful the man was made. Then she blinked. Had there just been a change here, in terms of her job at Phelan Investigations?

Her turf, a steno chair and a desktop, a secretary office and a fat blue pillow sofa, had just enlarged to include a dilapidated Dodge and the city of Beaumont, Texas. Hadn't it? Mr. Wally that taught Business at Gatesville, was this what he would call "division of labor"? No—that was when you sewed legs all day while the girl next to you sewed sleeves. Still, she pondered this notion.

The car door creaked, reluctant at first, then *pop* flew open. She slid the key in the ignition and turned it. A rumble bloomed around her. *Uh oh.* Well, probably a lot wrong with this car, after all those collisions. Gash in the muffler, poor tuning.

Delpha turned into the Pig Stand. When the tray arrived at her rolled-down window, she tipped the sweating waitress and carefully papered her lap with napkins. She ate a hamburger, drank a Coke from a bendy straw while consulting her written directions.

Then she turtled the loud car around to the realtors' offices.

One owner refused on grounds of privacy. But the secretaries—if the bosses and agents were out with clients, which many were, they hardly let her finish her story. They passed over the Sold records like a pan of stale Rice Krispie bars.

Around quarter to five, she came to the home office of Kirk Properties, situated in a remodeled garage attached to a neat yellow ranch house with a porch swing. Strip of fluorescent light illuminating a mustard carpet, gray file cabinets, rows of Kirk Properties calendars on both walls going back twenty years. Each calendar featuring a woman in handsome middle age, softening and thickening until there sat the proprietor herself, sixty-ish, a dome of hennaed hair and powder in the cracks of her face. She was in greeting mode, her hands lightly clasped in the air over her desk like a catalog model in white gloves.

"Good afternoon, young lady. You and your husband in the market for a new home? I'm Nan Kirk, and I'd be pleased to help you find one."

Delpha said her name and politely asked if Mrs. Kirk kept a record of all the houses she'd sold in the past year.

"Well, I do,"—the woman peered into her face—"but what would you need it for?"

She was looking for a single man who was so mad at his family he'd moved and legally changed his name from theirs. She worked for Mr. Norville, the attorney of the man's father. That gentleman was ninety-three and not well. He wanted to reconcile with his son.

The hand model pose collapsed. Mrs. Kirk laced her hands against her bosom. "Well, family's all we got for sure in this world. What did he change his name to?"

A curl-tailed pug dog scrambled up into the woman's lap, craned its neckless head, and confronted Delpha with goggle-eyes.

"That's the problem, Mrs. Kirk. The father doesn't know."

"Now isn't that sad? I only sold two houses to single men in the last year, and one of 'em wasn't but twenty-four years old. Doesn't seem like his daddy would be ninety-three." Mrs. Kirk bent down and pulled out a lower desk drawer.

A side door flung open, causing Delpha to reel back, and a pigtailed teenager leaped through, singing, "Nana Nana Bo Bana, Banana Fana Fo—"

"Aileen, you idjit, this lady and I're talking here. Excuse yourself."

The girl's short pigtails were the color of a peeled sweet potato. They were cinched high on her head like a pair of foxy ears, the back of her hair fallen down from them. She wheeled toward Delpha, revealing a freckled nose and a bold chin, and stopped short. Either she'd been fooling with a makeup pencil, or she had two genuine beauty marks, one black dot under each wide green eye.

Mrs. Kirk had retrieved her Sold information and was gesturing toward Delpha's legal pad. Delpha held it out. The older woman copied down names and addresses, reading each syllable aloud, and then passed back the pad.

Delpha glanced over at the teenager. The girl had been gaping past Delpha, her forearm and an out-turned palm shielding her chest, but her arms dropped, and her eyelids fluttered, shutting away the beauty marks. She had gone motionless, her eyes fixed unwaveringly on Delpha, who asked, "Is she OK?"

Mrs. Kirk swiveled toward the girl.

"Oh Lord. She gets these…thoughts, ever once in a while. Aileen, go on back in the house and do your homework, honey."

"I'll be on my way," Delpha said to Mrs. Kirk. "Thank you very much for the information. Mr. Norville will be grateful."

"Huh uh. Huh uh now. You're kinda a sight, lady. But

to start off with, you're fibbing 'bout Mr. Norville." Aileen wafted over and grasped the side of Delpha's hand. The girl was talking in Delpha's direction rather than to her. She lowered her head again—the pigtails poked forward—and pressed the bone of Delpha's little finger.

"You saw the worst thing, didn't you. I can tell because I did once, for just a little bitty bit. I saw a man that had this black rim around him. Like the opening to a cave you wouldn't never, ever go in. Scared me to death. Hey, that thing's way far back from you now. You should keep it back there."

The pug dog hit the floor and pranced desperately around the teenage girl's bare ankles. "You just turned your head quick and saw it, right? That's what happened to me. On a man at the racetrack when Pawpaw and me went." Her head tilted. "Wait a minute. It came closer to you. Real close. You understand what I mean?"

Delpha had chilled, standing on the worn carpet with calendars of years on years on her either side. "Maybe."

A flushed Mrs. Kirk shoved back her chair, saying, "'Scuse us. My granddaughter needs a drink of water."

"I don't either." The girl squeezed Delpha's fingerbone and glanced at her face then, awake. "But listen, lady, that's not all. You really...you know you got this—"

"Aileen! Aileen, go on in the kitchen, honey. Now."

The girl huffed, dropped Delpha's hand, and grabbed up the begging dog. "Any-way. Nana Nana Bo Bana doesn't have what you came here looking for. That thing's not at our house, thank you, Jesus, Mary, and Joseph." She scooted through the side door rocking the pug in her arms.

Mrs. Kirk was still standing behind her desk, which Delpha read as a sign she should leave. She couldn't yet. "What'd she mean by all that?"

"Just one minute here. What fib did you tell me, Miss... what was your name?"

"Delpha Wade. I work for a private investigator, not a lawyer, and we're looking for someone, just not how I explained it to you. That was the lie. Your granddaughter see either of those single men you sold to?"

"I don't know. She's in and out the office. Listen, Aileen had some troubles in her little life 'fore we stepped in and took her away. Sometimes she makes remarks we...we don't understand what she means. That's nothing I care to discuss with a stranger. Now is there anything more I can do for you today?"

"No, thank you, Mrs. Kirk. I apologize for lyin' to your face." Delpha stuck out her hand.

"Well. Guess that's part of your business." Mrs. Kirk wrinkled her nose, but she shook hands, one businesswoman with another. When Delpha offered her a cramped smile, admitting, "Have to say that it is," the woman dropped the unfriendly expression.

Delpha's smile became fuller. Not a grudge-holder by nature, Mrs. Kirk.

"Truth is, I don't mind so much Aileen runs in and out of here. What am I doing so important? We've raised her since she was seven. Turn around, she'll be grown." Mrs. Kirk straightened some papers. "Her granddad and I discourage the funny thoughts Aileen gets. Scares him. Me, too. But that doesn't mean I don't believe her. She's been right too many times." Mrs. Kirk jutted her chin.

Delpha took that in. "Not judging, believe me. Knew a girl once could read a worried person's mind. But your Aileen's in a bigger league. Thank you, ma'am."

Mrs. Kirk's smile quavered with gratitude and dread.

Aileen was not drinking a restorative glass of water. The
rain had paused, and she was out in the oil-spotted driveway
peering into the Dodge. "I like this car, lady," she said. "Fast.
Is it yours?"

"No."

The red-haired girl's gaze passed over her. "Not fibbing
about that."

"No, I'm not. Answer me something, OK?"

Aileen skittered away from the car window into the yard.
Poked both sets of fingers into her tight jean pockets and
looked off across the street to where an optimist neighbor was
pinning wet sheets to a clothesline.

"If I can. But only if I want to."

"Fair enough." Delpha leaned against a fender. "That
black thing you were talking about. Was it on the man or
was it loose? Is that—can that black cave get on the inside of
people?"

"You did see it. I knew it!" Expressions tumbled over
Aileen's freckled face: satisfaction, vindication, a shudder.
The girl's gaze attached to Delpha. "Inside of a person? Man, I
don't know. Wasn't in you."

She stood for a good minute, eyes unseeing, nose up,
as if sniffing a patch of air that was a channel to the air of
everywhere else.

Delpha felt a mild jolt. Aileen reminded her of herself in
the hospital, lying still, gazing through the windows to green
treetops so as to leave behind pain and clatter.

The teenager turned to Delpha. "The point is, duh lady,
I wasn't *sposed* to see it. It was an accident. Now you, seems
like it showed itself to you." The smooth brow furrowed as
she stared, the emphasis of the double beauty marks startling.

"But, look, there's a…you know a little tiny girl's following you?"

Delpha didn't move. Softly, "No, Aileen, I didn't know that."

"Welp. Not now. But I swear she was there in Nana's office. Wore a little blue smock."

"Who is she?"

Aileen angled away as if to escape, and then irresistibly back again, so that she appeared to perform a rippling dance move. "I wouldn't know if you don't. Hey, you come again let me drive that car, OK? Friday I'm a get my learner's permit."

She twirled away. "Bye."

VIII

PHELAN HAD DECIDED that an hour or so spent on
Louisiana birth records might not be a waste of time. Might
provide a fallback in case the house search did not uncover
Rodney. By finding baby boys born two years apart in the New
Orleans area, 1898 and 1900; they could find the Bell brothers—
Rodney's real name, parents' names, maybe an old address.

Phelan hit up 4-1-1 to ask for the number of the Louisiana
Vital Statistics Office. After hearing his request, Vital Statistics
informed him he needed State Archives, which resided at the
Secretary of State's office. He duly connected with this office,
was transferred, and held while Louisiana Archives in Baton
Rouge searched out the proper clerk.

A voice like a trellis twined with honeysuckle identified
herself as Louisiana Archives and wished him a good morning
so fragrantly that September 10, 1973, rainy or not, became a
very good morning. Phelan gave her the name of his business,
his location, and said what he wanted.

The clerk interrupted his request: he wanted *wha-at?*
All Orleans Parish births for 1898 and 1900? Couldn't he just
supply her a surname? He was afraid he couldn't. *Ga lee*, he
didn't know this was gonna run him a arm and a leg?

State office. Why wasn't it free?

"Oh, honey. This is Louisiana. *Nothing's* free to Texas."

"All righty then. Tell me what I owe you. Who'd begrudge
you a dime, Miss?"

A laugh. "Watch out who you Miss-ing, Sugar-mouth.

I got eight kids. Listen, gimme your number, I'm on have to call you back just to tell you how big a check to send us. Gotta count the pages."

When Mrs. Louisiana Honeysuckle called back with the amount, Phelan jotted the number and squinted at it. Not a fortune, but sure seemed steep. He grimaced and, equipped with a Louisiana-addressed envelope, trotted off to the bank to buy a money order so they wouldn't have to wait for a check to clear. Shielded his head with newspaper on his run to the car, which took care of reading any unpleasant headlines about the White House today. Phelan slotted the envelope with the money order into a mailbox and skidded into the office just in time to catch the ringing phone.

On the line was the manager of Bellas Hess, a rambling store that aimed to be your one-stop shopping. Except it didn't sell liquor or food, so that threw a lot of its Beaumont, Texas customers into two or three-stop shopping.

High-ticket items—TVs, stereos, cameras, car tape decks, handguns, shotguns—were walking out of the store. It was happening at night, of course, they'd find the stuff gone the next day. Only the manager and the assistant manager carried keys, Ralph Bauer, the manager, told Phelan. Yes, they kept the keys with them at all times. Headquarters was planning on adding more security, fancier cameras and monitors, but the manager had seen one of Phelan's ads in the *Enterprise*, and he thought maybe they could fix the problem before the company went to that expense.

"Be real good if the problem got fixed fast," he said.

Ralph wanted it fixed on his watch, get a backslap and a head-rub from the company. Phelan understood that.

"Our current schedule's pretty busy, Mr. Bauer."

"Aw, now." The man pushed out a heavy breath. "I was hoping for quick."

"OK, I tell you what. We're waiting on some records, so I could work you in right now."

Silence. Then, a happier tone. "Hold on, lemme go check on something—"

Bellas Hess's manager came back on the line to report that, all right, the job could be started this afternoon. He was at the store right now in case Phelan wanted to see the lay of the land, so to speak.

Phelan'd been in Bellas Hess before. The land lay flat like every other big store he knew, a concrete plain broken up into corrals, each with a cash register and a minimum-wage captive. 1973's hourly ran to $1.60, been stuck there five or six years.

"Six p.m. is fine, Mr. Bauer," Phelan told him. Now he'd have a while to dream up the plan. He hung up, lit a cigarette, and plotted out the next few days. Then closed his eyes.

Two jobs going, and the first was, if not a piece of sponge cake, then simple—an earnest, stuffy old guy looking to be reunited with his slippery brother.

And Delpha was back. She was back.

Though he had almost lost her again on the very day she returned.

An hour after Bell's departure, the mail slot had clinked, and a couple of letters had dropped onto the floor. With a light step, he went and scooped up the two envelopes.

One white and windowed, one an unbroken expanse of luscious French vanilla. When Delpha's hand closed on them, Phelan had recalled that the mail was her job. He let go, then scanned the return addresses.

Gulf States Utilities. Griffin and Kretchmer, Attorneys at Law.

"Pay 'em both out of the account," he said.

"No sir. I'll pay this one." Meaning Griffin and Kretchmer. Which would be Miles' bill.

He looked at her. "You're *not* calling me sir?"

Without moving, Delpha seemed to resettle herself on her feet. "Didn't mean to *sir* you. I just meant that I really meant this bill was mine. Mr. Blankenship worked for me. *I* owe him."

"I called him. This was a contract between me and Miles."

"Contract is lawyer and defendant. Ask a judge."

"Defend—you weren't a defendant. You weren't even arrested. He's my friend, Delpha."

"He was my lawyer."

"My name on the envelope and—" Phelan covered her hand with his right one and slid the envelope away with the left. He tore it open and displayed the letter. "My name on the bill."

Uh oh, she rose to her full five foot six, her slender neck elongated and her chin curved down.

"We both know his time went for me."

"And we both know you were working for Phelan Investigations when it happened. But listen, aren't you...are you on the hook for a hospital bill, too?"

Her face went blank. "Joe Ford sent the hospital's Indigent Fund my parole papers. Now I get that he thought he was doing me a favor, and truth is he did. But he coulda asked."

She walked over to her desk, pulled open a drawer, and came back thumbing the pages of her miniature dictionary with the red plastic cover. Peering into it.

"First time I didn't have a lawyer because I was indigent. Wasn't no law then said I had to have one. Fact, there was a law said I didn't have any right to one. And you know what happened."

He nodded.

"'Indigent,' that isn't...the sign I wanna keep dragging around."

Phelan was beginning to feel like dog food.

She flipped the tiny pages around to him.

"See there? 'Indigent' means 'deficient in what is requisite.' And 'requisite,' if you look that one up—and I did—it means 'whatever is called for.' Isn't that some word? Requisite. Whatever's necessary. So 'indigent' means whatever it takes, you don't have it. People don't like people that are indigent, Tom. They think they can catch it."

Phelan surrendered the vanilla envelope. Lips pressed, he glanced over at her determined face and downward, to where the miniature dictionary blurted its judgmental words. He was not seeing it that way at all. Phelan's hand had fallen on her shoulder and, well, held it. A verification—on his part anyway—that on the day Deeterman came at her what was requisite was the blindest kind of will, and she had had that, and she was here now in one piece.

But her shoulder had tightened, and he had let go.

IX

DELPHA DROVE AWAY from Kirk Properties. She turned into an abandoned parking lot and sat, thinking about Aileen, balancing what she didn't understand against what she did: Aileen Kirk against Dolly Honeysett.

Dolly was eighteen when she came in, like Delpha, and not full of rage as Delpha had been, but full of guilt. She had answered her mother's screams for help by swinging a loaded kerosene heater at the back of her step-father's neck. If he'd been making off with his wife's purse or Pontiac, Dolly could have walked—by using deadly force to protect property. If she'd swung with less fright, if she'd just conked him, she'd have been sent home with her mother. But the man was only beating on his wife, not stealing from her, and in court the mother recanted. *Why, she'd never urged her daughter to* burn *George with the heater, she was a loyal wife, you ask any of her neighbors. George, he'd a been sorry later, bless his heart, he always was sorry. She certainly didn't mean for Dolly to set fire to him like she did...*

The Defense leapt howling onto his polished Florsheims and tried to sandbag her with her Grand Jury testimony, but the sobbing witness overran him like a hard rain overruns a ditch. The defendant sat stricken, her wide mouth downturned. Once the judge banished the sodden mother from the stand, the State of Texas went to town on Dolly.

Or that was the story.

Aileen Kirk looked nothing like Dolly Honeysett. Inside prison, Dolly's white, five foot one, pudgy body faded behind other inmates'. She occupied no fixed spot in the chow hall, only nomadic outposts on the peripheries. Her upper lip was long, her nose a small knob high above it. Her brown hair, rubber-banded into a rat-tail, started off the morning flattening a pair of prominent ears that soon fought their way to freedom. Who came in with Dolly Honeysett were three other women and the good fairy Glinda, and it was maybe six months before anyone put that together. Nobody wanted to, did they? Glinda, named by an early recipient of her magic, was a positive force in their unit of Gatesville, even if you couldn't see her. Because you couldn't see her. Glinda divined a need and delivered tokens to the poor in heart. These items were puny and a surprise and their juju all the stronger for that.

A woman whose parole had been denied slumped back to her cell to find just inside the bars, a Baby Ruth resting on the smooth surface of her special favorite, a banana Moon Pie. A month later, one going up for a parole hearing and climbing the walls about it discovered three packs of Luckys. Wasn't her brand, but the omen heartened her. Maybe a couple months after that, a laundry worker losing her looks and her grip picked up a squat pink bottle of Oil of Olay. A young one, twenty-three, worried about her ten-year-old son, explosive about her lack of telephone time, found stamps and three four-packs of envelopes. Write him letters? Well, maybe. If somebody would spell for her.

These were items anyone could buy at the commissary or receive from a relative. Not like a lacy negligee or a ride in a Cadillac convertible or an honest embrace. Something like that, though. This was all during—Delpha had to concentrate here—1965 or '66, when they got used to hearing that name, Vietnam, on the radio. When one of the Beatles said the four

of them were more popular than Jesus—didn't that remark
get some dedicated chow-hall discussion? The gifts went
on through 1967, the year that started off with the spirit of
dough-faced Jack Ruby whistling past the bars of Death Row.

Conversations about Glinda, like conversations about
lottery-winning, were pleasurable in themselves. The
speculation, the secret glances, the proposing and dismissal of
names. People started calling out to Glinda that they wanted
some Fritos and bean dip, some Dragon's Blood nail polish,
an ice cold Grapette, then they got crazy and wanted parole
and a Thunderbird car, a snuggle-date with Rock Hudson.
Women cried out for everything impossible. After an upsurge
of such craziness, Glinda did not come for a long time, and
speculation grew that whoever she was had left Gatesville.
Then she came again, and once that news had circulated,
people seemed relieved, content to hush-hush her name.

In summer, in the scorching middle of it—the coarse
white uniforms weighed like wet concrete on their backs
and thighs, and the news outside was that the pretty boxer
Cassius Clay, Muhammad Ali, could be headed for prison—the
warden summoned Mary Buell, a black inmate, so that two
Marines could notify her that her son had been killed in battle.
Afterward, a chaplain ministered to her in her cell. A funeral
could not be arranged until the body arrived, no certain time
was given, and there was no consoling the shrieking mother.

Had her son died in a car wreck or a forklift accident, her
lack of consolation would have remained solely her business,
and her shrieks the burden of her neighbors. But Ernest J.
Johnson was the warden then, a veteran who'd been frozen,
starved, and shot at a place called St. Vith, and when an
African Methodist Episcopal pastor in Temple volunteered to
hold an interim service, the warden arranged it. To Ernest
Johnson one thing only divided men more surely than skin

color, and that was *Semper Fi*. Two other inmates had sons in the Army, and a question meandered to the warden. Could the funeral service be opened to the unit?

Friends of the bereaved took the right-side pews in the stifling chapel, and white inmates, including the two other servicemen's mothers, filed into the left. One of those must have been a Catholic because she stayed on her knees the whole time, though there was no cushioned rail to kneel on. A Gatesville funeral home had donated fans, and these were passed out to all and gratefully used. Not until the pews had settled did the mother of the fallen Marine advance down the aisle in prison white, her face gleaming with tears and sweat. Mary Buell was supported by her two sisters, accompanied by the young soldier's teenage sister and his small brother. From the first step onto the chapel linoleum, there were wails and weeping and folding and contorting, thrusting arms and beseeching the Lord.

Looks passed among the inmates on the left side. Many of them had not seen black women freely carry on like this, it was a strange window they were seeing through. Ridicule rose up. Most swallowed it. One girl who sniggered took a swift elbow to the ribs. Though this greeting of death was different than what most of them were used to, they sweated in silence. A lot of women in there had sons. Didn't matter if they were two-year-old babies. Or six years old or ten. The white inmates saw a mother beset with the mother of all fears, and it had come-to-be, and they feared it for themselves. A moan broke out from the chapel's left side, mingling with those from the right. Then another.

Delpha had been to one funeral: her mother's. That was a tight-jawed affair. This was something else, but what? The black women and girl, the brotherless boy, made their way toward the altar as though barefoot on shattered glass, and Delpha distinguished two things: the suffering of grief and the expressing of grief. Both were real—she read that in Mary Buell's murdered eyes, in the sisters' clutching and entreating. The griefs were intertwined, as if Agony itself were crawling down the aisle, one bloody body with many arms and voices.

Afterward, when Mary Buell was escorted to her cell, she found just outside the bars a jar of the flowers that grew haphazard around the prison garden: milkweed. A gallon glass jar, de-labeled and buffed to a crystal sparkle. Its tin lid was poked with holes, the jar filled with a green leafy stalk sprouting purplish-pink florets. Mary picked up the jar. Jostled, a Monarch butterfly arched gold-red wings and flitted to another floret. An inmate heard Mary murmur that her son was found. She lifted her voice. Her Clayton was not lost in a foreign land, he had waked up in the mansion of the Lord.

To Mary from Glinda.

That was how they caught her. An inmate near the garden had been struck by the sight of a girl with a yard of cheesecloth, creeping and pouncing, chasing and swiping like a lunatic. She didn't know the girl's name was Dolly Honeysett, she called her "the one with the Dumbo ears."

Soon enough, some girls cornered Dolly. *Was she the one who gave people stuff? Was she Glinda?*

Dolly shook her head.

Hit on the shoulder she said,

No.

No.

No.

No.

Then *yes.*

Why on earth?

Dolly shrugged.

Why did she do that?

Backed up against a wall, she stammered maybe because it helped some.

Some what?

What did she mean, helped?

Helped what?

Well, because she had to do something to make up for misunderstanding her mother. For burning George's head. Her prayers were dry. The only thing she could figure to do was give something to another person who needed it. Certain people, it was just large in their face what they needed. After she left her offerings, Dolly had found that, for about as long as a kitchen match would burn, she felt clear.

There was no magic in this answer. Some people didn't understand it. Other people did. But nobody talked about Glinda anymore, not like when she was a mystery. Whichever sad people received candy or Lipton tea bags or pink Suave shampoo mumbled thanks to Dolly, and that was that. Until— wasn't too long after Otis Redding had plane-crashed, was it, Christmas, 1967—Dolly's trial attorney with the polished Florsheims, his legal vanity torpedoed by Mrs. Honeysett's image-burnishing perjury, assassinated the woman's character in a parole hearing. He managed to spring the obedient girl who'd swung the gas heater.

Goodbye, Glinda, goodbye.

Both Dolly and Aileen stuck in her mind, Delpha understood, because they saw things others couldn't, but Aileen craved the spotlight on herself while Dolly had shined it on others. Really, the girls were opposites.

Like Delpha and Isaac.

Back in the late spring Delpha had had a lover, a college boy mourning his dad. She'd unlock the Rosemont Hotel's kitchen door around eleven and let in Isaac. Him almost twenty, astonishing her with his open nature; her thirty-two, a wary ex-con—not that she told him that. What fiery nights they'd spent up in her room. They had gone slow, touching slow, had lingered learning each other's bodies. Other nights they were wild, pushing. Tall, a shade stooped, and crazy to learn, Isaac was in the flush of leaving boyhood. Delpha, lifting the floodgate prison had locked, had known that craziness, too. Until summer was almost at its end.

Last week, Isaac had sent a shiny postcard of what looked like the biggest brick church she'd ever seen. Princeton University.

Dear Delpha, You were right that I had to go back, the card said. *And you were wrong, too. I don't understand how that works, but I miss you. Isaac.*

She'd kissed the handwriting side and put away the card in the night table's drawer.

Delpha shook her head as a misty gust blew leaves across the vacant parking lot. Her hair brushing against her cheeks, she turned her mind away from Isaac, from Aileen, to the right now. See there—her blessed focal point: the line between treetop and sky. Then down, to a fan of broken brown glass on the cracked blacktop, the orange stars of sweetgum leaves. She breathed out. Placed her hands on the wheel.

Tomorrow either she or Tom would finish off the realtors' offices, then they'd have a list to work from—names of men who'd bought homes, and one of them just might be Xavier Bell's missing brother Rodney. What if Rodney wasn't on that list? Well, they'd try something else. Delpha sighed.

What you always do. She put the car in gear.

X

BY SIX O'CLOCK Phelan was out on the Bellas Hess floor,
selling cameras, tape decks, and televisions. He was boxed in
behind a little corral of a counter with a nineteen-year-old
named Ben. That night he'd sit in his dark car in a mostly-
deserted parking lot at a judicious distance from the back
door. That would be his post, in view of the loading dock. A
store security guy would cover the locked front door. The
manager had furnished them with a pair of walkie-talkies
from Radio Shack.

"How come you get to walk all over the store and Ralph
doesn't chew your butt?" Ben complained when Phelan
had rambled back into the corral from reconnaissance. The
teenager glared at him from Buddy Holly black plastic glasses,
hands planted at his waist where his hips would have started
if he'd had any. His black gabardines were staying up courtesy
of a workhorse belt.

"You're so sharp with the merchandise he can't spare you."

Ben's sull reduced a little. "Well, I tried to teach you."

Phelan stared at the kid. Ben went over to the other side
of the glass counter and polished.

Ralph the manager had introduced him to the staff. The
assistant manager Dean was a short, squat young man with
thinning blond hair and a dog-like expression. Ralph had
wanted to let him in on Phelan's role, but Phelan had shaken
his head no. There were girls and middle-aged women, both

black and white, behind the counters, and an old man janitor for spills. A food area where two bored boys speared hotdogs off a heat-lamp griller, and handed over potato chips and Cokes. A loud, friendly pharmacist in the pill house with a pretty girl out front ringing up the white prescription sacks. Phelan's guess was the stockroom, since they were the ones handling boxed goods, appliances, knowing the inventory, what was coming in. He'd have to make it back there. Meanwhile, Ben with the slicked-down hair was the only man on the floor proper. And it was easy to get him to talk about himself.

He was the next Ansel Adams, he told Phelan, looking for the impress-o-meter to register. The name rang no gong with Phelan, but he nodded anyway. Ben told him about a trip to Big Bend and all the boulders and wildflowers, jackrabbits and scorpions and sunsets he'd taken pictures of. He'd got an A in his Nature Photography class at Lamar College, and his teacher said some of his shots were good enough to sell.

"Ever take pictures of people? Action shots?"

"Sure. And print 'em. Got my own darkroom."

Phelan filed that info away while Ben enthused about his series of the Southeast Texas State Fair. Tattooed carnies, couples Frenching, kids with cotton candy stuck in their hair, teenagers freaking on the Tilt-a-Whirl. He was so wound up that Phelan had to step up to a customer and badly advise him on what camera to buy.

"No, no, this one's better," Ben cut in, demonstrating features until the customer backed off and pulled out his wallet.

Apparently soothed by getting to speak his piece to his new fellow employee, Ben turned to Phelan afterward. At length and kindly, he repeated the specs for every camera set out around the case and in it.

A sliver of Phelan's brain attended, the rest of it mapping out the employee in each station. At break time, he made it a point to wander past them, have a casual exchange. Smoked a cigarette with the stockers in the back, two black guys in mechanic's jumpsuits who had nothing to say until one of them noticed his missing finger. Then they worked up a brief conversation about one of them's cousin, a machinist who'd cut off both his thumbs last month.

Phelan winced.

The other guy hooked his chin and said, "Got to git back to work." His friend, shooting a glance at Phelan, ground out his cigarette on the stockroom floor.

The pharmacist, Ted Something, phone cradled between ear and shoulder, set out sacks like a short-order cook. Hung up and jawed Phelan's ear off with baseball predictions. No hope for old Yogi's Mets, even with Seaver and Mays; might be rallying now, but they'd choke in the end. Reds would skin 'em alive. Hotshot Nolan Ryan's arm wasn't made for the long haul.

"I don't know. Man's pitching a hundred miles an—" Phelan put in, but the pharmacist answered the phone again, scribbled, hung up, and started in on the player for his money, Pete Rose. Hank Aaron, well yeah, he was edging the Babe's record, but he'd choke, too. Streak would putter out. Guy was thirty-nine years old, staring forty in the face. And over the winter—

"Oh, c'mon, man, Aaron's almost to 715 now. Hit Number 711 already," Phelan said.

"Almost only counts in horse shoes and hand grenades. Now, that Pete Rose," the man planted a thumb in the air, "he's my darlin." Statistics spilled as he jiggled pills from jars into the little plastic canisters.

Phelan continued his tour. He didn't take pills, but if he did, he thought he'd get them somewhere else.

The rugged lady in Sports was knowledgeable about handguns in the case, also shotguns racked on a wall and fishing tackle. Set her trousered leg on a lower shelf and recommended lures: baby wrigglers, husky plunkers, underwater minnows bristling with hooks. She hefted a double-barrel to her square shoulder like she needed to hold off Housewares with it.

Housewares was Mabel, a fifty-five-ish saleswoman who wore her dyed, flat-black hair in a time-warp pompadour with sausage curls, platform shoes with a big painted toe sticking out the peephole, and a scalloped apron over her dress. Canteen girl from *The Twilight Zone*.

"Nice to meet you, honey," Mabel said, not shaking but patting the hand he held out to her. "Your wife likes baking, pick her up one of these Corning Wares with the blue flower decals. They're on sale."

The two boys penned inside the snack bar not far from the store's front door sleepily resisted conversation with anybody but each other. The chubby girl in makeup had her fingernails all painted different colors. Seemed to have a lot of visiting friends. Phelan bet she was throwing in freebies with the rung-up items, but that wasn't what he was there for.

After closing, he suffered Crandall, the security man, who was in lust with the walkie-talkies.

"Hey, Tom, your daddy ever sic a hound on you?"

"Hey, Tom, you ever go out with a girl had hair on her nipples?"

"Over and out, Crandall, less you see somebody at that door."

"Well, pardon my ass and 10-4 that."

"10-4 this, too. Don't move an inch till I come get you. In person."

Phelan sat there till four-thirty a.m., slouched down in his car a few yards from the only light pole behind the store. All was calm, all was bright. He had plenty of time to feel all right about Delpha having not quit to find a less murderous job. He already knew how he'd have felt if she had done that.

Only one alarm. A dark sedan, couldn't place the model, had driven into the parking lot, done a loop, and exited. The driver wore a hat. Phelan had the feeling, from the slow speed of the loop, that his lone car was of interest, but that was only a feeling. Maybe the slowpoke was lost.

XI

HE CAME IN late. Delpha, cheered to hear that Phelan Investigations had booked a second job, leaned toward him as he sat bleary-eyed on the corner of her desk, describing Bellas Hess's inhabitants, speculating on possible culprits. The manager had drafted a list of stolen goods, brand names, and models. By the way, had Delpha ever heard of Ansel Adams? Photographer of nature pictures.

She shook her head. "I've got more realtors to see. With both us gone, Tom, nobody's answering the phone."

"Can't help it. Don't suppose you found Rodney's house yesterday?"

Delpha's eyes narrowed. "No. And you didn't catch any thieves at Bellas Hess."

"That's a negative."

They looked at each other. Delpha shouldered her purse and headed downstairs to the Dart.

By quitting time she was back in the office, inserting the twenty-seven names she'd gotten from the realtors into a file folder. She printed on its tab *Homebuyers*. Swelled with satisfaction, she rolled some paper and carbons into the Selectric and typed it up. Twenty-seven homebuyers, and one of them could be Rodney Bell.

There wasn't a Rodney or a Bell on the list—but that didn't mean he wasn't here under a different name. Xavier Bell had been right to mention invisibility. Family trait.

Nothing more she could do today.

But Delpha lingered, her pencil doodling across a yellow pad of names. If *Homebuyers* didn't pan out, she would check out old New Orleans phone books and city directories at Tyrrell Public Library. And if they didn't find a shop that had had a proprietor named Bell, they would need to have another meeting with their client.

Then Phelan could ask him what kind of strange game he and his brother were playing.

She was only paid to answer the phone from eight to five, but a little extra time wouldn't hurt anything. Delpha climbed the few steps up to Tyrrell Public Library. Had been a church at one time, anybody could see that. Its windows were arched, the largest ones glorious stained glass: pictures of flowers, maybe, or shells, blocks of grass and sky and ruby shapes, a crown and a cross. The library drew her, and not just for the books—for the building, rough limestone blocks, a towered and turreted castle fit for a river king. Close behind the castle ran the slow brown Neches.

The pine floor creaked. She crossed the fan of late sunlight let in by the stained glass, picked one of the little paper slips. She searched the card catalog for a book by that photographer Tom had mentioned. Jotted down a call number.

A little shyly, Delpha went to see her acquaintance, Angela, behind the counter. This was another reason she liked the library. Angela had acted like Delpha's friend, someone Delpha wasn't assigned to as in prison, and for Delpha their interaction had been novel and pleasant. She steeled herself to deal with a change, but mini-skirted Angela either hadn't read the newspaper's police stories, or she had her mind set on higher matters.

She snagged Delpha's scrap of paper with the call number listed and turned it around. "Just a minute," she murmured, "lemme do a little job training here. That's Opal, and she's got a lot to learn." She pointed a frosted white fingernail at a girl built like a teapot, her little breasts stacked on top of a midriff-roll stacked on top of apple-round hips.

"See this call number? Find that book on the shelf. If it's not there, see if it's checked out, and if it is, then help her find another book by that same author. Or look on the re-shelve cart. Got all that?"

The girl nodded and disappeared.

Angela beamed. She was looking especially gratified, peppy, and notable this evening in a pink-and-orange striped, spaghetti-strapped mini-dress accented by a cloth blossom tacked to a strap. Sparkly royal-blue shadow from her eyebrows to her lids traveled on around her black-lined eyes with the spiky false eyelashes. Her orange, vanilla, rose-petal, honeycomb perfume transferred itself as if on a dolly across the front desk and tipped over onto the spot where library patrons stood.

"That's some perfume."

Angela smiled wider, extended the white fingernail again and tapped it in the air. "Ding dong, Avon calling. I'll be happy to put you down for one. It's brand new. Called Sweet Honesty."

"Maybe next week," Delpha said. She did not sound convincing, but Angela didn't appear to notice.

"Guess what." The royal-blue magnificences twinkled from within.

"What."

"Mrs. Samson's husband fell off their roof and broke his hip, and she went on and retired early. Now I'm sorry for that, but guess who the new reference librarian is."

"I'm guessing that's you, Angela. Good for you."

"Thank you!" She preened toward Delpha. "The reference job should have gone to Mrs. Tilly, but she likes sitting still on her special pillow, so it's mine. I get a quarter-an-hour raise, and when people call and ask questions, I get to go and look up all the answers. I mean, mostly I have to take their phone number and call them back. But then I tell them the answers." Her smile, aided by white, even teeth more than the champagne lipstick, was triumphant.

"You mean people could call up and get you to find out things without paying you a dime?"

"Yes sirree, that's what I mean. Delpha, honey, you could call any reference librarian in this country and they'd help you! But not with a ton of stuff. I'll help callers, but I won't do kids' homework for 'em." Angela swerved her head right, then hard left. Her spaghetti-strapped shoulders moved along, causing the blossom strap to droop. She hooked it back in place.

"Just like, say, who won the World Series in 1922 or…or whether there's albino polar bears. Like that."

"Lemme ask you something."

Angela looked charmed.

"So you mean…could you call up a reference librarian in some other town and have them answer a question? Say, a local question."

"A course! That's what I'm telling you. That's what we do. There's…there's a whole army of reference librarians out there—every town in America."

An army. This was something worth thinking about. "I'm glad you got the job."

"Me, too. It's an advancement. You interested in advancement?"

Six months ago, such an idea would have been a jeer. To advance, you had to have somewhere to advance to. Coming out of the prison gates, Delpha did not have a where. Now she had Phelan Investigations, and she had performed an outside-the-office search single-handed. Was that advancement?

"I don't know. What could *you* advance to next?"

Angela's finger crooked. Delpha leaned into the solid block of Sweet Honesty. One set of black lashes swept shut and opened again. "I wanna run this place," Angela said.

Hearing a heart's desire, Delpha warmed. "You like books that much," she said. "I knew somebody just like that once."

The royal-blue eyelids compressed. "Honey, what I like is *organizing*. Oops, here she comes."

Delpha read the spines of the books Opal offered and selected one. "I'll take this one with me."

Angela nodded solemnly. "All right. Next, ask the patron if there's anything else you can do for them."

The girl's eyes shifted to Delpha. Delpha shook her head.

"Opal," Angela said, "it's best if the words actually come out of your mouth."

Delpha left them to their training. She gathered her purse and the one big, flat photography book Opal had found for her. Glancing up, she saw by the wall clock that she was late for dinner. She hoped that the Rosemont residents had not cleaned the trough.

XII

PHELAN SNAPPED STRAIGHT upright in the front seat of
his Chevelle, deeply knowing that the black car he'd seen in
the parking lot the night before had been a Mercury Montego.
His second thought, hazier but pinching, was that he had
dozed off. The car now noisily beetling across the parking lot
was not that dark sedan—it was a white van that backed up to
the loading dock and cut its lights.

He walkie-talkied Crandall to call the cops.

To Crandall's excited *When, man, when?*, he said, *Now.*

Scrunched down in the seat, Phelan expected some crony
to exit the back door, having stayed behind at closing. But two
guys sashayed straight to the door and unlocked it with keys
one of them took from a pocket. He watched while one heaved
a large box out to the van. He shoved that inside, and then they
went back for more. Six boxes, and boxes meant the stockroom.
As they passed under the wall-light on the building, though,
the loaders looked white. No hurry, not pushing themselves.
When both of them disappeared through the door, one after the
other, Phelan slid out of his car. He had on a black t-shirt and
low tops and didn't make much noise as he loped over to the
van, jacked the keys, and stashed them in a front pocket. He'd
already scoped out a shadowed place between the end of the
dock and the building wall, and he hunkered there.

One robber plodded backward with a refrigerator slanted
on a dolly and the two wrestled it into the van, dolly and all.

The other robber went back in with a gym bag and after a while strolled out again, set the bag on the dock, and relocked the store. He turned, couple of gold chains around his neck glittering in the wall light, and drew out a handgun from the gym bag, long-barreled piece of work, maybe a S&W .22. Laid one forearm over the other and aimed the long barrel at his accomplice.

Adrenalized, Phelan flattened himself against the wall.

Did *not* think it was gonna go this way. *Absolutely* did not. His gun was back at the office. *Way to go, Tom. Way to quit Boy Scouts when you were eleven.* Phelan Investigations' abundantly un-foolproof plan had run along these lines: observe, get descriptions, a license number, call cops, report to manager, collect paycheck. No shooting.

The guy with the long barrel drew down on his accomplice. A second later, pulled the trigger.

The gun said, "Boom!" and recoiled.

The partner's hands flapped to his chest, then collapsed downward one at a time, like two gloves dropped off a parapet. He staggered. Lurched step by step over to the gym bag, pulled out another weapon, snubbier, maybe a .38. He drifted down to a crouch, wobbled, and shot the first guy back.

#1—in and out of the glow of light over the door— stumbled backward, ambled around, tripped and skudded to one knee. Fired.

#2 ducked as he shuffled a sloppy zigzag pattern, his feet stopping almost at Phelan's head, at the dock's end. He trudged in a circle for a few turns then lumbered forward. Sank onto the dock and rolled once lumpily, like a Long John donut onto a plate, hoisted himself up, and fired.

The first guy slouched over to him and on the third try nudged #2's .38 aside, and executed him. Muzzle to skull. Click.

Dropped his gun back in the bag, said, *Th'ow it in, man.*

The other guy tossed his, clunk of metal on metal. Flashes of a lighter. Red dots appeared. Holding the smoke, then letting out clouds that drifted toward Phelan, who'd known who they were soon as the gun said "BOOM!"

The snack bar boys.

After a while, one giggled. Then the other giggled. Two grand larcenists at leisure.

Phelan walked out of the dark and into Looney Tunes.

The two boys jumped. Red dots arced to the ground. One of them ran in place for a few seconds before his feet grabbed purchase and he leapt off the dock and scrambled for the van. The other, minimally more coordinated, snagged the gymbag and beat him to the passenger seat. Doors slammed.

Then the van instantly did not peel out.

Phelan leaned against the dock behind it and slapped a mosquito drilling his neck. Weird. His very first job, he gets scratched by a raccoon and has to shoot a cottonmouth water moccasin. This one, he sits on his ass and lets people catch themselves.

Stay in that van, he thought.

The driver's door flew open so violently it hit its extension and boomeranged back to crush the boy's leg. A loud *Fuck!*, and they both managed to break for it. Maintaining their genius status, the two didn't take off in different directions, the thing Phelan was most hoping they wouldn't do, but started an arm-pumping, high-kneed gallop shoulder to shoulder across the parking lot. They were not track stars. Phelan caught them in twenty yards, two fistfuls of t-shirt, clipped one and stepped on his back to make him stay down. With the other he traded t-shirt for neck and squeezed so tight the boy went limp.

"Hey man, you know. Hey man..." the one on the ground whimpered.

"Stay down on that pavement, Snack Boy."

The kid kicked listlessly at Phelan, no hope of reaching him unless his leg developed elastic properties. The one he had by the neck rallied to flail backward at him. Aided by beginner's luck, a heavy ring whacked Phelan in the mouth. The sorry dance went on for all of ten seconds, until Phelan put his weight on the downed one's back and head-locked the other one.

When the red whirlies screamed into the lot, they found a three-part still life. One flat boy, Phelan, and one dangling boy.

"Where's your gun, Ace?" a young, blond cop asked him after he and his partner, a black guy about the same age, had handcuffed the two boys and stuffed them into the cruiser. The partner appeared to be memorizing the P.I. license Phelan had presented them with.

Phelan might be bitterly berating his weaponless self, but that evaluation was for private consumption only. Hiking his chin, setting hands on his hips, he said, "Don't need a gun for boys."

The cop gaped at him. Little yellow hair-pagodas flared out from under the cap. "You kiddin' me? Gun works good with boys."

His young partner tipped a finger toward the blood leaking down Phelan's chin, snorted, then returned to the license. "Johnny," he murmured to the other cop, whose gaze turned downward.

Phelan swiped his chin with the back of his hand. Aiming to project a quality of helpfulness, he offered, "Here's the keys to their getaway. They left doobies up on the dock. If you're interested." He dug in his pocket and tossed over the van's keys. The cops didn't even try to catch them. They hit the pavement.

They were examining Phelan, shiny-eyed.

"I seen you before at the station," said the white one. "You're—you're Chief Guidry's nephew."

"Proud of it."

The partner handed Phelan back his license. Bent over and scooped up the keys. Shifted his weight, scratched his temple in a fakey way. "That woman that works for you…wasn't she the one took out the kid-killer?"

Phelan sloughed the appearance-of-helpfulness. "So what?"

The blond cop raised a hand. "Hey, we're just, you know, asking. But hey, right on."

The black one side-eyed his partner. "Yeah, *Right on's* all we meant."

Pagoda-hair jumped in again. "But look…did we…uh… hear something about that not being her first 187? Another one, you know, way before our time—"

"So?"

"Sergeant Fontenot said it's true."

Phelan wasn't saying anything.

"Aren't you kinda…you know, nervous? I mean, man, if she wants a raise, you better give it to her." The young cop's cheeks puffed, then flattened at Phelan's continued silence, but his face twitched with the strain of not laughing.

"My grandmother used to tell me," Phelan drawled, "if you can't say anything nice, don't say anything at all. I bet y'all's grandmas told you the same fucking thing."

Both cops nodded, the white one begrudgingly.

"Less y'all got a questionnaire for me to fill out, I'm calling it a night, officers."

They waved him on, slid into their car, and jet-reversed to the dock, where the blond cop bagged the doobies. Then the cruiser hauled ass with the snack boys. Phelan stowed away his license and headed for his car. His cut lip smarted.

He drove around to the front of the store, where Crandall flung himself out of his Pinto, steaming to know what had happened. Phelan obliged him with the long version.

The short version was he'd just paid off Miles Blankenship. Or would have, if not for Delpha's pride. *OK, let that go.* Short version was that Phelan Investigations was about to have some jingle in its pocket. And its proprietor was about to sleep the sleep of the righteous.

XIII

PRESSING THE LARGE book to her chest, Delpha hurried down the library steps. Way past suppertime, and she crossed her fingers there was something left to eat.

These days Oscar Hardy was running the kitchen for a vacationing Calinda Blanchard, owner of the Rosemont, and opinions were split on this temporary power shift. All laxness in the rules had disappeared—late-risers bemoaned the cutoff of coffee at ten a.m. sharp—but the revised supper menu included a certain number of fried chicken wings with cayenne in the batter, a sweet carrot and raisin slaw that had caused a tug-of-war, and, instead of the canned fruit cocktail and store-bought sugar cookies Miss Blanchard favored for dessert, there had once been *hallelujah* red velvet cake with cream-cheese frosting.

Delpha had a soft spot for Oscar. On the night of the afternoon she'd arrived back at the Rosemont—walking bent over in a new white blouse—he had room-serviced a generous portion of his mixed-fruit cobbler with the butter-crumbly crust. "I read the papers," Oscar said, standing at her door, "and it look like you sure had a go-round."

Tonight Oscar had a problem.

Serafin, the gimpy dishwasher, had allowed as how he liked working very much for young Señor Oscar, who hired him even though his hip was not good. Serafin liked Beaumont—no ice from the sky here, no cold wind. He had sworn he'd return in a month. He'd raised the oval medal on a chain to his lips and kissed it. His mother was eighty-three, and the Blessed Virgin would heal her or She would take her to live in heaven.

Oscar griped to Delpha about this while he stacked up the dishes and she quietly put together a plate from what was left of dinner: no cornbread fritters or coconut sheet cake—but there was ham glazed with brown sugar mustard sauce, julienned green beans, and buttered cauliflower with a squeeze of lime. Mouth full, she heard his sad story. In the morning he'd take Miss Blanchard's Ford and go down to the unemployment office where guys sometimes hung around, and he was not enthused. Oscar's opinion of dishwashers was that they were like cats, either lying down on the job or slinking away without warning. "Drunk cats." He scanned the dirty kitchen and swore.

She swallowed several more heavenly mouthfuls, scraped up a spoonful of brown sugar mustard sauce, hearing him grouse, doing math in her head.

"Serafin be gone a month?"

Twenty minutes and some instruction later, a rainbow broke in Oscar's smooth face as Delpha tied on an apron and jerked her head toward the parking lot door. He offered a reverent hand to his heart, snagged his fancy shades, clocked out, and inserted himself into an evening with unforeseen possibilities.

Delpha ran hot water in the double stainless steel sinks, sprinkled in flakes and immersed the dirty pots, the greasy skillets, and the cake and muffin pans. They'd soak. At the sink by the corner Hobart, she scraped the stuck-on food from plates and silverware into a garbage can she'd pulled up to the counter, racked the dishes on their edges, set cups and glasses mouth-side down, silverware in a flat rack, and sent them through the dishwasher. Scraped the next tub while these washed, stacked them. This job might do her complexion some good—all that steam—but apron or not, she'd get wet and smell like bacon grease and cooked cauliflower. The concession Oscar had made to her recent wound was to line up all the tubs on the long steel counter so she wouldn't have to lug them around, just do the job assembly-line fashion.

She kept the back door open to the breathy night, latched the screen door so the warm breeze ushered in a little bug and frog bass line. Oscar had a cassette tape deck he used in the kitchen, but right now Miss Blanchard's radio was entertaining itself up on a shelf. Muffled TV from the lobby. The Rosemont favorites were Lawrence Welk ("Lord God, more frightenin' than *Night of the Living Dead*," Oscar shuddered), Disney on Sunday, *Gunsmoke* on Monday until football season arrived which it already had. Mrs. Bibbo, an Italian widow, had whispered to Delpha that Wednesday's star, Kojak, a husky, bald detective sucking Tootsie Roll pops, was one sexy man. Mr. Nystrom considered *M.A.S.H.* unpatriotic while Mr. Finn the ex-doughboy liked it, so there was division on Saturday nights.

At the end of this week, Chef/Acting Manager Oscar Hardy would pay Delpha $35. She'd negotiated a little more than minimum wage, and he'd pay her in cash money, under the table. No payroll taxes to run up and be paid over to the IRS. And, unlike the crop of dishwashers before Serafin, Oscar could always locate Delpha. She could promise she would neither nod off into a pot of butterbeans nor tiptoe away with a waffle maker, leaving the back door ajar to alley cats.

Tomorrow Delpha would call up Miles Blankenship's law office and talk to his secretary. She would learn that Mr. Blankenship booked $80 hourly (she got $2, with her hard-fought deal with Oscar), and, including coming and going, the attorney had spent two hours and some with her down at the police station. The "coming and going" and the "and some" counted. A month of dishwashing, along with her small savings, would pay him off, and that was more or less the time Serafin needed to guide his mother safely off to the Mother of Jesus.

That would be tomorrow's serendipity.

Tonight she wiped her forehead on her rolled sleeve then racked more plates and saucers and those damn ramekins. Stopped a second to dial up the volume on the portable radio. Far as Delpha could tell, the DJs played the same songs over and over. That organ-grinder *Tie a Yellow Ribbon* song started up, about the wife tying yellow ribbons all over an oak tree so her husband out of prison would know she wanted him back home. Delpha's eyes slitted. For sure, it was more likely to be a wife than a husband tying those particular ribbons. From reports she'd heard, which were 100 percent from women.

Should she want advancement, like Angela? Anybody would say she was the low person on the totem pole—but whose totem pole?—washing dishes, worst job at the New Rosemont Retirement Hotel. Is this how she'd seen herself after prison? Truth was, she had no one clear vision from those years, mired in boredom or anger or frustration, complaints swallowed, lack of hope. Waiting so ingrained that it seemed she waited to hope. Or had only fuzzy hopes. Get this, go to this, do that, end up better if she could. End up with something of her own, whether that be a safe place to live or a man or a child or faith or the ordinary regard of people who would come to know her. At different points during fourteen years, she had spent time trying to construct a picture of each of these. And more than a few nights hollow-bellied with terror that she might find nary a one and have to keep on living.

She'd had one vision: Never go back.

She hadn't, had she. So far. But it had been close, and the price had been high.

Each tub of dishes run through. Blasts of steam. Her hair plastered to her neck. Tub of clean, hot white crockery. Knives and forks and serving spoons. Let 'em cool before stacking in place.

She turned off the lights except for the pull-chain fluorescent over the sink. Stretched tiptoe and dialed till she hit Aretha Franklin singing *Do-Right Woman, Do-Right Man*, scrubbed up the grill, wiped down the counters, swept, and fetched the mop and bucket. Mopped and wrung. Prodded her no-longer-sore incision. Then she snapped off the radio and stood for a while in the clean.

She was not alone in this brick building. Maybe, all-told, twenty-five souls were tucked into this old place. But she was alone in this wide room, and she pretended. She pretended the side door to the parking lot and the door into the kitchen from the lobby sprouted iron padlocks, she pretended that all the retired people were upstairs in their beds dead asleep (though some wandered, some sat late in the lobby under a white-shaded lamp). She was pretending so that she could feel even more private. Felt nice, didn't it?

One blip of unease: would this pretending be good long-term? Was that a little like wishing yourself back in jail? She didn't know. For now, it was enough to know that the screen-door hook was latched on her side, no intruders. This wide, black-and-green checked linoleum floor was empty.

After she untied the apron and folded it, she stood in the big dim room feeling, unexpectedly, how slight a space she took up. How easy bones break and flesh tears.

She glanced toward the screen door where the skim of a darker shade passed. She flashed to Aileen and her pronouncement about the tiny girl in the blue smock. Delpha walked over and peered through the screen—no ghost-child out there, only night. And the trill of insect-song, a September breeze now entering into Oscar's orderly kitchen.

The black outline that had frightened Aileen—Delpha had known what Aileen was talking about. She'd seen it around the rims of the big man's eyes, seen it catch and kindle, spread to the center. Deeterman—Delpha had handed over the book he asked for, told him he could go. She would rather have been any place that day than there in the office of Phelan Investigations. If she hadn't done what she did, she'd a had to stand there and let him kill her, and that was the truth. The death they'd brought her down to the police station to explain, to judge her for—cops were always the first judges—that man had picked it. Decided the place for it, decided the time. She was there. He was who he was, she was who she was.

Delpha searched for guilt, and unlike Dolly Honeysett, she didn't find it. If that made her different than other people, then that's how it was.

XIV

RALPH BAUER, THE manager of Bellas Hess, was edging fifty, bloodhound face, but his graying brown hair had a cowlick back of the crown. He scribbled out a check, which Phelan folded into his jacket pocket.

The manager caressed the tie tack stuck through an exhausted blue tie.

"Bobby and Pete from the snack bar, huh?" Ralph sat down. "Can't ever tell, can you. Pete was an Eagle Scout."

"I was hoping it'd be Mabel from Housewares," Phelan said. "More interesting."

Ralph gawked at him. Phelan smiled.

"Oh. Yeah, she's that, all right. Candice!"

A girl waltzed in the door.

"Call in an ad for help at the snack bar. Then you go work it today."

The girl's eyes, bordered in one black line topped by a white line, widened into two little targets. "Aw, c'mon, Mr. Bauer, I got on my new dress." The pale gray dress was one of those tent ones girls were wearing; it stood out around Candice like a tin funnel. Ketchup and mustard, Phelan thought, might brighten it up.

"Go borrow Mabel's apron."

"Yuck. I don't want Taboo reeking all over me."

"Then splash on one of those samplers from makeup. We got to pull together now. You know what that means, hon?"

"Means I got to work the snack bar."

"Kids," Ralph said when Candice had flounced away. "When I was a kid, I couldn't get to work fast enough. Put two dollars in my mother's hand, I was king of Tyler County. But now it's everbody for hisself and hell with the rest. All the way to the top. That Watergate gang running the country, they held the truth under water till it run out of bubbles."

He took a long breath and looked up at Phelan. "Put it off long as I can. How'd they get in?"

"Keys," Phelan said softly, feeling sorry for the man.

The hound dog eyes sagged. "Keys. So it's Dean, my assistant manager. Me and Dean's the only ones with keys. And I'd've sworn on a stack of bibles about him."

"Not necessarily. I'll continue the investigation if you want, but you might save yourself a dime or two if you inventory the pill department. Your pharmacist, he's a live wire, isn't he. And the snack boys, they were on thirty-three rpm. Like chasing down spaghetti."

"Wait. Yeah. Ted mighta had the keys once when Dean was sick. Forgot about that. Oh God." The manager propped his forehead in his hand.

Phelan suggested Ralph Bauer call his headquarters and report that the situation was under control—and in only three days. That brightened Ralph some.

"Pill department comes up roses, you call me back. But Mr. Bauer, I'm betting you got this one licked. You let me know, you hear?"

Ralph Bauer called later to let Phelan know the pill department had not come up roses. Headquarters was happy and that was good, but the scene with Ted the ex-pharmacist was not one he wanted to live again. He thanked Phelan for his help. If he wanted to come by for a hotdog and chips any time, it was on the house. Oh yeah, and here was the home phone number of Ben from the camera department. Did Phelan have a pen?

He had to locate the kid in a dorm out at Lamar College. He spoke to a groovy young man behind a desk that had behind it a wall of pigeonholes with notes stuffed in the little boxes. The guy picked up a phone.

Ben flew down some stairs and, seeing Phelan, pulled up. The kid folded his arms and slouched hard-eyed behind the black-framed glasses, one joint of which was bandaged with electrical tape. Apparently, he judged that Phelan had made a fool of him.

Phelan omitted a greeting. Just told him, speaking soft enough that Ben had to inch closer, his real profession. Asked Ben if he wanted to develop pictures for his private investigation business. Phelan would pay the going rate. He didn't know what that was, but bet Ben didn't either.

Ben unthawed some at the word "pay." So…would Phelan have a job for him any time soon?

As a matter of fact. Did Ben have a car?

Ben nodded.

He have a zoom lens?

"I could borrow one."

OK. He'd need to find a quiet spot where he could survey sightseers in the bird-land marshes in the area. Make the rounds, there was more than one of them, but specially High Island and Anahuac. Phelan wanted Ben to range around out there, take some nature pictures. Pay attention to any elderly male birdwatchers. Nothing dangerous, ordinary stakeout except he didn't even have to hole up in a car. He would just play himself, a photographer.

At "stakeout," Ben's standoffish arms had fallen loose to the sides of his Dennis-the-Menace livery—striped t-shirt, cut-off jeans, black socks and sneakers. A preliminary glow settled into his eyes.

Phelan would pay minimum wage for the watching, same as Bellas Hess, but, as he'd mentioned, the going rate for the pictures. All photos had to stay private. Did Ben understand discretion?

"Discretion" stood Ben's pecker up. "Could I use black and white film? It's the best."

"Less there's a reason not to, use it. Like Ansel Adams. You know, Ben, this stakeout might take a week, might take two, more. Might have to miss some classes—"

"I don't care. My dad's making me major in accounting. I'll do it."

The kid seized Phelan's hand. He wrung it like Phelan had hauled him from a bayou full of benzene.

Phelan knew who Ansel Adams was now. Delpha had left a big rectangular library book on his desk. When he'd got around to it, he brought the heavy book to her desk, so they could both see what Ben had been talking about.

She leaned into the pages.

Sure enough black and white, as Ben had described. Craggy rocks. Twisted trees. Rivers. "Could be a cloud spilling down that mountain," Delpha pointed out, "'stead of a waterfall."

They leafed through several more photographs.

She traced a finger along the curve of the Snake River. "All these places and no people anywhere. Why these pictures look perfect, isn't it. One perfect picture after the next, and people'd throw the whole thing off. You think...when he put away his camera, he sat on the hood of his car till the sun went down, just him and the mountains?"

Phelan had raised his head and lowered it. They turned the pages, water like clouds, clouds like mountains. A river smooth as the last highway you ever want to drive.

XV

"GOTTA BE A mistake." They sat side by side in the Apollo
White office, receiving the mighty sunlight of the day. Phelan
stared levelly at the heap of papers in Delpha Wade's hands.
"Told her the years 1898 and 1900."

Delpha looked sideways at him. "You tell her not to send
more than that?"

"Well, I...no. I mean, I told her those were the years
we wanted. Didn't say anything about other years. Order a
Chevy, you don't tell the dealer not to send a Ford."

"Says here these birth records were compiled by the
Orleans Parish Volunteer Association in 1970. Bet they're
a nice bunch. And since we didn't have a last name to give,
Louisiana Archives sent you the whole shebang. You're
looking at a kindly favor, Tom."

Phelan shut his eyes and bracketed them with his hands.
"Do the math, OK?"

"Already have. Hundred and nine years' worth. Of
babies."

The copies spanned the years 1796-1905. The sheer
number of pages recording the births in Orleans Parish, the
thickness of the stack, caused Tom Phelan and Delpha Wade to
behold them silently.

"When I told Bell this was a heavy research case," Phelan
said, "I didn't mean this heavy."

"We don't need to go through all those pages. Look, if

you're seventy-five today, in September of 1973, then you were either born in 1898 or late in 1897, right? Same thing goes for Rodney. 1900 or late 1899."

"I don't know, Delpha. My idea, but it seems pretty far-fetched now. I was planning to start checking out the homebuyers on your list."

"Sure. You go on and do the homebuyers. I'll take the babies."

Phelan's head lifted. "Wait a minute, ding," he said. "My uncle E.E. grew up in New Orleans. Wish he still talked to me."

Delpha got up and dragged the client chair back to its designated position, across from Phelan. "His mama still around?"

"Yeah, she is. Why?"

"Talk to her. More details, more gossip. Ladies soak that up."

Phelan brightened. "Then I'm not asking him directly, am I?" He stood up. "'Scuse me."

Delpha went back to her desk while he closed his door and made the call. Fontenot put him through with neither greeting nor comment.

"Well, if it isn't my nephew Judas."

Phelan plunged ahead with his question.

E.E. cut him off. "You want some noise 'bout a old time antique seller in New Orleans? Down the quarter? What for you aksing me to do your job? Bringin' in that lawyer, you coulda made mine harder."

"And for that I 'pologize again. Not my intention. But... what I'm wondering is if you'd mind me calling Miss Estelle to ask her for any stories about those shopkeepers. Old folks know stuff."

"You wanna call my mama—merde!" E.E. shouted, and there was a sharp rap, just like a diamond ring punching a wood desk.

Phelan's heart stuttered. "Listen, E.E., how many times I have to say—"

"Yesterday's her birthday. Yesterday, damn it, and oh, she fuss when I missed it before. Man oh man…what is it you want again?"

Phelan told him as he let out lungfuls of breath, stealthily.

All right, E.E.'d phone her—only because of the birthday—and also so he'd have an excuse to be late for the Lions Club lunch. Maybe miss the speaker. His mother would know somebody that knew somebody that knew something, and he could guar-on-tee they would all be old-time.

"What about if they're dead?"

"Far's Mama's concerned, dead people's even betta."

Slam.

Phelan softly set down his receiver, stretched out his jaw and his neck. After a while, he got up and opened his door again, to let in some air same as the air in his office.

"He's not mad at you anymore?" Delpha asked him. "For the lawyer?"

"Naaah," Phelan said. He crossed his right middle finger over his index, signaling just how tight they were. His eyes were cloudy. He looked tired.

"E.E. told me once that I should know who I was, and if I had to fight somebody I should know who he was and if I did, I'd be OK."

She waited. He raked his fingers through his hair.

"So?"

"Far as the Bell case goes, all I know is who I am."

"Did a fast, good job at Bellas Hess, Tom."

Phelan turned to her, the statement like a stray fifty winking from a sidewalk. He got why Delpha's voice had unthawed Bell—warmth or regard or whatever it was the old guy felt when she spoke to him—it was not something Bell often encountered.

Delpha was staring down on the babies. Phelan walked over and read over her shoulder. After they'd both run their gaze over the second sheet, and the third, they looked at each other and smiled.

The break was this: births were organized alphabetically by surname of the married couple. Regardless of the birth year, all of a couple's children appeared under their parents' names, stacked one on top of the other. At a glance you could see that Lucia and Salvatore Marchetti had produced Domenico, Vincenzo, Anna, Andrea, Stella, Giuseppe, and Giuseppina over a period of sixteen years. Gender, color, birthdates. Phelan Investigations didn't know the surname, but they knew the years. Not difficult to ignore the unqualified and circle Moms and Pops making babies at the turn of the twentieth century.

"So why'd we get this first page? It's from the 1940s." Delpha turned it over, read out the note scrawled on the other side. "'I have always enjoyed talking to gentlemen with baritone voices. That's how I got eight kids.'" She looked up. "It's signed *Yours Cordially, Mayella Singleton*."

"Mrs. Louisiana Archives." His ego petted unexpectedly for the second time in one day, Phelan perked up. He gave the stack to Delpha, who picked up the heavy Selectric and set it aside. She lined up her pile, opened her desk. Phelan didn't know when she'd bought a ruler, but she had one.

He pocketed the carbon copy of *Homebuyers* from the folder on her desk. "I'm gonna go see if E.E. talked to his mama, then get a bite and go find out who these guys are."

"You know, you could wait till I finish the babies and find out who all's on both lists. That'd save you from having to run down twenty-seven people."

"Or I could find Rodney tonight, and you could shitcan the babies."

"Yeah. Like that idea better, I guess."

"Thought so."

"Isn't there a ballgame tonight?"

"Saturday afternoon. How'd you know I like baseball?"

"All your newspapers get folded to the baseball page. Like all Mrs. Bibbo's—you know, the old Italian lady over at the Rosemont?—hers get folded to the Watergate stories."

His head tilted to the side, he looked at her a second. "Don't imagine I'll finish twenty-seven homeowners tonight. If I don't, you can help me tomorrow. When you finish the babies." He grinned. "That beat-up Dodge drove OK for you?"

Delpha nodded, turned her gaze back onto the Louisiana Archives. Phelan clattered down the stairs. Footsteps halted. Clattered upstairs.

He told her to please lock the door when he wasn't here. Keep it locked. He'd ask Milton the dentist/landlord to have his handyman Calvin install a peephole and a bell. Tomorrow. Milton didn't, he would.

"Security," Phelan said to her stare. "Make me feel better."

XVI

PHELAN CHECKED IN at the station with a young desk
sergeant. Not Fontenot, who must be either lodged in the john
or home marinating pterodactyl wings in onion, garlic, and
crushed red peppers. Allowed past, Phelan tracked down his
uncle at his desk. He just couldn't leave it alone, could he?

E.E. raised his head and looked at him like he was a bell-
ringer for the Salvation Army.

Phelan located his gaze on the floor, so as to respond in
a humble fashion, and asked if his uncle had had a chance to
make the phone call to his mother.

"I did. You know, I'd forgot that at Christmas-time, she
used to work gift-wrapping at some shops in the Quarter.
She loved that pretty paper. And she loves talkin' bout those
shops." E.E. smiled in spite of himself. "Oh, that make her
happy, talking 'bout annés passés, I tell you what. Been a long
time since I heard Mama laugh like that."

E.E.'s smile felt like a break. Was funny how some people
didn't get themselves, wasn't it? Talking to E.E. made you
smile back, laugh, feel a little yank below the breastbone
cause you wanted to be with him or be like him. Phelan
didn't have to stretch to understand that his uncle's mother
was jubilant to have her son on the line for as long as she
wanted, for once.

E.E. had prompted her to remember the shops that sold
old stuff—pistols, swords, rare coins, furniture—not dago

fruit-sellers, no, Mama, not artists with funny clothes or painters with splattered ones, teashops, and all the food, oh the cafés, *cher, les restaurants...* He did a creditable and fond imitation of Mrs. Estelle Guidry, who had recalled merchants with relish, if not precision. Here and there he broke into French and Phelan hung on best as he could. Belatedly, he drew out a notepad.

Well, she had a personal friend, Miz Smith, who ran her shop down there for years and years, sold heavy furniture from estate sales and estate jewelry, pictures in gilt frames, and what all. Bless her, she passed this summer, but long time she'd been retired. So nice... Nother sold coins and swords and such, he had a son came back from the war with medals, the other war...she couldn't remember the daddy's Christian name. Mean old pot-bellied man wore his trousers too short...come to her in a minute. There was Mr. Wertman, the Jewish fellow. Then there was Georges Athene the bachelor, ooo wasn't he a rogue, chased after the married ladies, run a mile from the single ones. Anton Hebert, now she had been a friend of his wife, Eugenie. His first wife. He had a second one, too, Vera, at the same time, and neither wife ever made a fuss 'bout the other. Did good business, Monsieur Hebert. Les marchands, didn't they all love money, though?

His mother had had to hear about the grandchildren for a good while. When they finally got back on the topic, she lamented the number of shops that now sold ticky-tacky tourist junk. She added that two of the old shops, Mr. Chamberlain's and Mr. Hadfield's, were still in New Orleans, run by the children now. One other, Mr. Wertman's, had moved away somewhere, maybe during the war, after the war, around that time, to Texas, to Beaumont, she thought, where E.E. was. One poor soul had hung himself, but he ran a tailor shop. She asked him if he wanted tailors. And when he was coming home for a visit.

E.E. came out from behind the desk to hand Phelan the sheet of Beaumont Police Department notepaper *Dedication Integrity Honor* with five names scrawled on it. "Here you go. I got work to do." Then he cut off the blood flow to Phelan's brain by squeezing his neck with one thick arm.

Phelan hugged his uncle back.

He light-footed it back to the office to find Delpha still there, told her he was going out again shortly to pursue the homebuyers. He ripped out his own note on Mrs. Guidry's memories and stapled it to the police notepaper, handed both to her and started for the door. Half-turned back.

"Don't lose it," he said, just to watch her roll her eyes. He was rewarded.

Delpha Wade would not lose a paper, he knew, she'd install it in a file folder, label the folder, and place the folder alphabetically in the gray file cabinet. Going down the stairs, Phelan felt a pang, funny and not. If he were to make a list of all the things that to him meant freedom, office supplies would not be on it.

XVII

AT NOON, DELPHA unwrapped her pimento cheese sandwich, sliced tomato sprinkled with salt and pepper, bread and butter pickles. She ate and sucked her fingertips, then went over to the Rosemont, snagged some napkins, and bought an ice-cold Coke in a bottle. Oscar took her money, reminded her, *Bring it back, hear*?

If Calinda Blanchard had been in there running the kitchen, Oscar wouldn't have cared about the deposit on any Coca-Cola bottle. Delpha could return it to its wooden case of empties, or she could blow it to pieces with a pump shotgun. Add the bottle to Oscar Hardy's watch, though, and he would hunt you down for it.

"Miss Blanchard's loving you," Delpha said, smiling with one side of her mouth.

"I'm loving me," Oscar said and dropped her quarter in the petty change box.

"You after advancement, Oscar?"

He fixed her with a serious look. "So I'm keeping track of food costs, so what. It's what a chef does. And knowing that—that's initiative. You hadn't had any chance of that, where you been. But dig it. How much opportunity you see at the Rosemont?"

"Miss Blanchard's past seventy. You could manage the place for her. Fulltime."

"You sound jus' like my mama. *Jus'* like her. Listen here,

Miss Blanchard die, hotel get sold, probably tore down, and I'm on the pavement without a Thank You card. You know how many fancy restaurants they have in Houston?" Oscar pivoted around to the counter, reached over his mirror sunglasses and perched them on his nose, showing Delpha her distorted reflection in emerald green. He struck a proud pose. "'The future belongs to those who prepare for it today.' Malcolm X said that."

Delpha cocked her head.

Oscar's pose deflated as he laughed, "You look like that RCA dog in the old-timey advertisements. And, hey, that saying's not for you, hear? Just something I'm thinking 'bout. I mean, I am twenty-*five* years old, and I got my future glasses on. The New Rosemont Hotel is not in their forward view." He set the shades back on the counter. "Pork tenderloin for dinner. Sage, bay leaf, little clove. Best not miss it."

That's not for you. Not for you.

What's not for me? Future glasses?

Delpha drank the Coke stretched out in her office chair, ankles crossed. Odd that of the young people she knew best—though she didn't know either well—both Oscar and Angela were focused on getting ahead. So was Phelan for that matter, or at least focused on his business succeeding. At thirty-two, older than all of them, she found getting ahead was kind of a complicated idea. Theirs was not the angle she was seeing it at.

She'd known a number of women on the inside who had focus. Just not your regular one. Their passions did not lead to advancement. Maybe to...headway.

During the time Delpha had worked the prison's infirmary, anybody sick enough to need a surgeon got carried out to a hospital. A new girl on kitchen duty drenched herself with a sixteen ounce bottle of vanilla extract and fed her sleeve to a gas burner. No infirmary for her, took her straight from the kitchen floor. Infirmary dealt with less terrible injuries: sprained ankles, black eyes, strep throats, lacerations, bites, infections, flu. Also hopeless cancers. If a hospital could do nothing for you, no reason to charge the state. You passed in the infirmary.

An inmate named Fayann Mackie had developed breast cancer sometime in 1962, had had her breasts cut off in a hospital and been brought back to Gatesville aching and scar-chested, with a couple falsies in her bag. Her mama had passed from cancer and her Nannie and already two of her four aunties, and she harbored no pretty dream that old Raw Bloody Bones would skip her. Delpha nursed Fayann during her recuperation. She got better but could not go back to hauling around wet sheets, not with missing chest muscles. They sent her to the library, where she sat titless and sullen, until she pulled down a handbook of anatomy from 1930 and began to leaf through its pictures.

The illustrations that had skin were white people, all of them, but most illustrations had no skin. Underneath, the bones and veins and muscles were shades of gray, black, and white. Fayann recognized that these pictures also applied to her body, that her bones and veins and muscles were placed in this exact, same way.

She had a ball of pure bone in her shoulder. Her muscles over it, beneath the skin, were long thin stripes. In the drawing of the whole skinless arm, the muscles looked loosely braided and tucked, tied together like a white woman's hair.

Some illustrations in the book shocked Fayann. Drawings showed half a person as though sawn through. There was the side view of the middle of a man, an egg in clear sight inside the one ball, his limp talleywhacker with a stripe down it that ended at the hole. Bone endings looked like Fig Newtons. A brain was missing. A man angled back his head and offered his throat, skin peeled away to reveal tubes and spidery veins.

The chapter "The Female Organs of Generation" transfixed her. There it was, the slit drawn large with curly hair like black flames and the outside parts labeled. Another illustration displayed the sawn half of a woman. She oriented by the exterior: a curve of butt to the right and the springing bush at the left, but the inside was foreign shapes, packed, stacked, and folded. The scratched-metal shelves of books surrounding the librarian's desk lifted, rotated in a dizzyingly slow, full circle, and set back down.

Her womb was a thick, folded pancake, hers, Fayann Mackie's.

She was helping another inmate locate a romance novel when a guard strolled by her desk, where the anatomy book was opened to "The Hymen." Five slits, each differently patterned in its center. When the guard deciphered what he was seeing, he chokingly confiscated the book on grounds of horror, the assistant warden pinning on the charge of obscenity. This warden ordered a survey of the library after that, and that book was thrown out, but it was too late. Fayann found another book. She could barely interrupt herself from her own book to stamp yours. She abandoned her path of surly hopelessness and climbed up onto the hard dirt of a divergent road.

The books with romances showed her feelings she knew, acted out in fancy houses she didn't. It was the feelings that mattered, not the houses. Business books and *Nancy Drews* were dull, Fayann set those back. Slow going, but she read the one where the man got the poor girl pregnant and then drowned her so he could marry the rich girl. Maybe she hadn't seen outright murder in that situation, but she had known plenty girls left in the dust for a whole lot less than a rich daddy. She was about to re-shelve *Tarzan of the Apes* because of the author's running off at the mouth when she got to the sentence that said Lord and Lady Greystoke sailed to Africa. About Africa she was curious, so she kept on. Then the captain beat the old sailor, and the little old sailor's huge, fierce friend, Black Michael, beat down the bully captain, and Fayann exulted, hooked. When she finished *Ann Frank: Diary of a Young Girl*, she cried with her forehead against the cell's block wall, for wrongness and for waste that could not be measured. And for herself.

The cancer resurged in 1966, and Fayann's tough, folded pancake was removed, and more. Delpha, who'd rotated through the kitchen during '63 and '64, was again in the infirmary. She cleared Fayann's drainage tubes, cleaned her incision, supported her to the bathroom, and stayed next to her as Fayann, hunched and talking, crept around by sliding the flat of her hand along the infirmary wall. Talked to Delpha, to other inmate patients, to the walls. Well before then, Fayann had been set afire by a scuffed book from 1901 titled *Harriet the Moses of her People*. She'd paged through two decades of donated *Book of the Month Club's* to hit upon the one story called *Black Boy*. There it was—the everlasting meanness and scorn, the being held down, the doing what you have to, the hunger.

The hunger, Fayann knew where she was now. *I could be in a book like anybody else*, she assured Delpha, as she reached out, *like you, white girl* and jabbed the younger woman's shoulder. She weighed one hundred and one pounds, and her dark eyes snapped in their deep sockets. If she heard any patient or C.O., any attendant, including Dr. Yount, including the doctor his almighty self, call an inmate the usual word or any of the ugly terms that were supposed to be cute, Fayann hauled herself up in bed and corrected: *Black*. This was the line she chose to stand on, from which she could not be moved. In her clotted voice, *Black, she is a black woman.*

Fayann's change of language, at least in the infirmary, at least in her presence, was accomplished. Delpha was a keen student of this stand. She heard Fayann's call for respect, but that wasn't all. How did this declaration from one black inmate contain the rest of black women, a continent of them, alive and dead? How? To Delpha's ears, it did. What did that have to do with her, a white girl raised in swampy bayous, in jail for years to come?

Delpha sat her frail patient on the side of the single bed, went to get her some water. Brought back the glass and helped her tip it up. Then she laid her down, fixed her sheets, all the time digging at this way Fayann had found. Without having one thing people usually cried out for—money or position or a true sweetheart, a ripe body, freedom—Fayann was weighing in with her life. To herself first of all.

Second, to anybody who had ears to hear.

Delpha finished the Coke and set Oscar's bottle down beside her purse. Advancement in the way others thought of it was not her aim. She better understood headway. That meant moving forward on your own terms. To a place you recognized but maybe others didn't.

She took up the trusty green ruler, and though it was still light outside, switched on her desk lamp. These proper office tools fortified her. No fluorescent tubes spewing out light too bright to relax under but too shadow-throwing dim to read by. No headache-light. Clear yellow light falling on the children of Louisiana.

XVIII

AROUND THREE-THIRTY, FOOTSTEPS sounded on the stairs. Fast ones. Delpha leapt up, eyes locked on the door, a pencil gripped in her hand.

A rattle, and Phelan elbowed through the door, smiling, with two Dixie cups of ice cream and the little wooden paddles. He took note of her, and his smile slid off. He said only "Break time," walked over and gave her the cup. She thanked him. Pretty soon he was shuffling through desk drawers, and she was back to rustling pages.

Some new disturbance in the air caused Delpha to lift her head. She glanced around the office. Stretched to see Phelan at his desk. Her gaze passed over the window, the rounded, sea-green chairs. To the door.

The doorknob.

She took three quiet steps to Phelan's doorway. He looked at her, and she inclined her head toward the door.

The doorknob was rotating incrementally.

He was up and laying both his hands on her waist, pushing her efficiently and rudely back into his office space, and he was in front of her and moving forward as the tumbler clicked.

A head with a sunburned nose poked inside the door.

"Hi, Tom. Or should I call you Mr. Phelan? I mean, now you're kinda my boss. I mean, you are my boss."

Phelan concentrated on the face. His weight settled back on his heels.

"Ben. Took a second to recognize you. Come on in."

Flash of acknowledgment from Ben the Bellas Hess photographer as he entered. His whole face was red. "New glasses. My dad wants me to keep my eye on the bottom line." He gave a laugh, then strangled it. "That's a joke. Just not a funny one."

The boy had jettisoned not only the Buddy Holly specs but also the striped t-shirt. Moved on to wire rims and painters' pants. No paint smears but various stains, and his formerly slicked hairdo had not been slicked today. Or this week. Phelan did not comment further on the transformation. The kid had just needed new glasses. Couldn't be the influence of *stakeout* and *discretion*, could it? Not to mention the art of photography. His daddy would not be liking that.

"Reporting, sir." Ben saluted and handed over a black portfolio. Straightened up to his full height.

Had he grown?

Phelan waved Delpha forward. "Delpha Wade, Ben the photographer," he said, and the two exchanged faint hellos.

Phelan unlatched the portfolio. Instantly, Ben was at his elbow. "OK, here's several batches. You get the most people on weekends. Obviously."

Phelan didn't look up. "You went every day, didn't you?"

"Uh. Yeah. Made the rounds, hope you're paying gas. Date and site on the back."

Phelan laid the case on Delpha's desk, which she occupied again. He lifted the stack of stiff eight by ten black and white prints, edges curling a little, shuffled through them. Tall stack. Birds. Kid hadn't been able to resist, and damn if he didn't have an eye: a flock of flappers, wheeling toward a tree, a messy pelican taking a bath, shaking a million diamonds from its outstretched wings. The Gull Air Force, two serious wingmen flat-out over the water.

Bird-watchers. A woman in a scarf with binoculars, up on the observation stand. A stocky ranger, gesturing into the distance, over the marshy land toward the bay. Kid with a stick and a hopeful *what can I kill?* expression. A man with a camera mounted onto a tripod, whose bucket-like hat had a down-folded brim. A teenage boy closer to the watery ditch had somehow managed to stick out his tongue and grin at the same time. At the camera.

"Way to keep a low profile, Ben."

Ben's face flattened a little but shaped up again once he interpreted the sarcastic pucker of Phelan's lips. "Can't keep a low profile with a guy," Ben tapped the teenager with the impishly protruding tongue, then tapped his temple, "who hugs you."

"Guess not." Phelan studied the teenager, then passed on to a girl in short shorts glaring resentfully into the camera while an older woman loomed over her shoulder working wide-open jaws. Phelan fanned the rest of them, went back to the girl.

"Nice one. Funny."

"Cute when she smiled."

"Aren't they? OK, wait a second…" Phelan jogged into his office and pulled out a mustard yellow packet from his top drawer. Came back and fanned out the photos of Bell he'd snapped from his landlord the dentist's window. Then he chose Ben's photos with grown men in them, plopped them above his small snapshots. Maybe a man who looked like Xavier Bell was one of these birdwatchers.

"Anybody look alike to you?"

Ben came over and interleaved them, one of his, one of Phelan's, side by side. Adjusting their edges minutely, he said, "Wow, I see why you hired me. I could blow any of these up but they'll be fuzzy." He leaned forward, squinting. "Maybe that guy." He tapped the man in the bucket hat. "But I don't know. Nobody really jumps out."

Then, by degrees, Ben's compressed features began to relax. He pecked his finger at Phelan a couple times before he found his voice.

"Wait a minute. Yeah, wait, lemme take the negatives of these." He peered into the packet to make sure the negatives were there. "I'll blow them up and measure."

"Measure what?"

"Nose, ears. I read a whole article on it once. In old-timey France, they measured prisoners to keep track of them. There's a name for it. After the guy that thought it up."

Phelan waited, but Ben didn't come up with it.

"Well, so photographers do this. Not cops?"

Ben looked like he was trying to remember, or he was deliberating or debating himself or stalling. One of his eyes was squeezed almost shut. Then he stretched out his chin and raked his hair off his forehead, though it wasn't long enough to cover his forehead.

"Yeah," he said, "yeah, photographers... Yeah, we can do that." Offhand. Very offhand. But he stacked his own photos back in the portfolio, tossed in Phelan's mustard packet, snapped the portfolio's latch and disappeared.

Leaving a contrail behind him.

XIX

ONCE WHEN HE was twelve and a half and mad at the
world, Phelan'd swiped his mother's keys and gunned down
to the port where he took off his shoes and jeans, tied the
pants around his neck, and waded out into the turning basin.
He was a pretty strong swimmer and the ships were close,
though the soaked denim immediately changed into an iron
collar dragging at him. Still he pulled out, stroke by stroke,
until he'd reached a hull. He treaded water and hollered up at
the skyscraper. Nobody to holler at, but he kept on until his
chilled elbows refused to bend properly and his tiring arms
pushed at the heavy water like balsa oars. A dark head peered
down from the deck, stories away.

"Hey," Phelan yelled. "Take me on!"

A sailor with one eyebrow shouted down at him in some
gargley language. Phelan pointed up toward the deck. Another
head appeared beside his, and they both yelled at him a while.
One held up a palm and pumped his fist into it and they
laughed. Then both heads whisked out of sight. Phelan was
dumb enough to think maybe they were fetching a rope ladder
to toss down to him. But a bald head imprinted with a stern
face craned over the side, and the original two scuttled back,
frantically flicking their hands at the boy in the water.

Cold, water-logged, swallowing oily river, Phelan
chopped back considerably slower than he'd plunged toward
the ship. Some essential core of dignity and ridiculousness

forbade him to jettison the concrete jeans. He was bull-horned before he made shore. Phelan got his wish, hauled up into a boat. Only not a floating city sailing away to a foreign land, but a dinky speedboat manned by water police. Language he understood well was barked into his face. Phone calls were made while Phelan dripped on a linoleum floor. Barefoot. But not bare-assed.

E.E. wasn't chief then, just Detective Guidry, but he brought with him into the cramped port office a Napoleonic professional courtesy and a merry stir that lured people to him, including a couple jokes about the law firm of Boudreaux, Boudreaux, Boudreaux, and Boudreaux. Phelan had been shucked out of that fix like a Gulf oyster from its shell.

Being crossways with E.E. had been the shits. But he didn't regret the lawyer for Delpha.

He was working his second shift on the homebuyers. Supper was a good time to call. He asked directions or offered a phone book or pretended he thought his friend Carl lived at the address. So far, he'd seen seven more homeowners, all white, and missed three, including a Barton Hebert, who didn't answer the doorbell. Of the seven, five were thirties-forties-fifities, not old enough to be Rodney. One was old enough but in a wheelchair, his door answered by a daughter with a tower of Jehovah Witness hair that could have homed a gopher. The next—Phelan had to track the Beegees *Don't ask me whyyyyyyyy I love you and that's all I can say* around to the back yard to locate the owner—was in his early twenties. Guy was at least five years younger than Phelan's twenty-nine, and he had a beer in his fist, a smoking barbecue grill, and friends lounging all over patio furniture.

Fortunate son.

At seven-forty, Phelan pulled up to the curb of 7937 S. Sarah Street, the house a Mitchell Smith had bought in July.

Tidy ranch, its white window-trim half-painted over a beef jerky color. This was a modest neighborhood, couple potholes in the street. Chevy in the driveway. He touched his hand to the hood as he passed it. Cool. He knocked.

The door opened. The black man standing behind the screen wore khakis, a short-sleeved white shirt with sweat stains, striped tie loosened at the neck and a pocket protector that held two pens. Average height, late thirties. A cooking smell wafted out—fish.

"Mr. Michael Smith?"

"Mitchell. What can I do for you?"

"Mitchell," Phelan corrected himself and held up a phone book. Bunch more in the back seat. "I'm from the phone company. We 'pologize for being so late to get this to you, but here you go."

The man opened the screen door. "I got one. They left one when they put the phone in. But I'll take this one for my grandmother. Y'all hadn't brought her a new one." One of his eyes became narrower. "Hadn't brought one to nobody on her whole street, and they called y'all, too."

Phelan handed over the floppy book. "What street is that?" He was shaking his head, lips pursed as Mitchell Smith gave him the name.

"I'll report that. My supervisor, he's always getting names or streets mixed up. But his brother-in-law's district manager." Phelan quirked his eyebrows and pulled his lips to the side.

Mitchell Smith's eyes equalized. "I hear you," he said.

Phelan doubled back around to an address six blocks away to see if Barton Hebert was home and found a different scene. Now there were a lot of cars out front. Mr. Hebert was home. Late-thirties, rumpled black suit, reddened eyes, a haunted third-grader clamped to his hip. Black-dressed people behind him sitting and standing with plates of food in his living room.

Phelan pushed it, five more addresses. Chris Johnson was a tight-faced woman in her forties with fighting kids. Jim Anderson had so many trees in his yard Phelan could've used a machete to reach the front door. Which nobody answered. The last three didn't appreciate being peeled away from TV shows and symphony music swelling from a record player. Two the wrong age, the third the wrong race—seventy-ish but Filipino or Hawaiian or something. With female company. Annoyed.

Phelan was annoyed himself. He excused himself back to the Chevelle.

XX

AS REQUESTED, DELPHA had gotten up and turned the lock on the door to Phelan Investigations. Then squared up the stack of Xeroxes, took her pencil, and repositioned her green plastic ruler. She breathed a large, clean breath, settled into her chair.

She inched down the smeary page of births, ever alert to 1898 and 1900. Easier if the list named only City of New Orleans' babies. But this was the whole of Orleans Parish.

She sat up, her brow contracting. Then dialed the library, asked for Angela and when she came on, said, "Hello, this is Delpha Wade. Am I speakin' to the reference librarian?"

Happy squeal. "Sure are. What question can Tyrrell Public Library's reference department help you with this evening?"

"Wanna know how big Orleans Parish in Louisiana is."

"Buzz you right back."

Marie, Maria, Mary, Mariette, Miriam, Marianne. Glad she wasn't hunting for girls. The boys' names were more varied...the phone rang.

"Hey, Delpha. Orleans Parish covers three hundred and fifty miles."

"And didn't even get out of my chair. Thank you, Reference Librarian. You gettin' lots of stuff to find out?"

"I tell you. Just had a question today about birds that roost on your gutters so either you get stuck with them chirping all the time or you murder 'em. I can tell you how to do that, by the way."

"All this power's going to your head, Angela."

"Isn't it great? My head's like the Goodyear blimp. Bye now."

Delpha marked her place. She took off the black flats and tucked a leg into her chair. Quiet in the office, inside these fresh white walls, minus Phelan's simmering energy. The occasional siren, honk from the street a floor below.

Back in early April she was just out of prison, and the businesspeople at the other end of the job ads had whisked the door shut on her eleven or twelve times, one after the other. Six weeks later, when she had the interview with Mr. Phelan, she'd have agreed to type the Houston phone book and hum *Froggie Went A-Courting* as she typed, so long as she got a job. Delpha was reminded again of how things moved along. Even her. It was just, now that she had work, she wanted more.

She determined that was not advancement exactly. Not in the way Angela meant it. Angela had ruling on her mind. Maybe Delpha was a little more like Oscar. Oscar was thinking *Boss,* but he was also thinking pork loin, shrimp remoulade, apricot bread pudding.

Delpha didn't care about Boss. She was pretty sure she wanted her work to have an end that made her feel satisfied. That was it. She wanted to feel curious about what she did, interested while she did it—if interest and jobs could go together. They had for Fayann Mackie.

At nine o'clock she was starving, but she had them all. All those turn-of-the-century baby brothers. That's what she'd label this list: *Brothers,* when she typed it up.

And…there was something she hadn't done. One thing, filed back in her mind. Something.

Well, tomorrow. Now she was going back to the hotel. Heat up a plate of pork tenderloin. Good that she was doing Oscar this dishwashing favor—or she'd be out of luck. No special dinners on his watch. Somebody might could sneak into the pantry, heist a jar of dill pickles, mess up Oscar Hardy's food costs. Which would mess with Oscar Hardy's Do-It-Yourself chef education course.

That tenderloin—saliva filled her mouth. She gathered her purse and the empty Coca-Cola bottle, locked up, hurried down the stairs, looked both ways before she crossed. In the middle of the street she remembered. Delpha spun in the headlight of a motorcycle and ran back up the stairs.

The phone rang as she was pulling open her top drawer. She hesitated then picked it up. "Phelan Investigations."

"My word, aren't you keeping late hours, Miss Wade."

She stood up, glanced toward the window. "Just leaving, Mr. Bell. Can I do something for you?"

"Is Mr. Phelan making p-progress on my case?"

"He is. We're checking out every single man who bought a house in the last eighteen months or so. Mr. Phelan is…has been out doing that today. Anything else you'd like to add, that might help us find your brother?"

There was a silence.

"There are things…I neglected to tell Mr. Phelan. You sh-shouldn't withhold from allies, should you?" He was stumbling over some words, drawing out others.

Crisply, Delpha said, "Not if you want your allies to do their job."

"Of course. It was wrong of me."

Delpha gave a large nod, saying nothing.

"All right, I told you I wasn't angry at Rodney for getting an allowance while I went to the store every day. That wasn't true. I was angry. But you should know, Miss Wade, I suppose this is what I want to say, I would call Rodney in the years I could still find him, and when I heard my brother's voice, the anger vanished. I so wish he had felt the same. Oh, I w-wish he had. Once, I stood there with the hall phone in my hand, choked up, and I caught sight of a man's face in the mirror by the hat rack, and I thought, *That poor man is b-broken, that's his problem*. That man was me, Miss Wade." Surprise lingered in his voice. He waited, maybe for some exclamation from Delpha.

"I'm real sorry, Mr. Bell. That must have upset you. But—"

"That's not all."

"Excuse me, go ahead."

"Rodney will have a friend with him."

After a while Delpha said, "A friend."

"A younger friend."

"Boyfriend?"

"Friend. Are you...you're not all alone up there?"

She did not turn her head to glimpse into Phelan's office where a man had tried to kill her. She didn't have to. She could feel the shadow of his bulk. Which, according to Aileen's description, was something more like the rim of a cave. Delpha pitched her mind away from either shape, then pitched her voice: as if inquiring about an admirable accomplishment, asked, "Now how did you know we'd be here this late, Mr. Bell?"

"Why, I...I...just passing by a while back and saw the light on up there."

Delpha's head jerked toward the door. Had she locked it? "And you're home now, Mr. Bell?" His contract listed an address on Calder where he was staying. Not all that far from here.

No, she had not locked it.

A belch, muffled. "I bl'ieve you told me you had not seen 'The Thirty-Nine Steps'? The Hitchcock film? It *m-made* his reputation. You might be interested to know that its villain is missing half his pinkie finger." A chuckle. "Your boss is missing a middle one. I saw that right away. And the similarity between you and Miss Madeleine Carroll. Well. Don't you think it strange I didn't recognize my own face in the mirror? Uncanny."

Uncanny? She'd call his behavior feeble-minded. Some kind of sleep-walking. She pressed her growling stomach. "It's strange. I'm afraid I need to—"

A clinkety sound, followed by a crash, a piercing exclamation, and a crack as the receiver hit the floor. She could hear him at a distance. The slightly drunken drawl disappeared into a string of curses edged with piteous shrillness, as if he were on the verge of tears.

"The whole damn pitcher…"

"Are you all right, Mr. Bell? Mr. Bell?"

Dial tone.

Slowly she hung up, understanding their client was feeling sorry for himself. He'd stated his aim as a reunion with Rodney, but he must crave sympathy, too. Consolation? A bond? Well, that result wasn't the responsibility of Phelan Investigations. Delpha herself had discovered, by means of a few nasty lessons, that self-pity got in her way.

She went straight to the door and locked it. Making a mental note to buy an extra-extra-long cord for her phone, one that could be coiled out of sight under her desk, but that would allow her to reach the door, should it be necessary to hold onto the receiver and throw the lock at the same time.

Then she returned to her desk's top drawer.

It was there right where she put it. The piece of notepaper from a police desk pad that Phelan had brought back. The New Orleans people his uncle's mother remembered—French Quarter shopkeepers Mrs. Estelle Guidry had known, ones with merchandise like the shop Xavier Bell had described: swords, antiques, art, coins, pistols, jewelry. A dart of excitement hit Delpha. Look at this! The names Smith and Hebert were on Mrs. Guidry's shopkeeper list. They were also on *Homeowners*. And Mrs. Guidry had recalled three additional names.

She tucked this notepaper back into the drawer. It would have to wait. She had an urgent date with Oscar Hardy's cooking. She scooped up the Coke bottle and her purse, unlocked the door, locked it back, and ran across the street.

Delpha climbed five steps, not thirty-nine, into the Rosemont. An unusually rowdy crowd of TV-watchers was carousing in the lobby. Shouts hurled toward her. Blinking against several voices, she made out that Billie Jean King had just won the Battle of the Sexes tennis game against Bobby Riggs in the Astrodome.

"Girl's a bearcat!" Mr. Finn announced.

"She's a phonus balonus!" a sour-faced Mr. Nystrom barked.

In the pause that followed that opinion, Mrs. Bibbo said, "She clobbered the blabbermouth." Why hadn't Delpha been here to watch?

"Damn," Delpha said, "forgot."

The match was everywhere in the news, and she'd meant to watch. Well. She hiked her thumb in sisterhood with Mrs. Bibbo, went on into Oscar's post-dinner, off-limits kitchen. Tubs of dishes, crusted pots and lids, skillets, and crumby pie pans piled, the linoleum greasy and splotched.

Her stomach was eating itself. She put two fat slices of tenderloin, some gravy, a pile of black-eyed peas on to reheat. If there had been biscuits and slaw, these were gone, but Oscar had reserved her a pale yellow slice of lemon icebox pie with the graham cracker crust, the last in the pan. Perched on a stool at the chopping table, Delpha ate the pie first, saliva squirting with the sharp savor of lemon. She tamped up the crumbs, licked the fork, eyes closed. Oscar used real lemons and grated some peel on top. When you hoped in prison for anything good to come, you never thought of lemon icebox pie. But it was not a trifle. Right now, in this all-by-itself moment, lemon pie was the way.

She finished off the tenderloin and black-eyed peas. Delpha drank a glass of water straight down, then tied on an apron and took hold of the first tub of dirty dishes. All hers to set right. Her own kingdom of straw to spin and a new set of tools to hand: scrubbers, Hobart, broom, mop, Lysol, and muscle. She'd be here a couple hours. Made for a long day, yes it did, but the idea of weeks, stacked up against fourteen years, put a lopsided smile on her face.

There was this commercial the radio shouted over and over: *SSSaturday Night! SSSaturday Night! Gold-en Tri-angle RRRace-way!* Might she want to go to that raceway sometime—sweat in the bleachers, wave off the diesel exhaust, shield her ears from engine noise and crackling loudspeakers? Only because she could. But not yet.

What would she do on Saturday? She might could walk down to the Jefferson Theatre and see the picture show. Might could take a bus out to the Gateway shopping center and stroll through some stores, maybe that nice one, The White House. Look in every window. Ride the bus back. Later, sit on a bench by the port and gaze at the moonlight water and the ships. Or she could put some gas in the Dodge—she did have those keys—and drive down to Boliver. Cross the swing bridge that she and Isaac had crossed back in summer, when the roadside was scattered with primroses.

XXI

WHY IS IT you touch one woman she feels ordinary like a
cousin or a nurse who checks your blood pressure or some
lady at the bank who trips and you catch her elbow—but
you touch another woman, and she's live current? Phelan
suspected the answer might have to do with him, but that
avenue remained murky, and he let it stay that way.

OK, chemistry, what *was* that? Horniness, for sure. Partly
her shape, the way the waist sets in, the lift of her breasts, if
she smiles at you, how she smiles at you, what she means by
it, not that you know, but sometimes you do.

The day he met Delpha, no smile until she understood she
was hired.

He considered the idea intermittently while also drinking
Miller High Life and watching the Braves. Game was broadcast
from the climate-controlled Astrodome, subtracting fifteen
degrees from this Saturday's eighty-seven, and adding that
shazam neon scoreboard Houston worshipped. Fans were
warming up for rambunctious. Closeup of the bullpen and
Dave Robert's heater colliding with the mitt like a round from a
bolt-action rifle.

The Braves went down 1-2-3 in the first inning. Second
verse, same as the first. Astros had magnets in their gloves.
Top of the third, *all right*!, Casanova homered, Garr singled
and, little wings sewn onto his cleats, stole second. Died there.
Phelan grumbled. He should be rooting for the Astros, home
team ninety miles away, but they didn't have Henry Lee Aaron.

April 1954, the year Tommy Phelan was ten, the year Joe DiMaggio married the goddess—Coach Peterson distributed uniforms after practice. Bobby Peterson got 6, which'd been Stan the Man's number, and his twin Casey got 7, Mantle's. Naturally. Their dad was coach. When Ron Whitaker got 3, the Babe's number, he did about twenty somersaults across the field. Phelan, standing farthest from the coach, ended up with number 44. That was neither good nor bad—he'd seen the card of a player named Cavaretta, racked up some MVPs during the war—but Phelan was not kissing dirt over him.

There were *things* about Delpha that made contemplation complicated. That day when he'd touched her, a charge surged through him, belly, dick, thighs—just from the skin-to-skin. That was a complication. And the major thing was that they worked together and that was working out excellent as far as Phelan was concerned, so best there be no complications. He could make a mistake, their beneficial association could go south. This was one of the major things, anyway. That was it—his brain pinpointed the core problem: Delpha had *several major things.*

In the second, Hank had grounded out, but top of the fourth, he'd be up again. Phelan was already leaning forward, squashing his hands together. George Herman Ruth had blasted 60 homeruns in 1927 alone, his all-time stood at 714. Mr. Aaron had racked up 711 career homeruns, and was reaching for 712, but Roberts the pitcher was a southpaw, and Hank hit the righties.

Here he came. Crowd noise jacked up, the passionate chatter in Phelan's living room jacked up. Settling in over the plate. Those hands high, letting two go by before his hip and front foot slid forward, bat came down fast...*wham*, grounder. Short hustled, scooped, burned it to first. Phelan kicked the coffee table, and his green aluminum ashtray hopped facedown onto the carpet. *Shit.* He went and swept ashes into his hand so they wouldn't burn down the duplex, dumped them back in the ashtray, face locked on Baker. Single. Johnson and Lum singled and Johnson got squeezed between second and third. Helms and Rader having way too much fun, heckling him every doomed step: take off toward third/toss, run back toward second/toss, try for third again/toss, *tag you're it, dugout, baby, and don't you come back no more no more.*

Phelan sprawled back on the couch, ashing it, having forgotten about his dirty hand.

Starting in 1955, jersey number 44 had raised from nothing to OK and eventually to great because a Milwaukee right-fielder with that number started making big noise with his bat. Eleven-year-old Phelan's spot was also right-field. He was heartened by the novelty: luck had befallen him. That felt good. Even though Aaron was colored and he was not, he hung on to 44. When he found out that Henry Aaron had the same birthday as he did, the connection took on voodoo. Hank's swing could cause Thomas Phelan's brim to overflow.

He himself, even by eighteen, was just your average hitter. No call to strut, no need to cringe. His talent appeared to be right field. Tommy Phelan caught balls. He ran into board fences catching balls. He flipped over chainlink. Trampled parents in the bleachers. Dived and nabbed the ball on the fly, grass-surfed on his face for a few yards. Tripped and fell, twisted and caught it bare-handed. Once climbed a wall like The Fly and pushed off, launching his glove up to the ball. It wasn't exactly athletic prowess that made him an entertaining outfielder. Tommy Phelan just didn't like to give it up.

Top of the fifth, Casanova up again. Fly ball. Left fielder ranged back back back and plunk into his glove, damn. Bottom of the inning, the Astros' Metzger tripled, drove in two runs. Their game now. Cedeno popped up to center, and

Watson's dinky grounder was slurped up and smoked to first. Skinny Metzger got stranded out in thirdland. Astros trotted in, the Braves out.

A major thing about Delpha was her history, prison, the violence she'd suffered and done. What had happened, he reconstructed, was Ben the photographer had turned the doorknob too slow, and Phelan had put his hands around Delpha's waist to throw her out of the way of any Rodney that might be on the other side of the door. Backward from that was the day they'd argued over Miles' bill, and he had laid his hand on her shoulder. His thought, prompted by the dictionary lesson over "requisite," was that Delpha had had more than enough Rodneys already. He'd laid his hand on her shoulder, facing her, like he was between her and the Rodneys. He didn't have the right. And face it, Clark Kent, who said she needed your help?

She had looked at his hand, he noticed that.

Top of the sixth. Phelan put down his Miller and sat forward, elbows on knees, ordering and cajoling Perez to get on base. Perez singled. Phelan went to work on Evans, Evans singled.

Here he came.

When Hank entered the batter's box, Perez was dancing away and back to second, needling Roberts the pitcher, and Phelan was streaming patter at the screen. Hank took some practice swings, holding the bat a little closer to his chest than usual. Settled in, hands high behind him as Roberts let loose, throwing hard. Hank's hip moved, his front foot stepping out, hands coming down and around, power of the shoulders, chest, power from the torso feeding the swing, *craaack*! Legs far apart now, back heel off the dirt, the man stretched out, head up-tilted, watching it fly. Left, lofting to leftfield like a goddamn bald eagle, going, going—Phelan was hollering—

that ball was gone! Number 712, up in the bleachers. The scoreboard ready for it, flashing 712! AARON IS NOW TWO AWAY FROM TYING RECORD AND 3 FROM 715!

Henry made the bases. Not until he rounded home did Phelan fetch another beer, clink it with an empty, and pull the injured coffee table back so he could plop his feet on it. He was flooded with the old familiar feeling that a smidgen of Hank's homer was Tom Phelan's, too. Silly, but that's the cool way it worked.

A pounding on his door, and burrhead Clarence, his fiftyish neighbor in the duplex, pumped a blast of bourbon into Phelan's face and ragged at him for hollering, every word of which Clarence was forced to overhear through their shitty common wall, Phelan should know—

"Hey, sorry, just got carried away." Phelan's post-homer smile lingered.

Clarence's mouth was round as a drain-hole. *What kinda messed-up shit was it that Phelan was over here rooting for goddamn Atlanta Georgia instead of the Houston Texas Astros, for Christ's sake? And rooting for a tar baby to beat The Babe's record? Sure couldn't call himself a true blue Texan. Was he even a real American? Huh?*

An instant concentration bunched behind Phelan's forehead. He slapped open the screen door *Bang*, knocking Clarence back, and filled up the doorway.

"Man, what you see when you don't got a Claymore."

The drain-hole puckered. Clarence jabbed him the bird and stalked back to his place. Couple seconds, his door exploded shut. The old turd must have got a running start and hit it with both hands. Well, his deposit money.

Phelan threw himself back on the couch. Fucking Clarence. Hacked his buzz right off.

Baker, Johnson, and Lum hit flies the Astros hoovered

into their gloves. Snooze-city at the Astrodome till Mr. Aaron rotated up again top of the eighth—and fouled out. The Braves pulled him, and that was the game.

There would be no Number 713 today.

XXII

DELPHA DID NOT go to the Jefferson Theatre to see the picture show on Saturday or stroll the stores or drive down to Boliver to fish. She did none of those things, and not only because she didn't want to see the September roadside bare of primroses. What she did, she did because, like Fayann with the anatomy book, she was interested.

Angela was off on Saturdays. Little round Opal trundled over a cart of old New Orleans phone books in a battered cardboard box. Delpha glided the heavy chair into the library table, sat down, and lifted the top phone book, the most recent, from the pile. She counted on the businesses and the business pages to find the shops like Xavier Bell's. Those she wrote down, even if a proprietor's name was not provided. She worked backward to the oldest telephone book, 1919, whose mildewed cover was illustrated with a naked man-angel standing atop the world, loops of cable dipping to hide his private section.

Then she turned to the musty, yellowed city directories for additional information. These directories, which began to be published a good many years before the invention of the telephone, compiled city residents alphabetically by surname. They did not separate out businesses but did give a citizen's profession and current address. By noting duplicated addresses, it was possible to see at a glance who lived with who. Would she come upon a Xavier Bell and a Rodney Bell, merchants, both residing at the same address in 1920? Both working at a shop on, say, Tchoupitoulas St.?

She found Charles Bell, fireman, and Bell, Merthel L., Mrs., boarding house, at different addresses and in different years. She ran her finger down Babcocks, Bethancourts, Broussards, Blancs, Blanks, and Blanques. Finally, Delpha had seven pages of shopkeepers who were even loosely associated with selling antiques, used goods, firearms. She ripped these pages off the tablet, set them to her right side, and began a new page. On this one she consolidated, so that names appeared only once with a parenthesis of dates for years of business.

She finished. And neither Xavier nor Rodney Bell had appeared as a shopkeeper on this new list, which she'd labeled *Merchants*.

Abruptly, noisily, Delpha scraped back her chair. She took a hike around the library to cool off her inflamed face. Past the other tables, the card catalog, patrons lugging books to the front desk, up the broad stairs to the kiddie section where silence did not rule. Children were milling and chirping. Mothers huddled with each other in a row of wooden school chairs. On the other side of the stacks were the miniature painted chairs with the straw seats. On one sat a maybe four-year-old girl dwarfed by an upside-down picture book titled *DICK AND JANE Guess Who*. A smirking girl around ten was slapping the book shut, snickering when the teary four-year-old squeaked "Stop it, Debbie!" and jerked it back open. As Delpha passed, she slowed to backhand the big girl's hands away from the book and flip *DICK AND JANE* rightside-up in the grasp of the small one. She stalked on, past a cloudy aquarium and back down the stairs.

Guess Who. No shit.

Scooting up her chair again, she glowered at the new *Merchants* page. Delpha told herself that just because the Bells weren't on it, that didn't mean the brothers weren't there under some other name.

But it did mean—100 percent, truly, positively, and for a fact—Xavier Bell had lied about his name.

His own name.

Still frowning, she sat back. After a bit, the sunlight entering through the cross and crown window mellowed. A new thought had occurred: not that Phelan Investigations had wasted tons of time because Bell had lied.

The lists had worked.

After *Homebuyers, Mrs. Guidry's, Brothers*, and now, *Merchants*, she'd discovered their client's lie. She sat up straight again.

Why make up a fake name if you just wanted to find your brother before you died? Why hamper your private investigator when you'd paid him a bunch of money? And if you were the brother, why move all around leaving a string of aliases—unless you'd done something so cursed you had to keep running? She remembered the peculiar, temperature-changing sensation she'd gotten as she led their client into Phelan's office. Maybe both Bell brothers were dangerous.

Careful with the old directories' loosened pages, Delpha placed the slim booklets back in their elderly box, standing them up in order. When she finished, she flexed her cramped right hand. So this was her Saturday, and she found that she didn't mind missing a matinee. Or staring at skinny mannequins through a store window. All right, there was no shopkeeper named Bell in New Orleans during these years. So which surname on her lists would turn out to be the brothers'? One of them would. This was the strategy of the lists: they were nets—Xavier and Rodney could not escape them all.

Delpha realized she was humming.

Froggie went a-courtin' and he did ride, uh huh
Froggie went a-courtin' and he did ride, uh huh
Froggie went a-courtin' and he did ride
Sword and pistol by his side
Uh huh

XXIII

ARRIVING AT THE office early on Monday, Phelan stopped short, surprised to meet the first user of the aqua pillow-chairs, which Delpha had pushed apart and angled slightly toward each other. Chafed brunette, breathing barely-tamped fire, high color on her cheeks. Petite woman, swallowed by a man's XL denim workshirt. A not-quite-toddler perched on her jeaned thigh: wisp-haired tuffy in overalls with fat, bare feet—slobbering on his fist.

Delpha said, "This is Cheryl Sweeney. She's kinda in a hurry to talk with you. Let me show you into his office, Cheryl."

Cheryl Sweeney had already shot up from the chair, her left arm hefting the child around the middle, horizontally. He didn't seem to mind. Her right hand crushed Phelan's. "Hi, I'm not really in a hurry, I just move this way. Caroleen Toups is my mother's cousin. She told Mom about you, and Mom told me. I have a problem named Frank."

At "Frank," the tuffy tuned up and had to be relocated to a shoulder, from which he glared at Phelan as his mother entered the office, headed to a client chair.

"Can I get you some coffee or a Coke, Cheryl?" Delpha asked, following. The baby rared back and wailed. Delpha's hand reached toward him and drew back. "Get him anything?"

Cheryl would take a Coke, and as for the baby, she disappeared him under her blue shirt-tent. The wail broke off.

Silence. Mild smacking. Definite sucking noises. Delpha took one look at Phelan's blighted face and set off to buy a Coke.

His potential new client turned her head as Delpha left, tossing back a raft of long, dark hair. She whipped around when the door had shut, started in right away, fast and grim. Woman approaching thirty, her prettiness suppressed by the hard lines of purpose, black eyeliner with a little tail on each side, lipstick worn off the heart of her lips.

"Listen, before I tell you what I want, you should know one thing I don't care for your secretary to hear. Don't want to say this in front of her and her get all shocked or righteous or anything."

"I wouldn't worry about that, Mrs. Sweeney."

"Cheryl, and hear me out first. Me and Frank have a deal. We can both go outside the marriage if we feel like it. Just can't see that person more than once. Number one is each other. You think that makes me a slut, you say right now and I'll leave because that is not how I look at it."

She dropped a space for his response, staring him in the eyes. Hers were hazel, edging green, sharp enough to score quartz.

"No such opinion."

"OK then. Frank's so good-looking, women can't see the ring on his finger. Harping on cleave-only-to-me won't get me anywhere. I let him have his. I go a round with some other man, Frank gets roaring jealous. And *that* keeps both of us interested, and me from going crazy."

"Got it," Phelan said lightly. "How can I help you, Cheryl?"

Her elbows lifted out as she brought her chest back. Faint wet pop of a seal broken, an aggrieved cry, a foot kicking. Cheryl shifted the baby to the other side, hands under the shirt, started in with her story.

The baby clamored over her.

"Crap. Dried up. I been weaning him, wait a minute."

Phelan gazed helplessly out the window to the street and the New Rosemont Hotel.

She brought out the baby from under the shirt, dug in her fringed purse, uncapped a half-size bottle with milk in it, and popped it in his mouth.

"Now then. Here it is," she said.

Last six months, Frank had had a new job. At first it kept him away three weeks or so, then back, then after a while, off again. Then the weeks-long shift changed to a once-every-now-and-then night shift: he left around ten and stayed away all night and some of the next day. He'd just got in today around noon. Still drunk but wearing different clothes than he left in—so that meant a shower somewhere. He smelled like beer, tried to bribe her quiet with a cooler of shrimp on ice. Sleeping now—and she wanted to get home before he woke up. No, he was not working a trawler. Nope, not on the rigs, either. He'd tell her that. Yes, he had money, a lot of money, and Frank wasn't stingy. She was driving a new Ford Mustang Mach 1. She wanted to get dressed up, she had a sparkly dress. They went to concerts and paid her mother to watch the baby—Steppenwolf and Willie Nelson.

"But what?" Phelan said.

"Won't tell me what he's doing. Will not tell. Wherever he's doing it, there was a woman there, at least in the beginning. I smelled her on the one good shirt he took with him. Like a mix of green apples and bait."

Phelan sat back. "And you wanna know who she was?"

"Not really. What I wanna know is if he's breaking the law, which wouldn't you say he probably is?"

Phelan would say *You betcha*, but not just yet. He shrugged.

"What's his regular job? Before this new one?"

"Upholsterer. His mama and aunt have a business, Spindletop Upholstery, do loads of commercial work. Frank's good at it, just believes a sewing machine isn't manly enough." Her eyes rolled to the top of their sockets.

A door opened and closed. Cheryl set down the baby bottle, accepted the Coke bottle from Delpha, and took a gulp. "He's breaking the law, you make him stop, Tom. I'll call you when he's going out again. Listen, I know your uncle's the police chief. You lay that on Frank. Twist his arm, blackmail him. Whatever you got to do to get his attention, I don't care."

"Any illegal activity, I have to report. You understand that, right?"

"Well, I guess I see that. What I'm asking is get Frank out of it before he's caught. I want my husband not in jail. Married to me, even if the bonds're a little loose."

She tipped back her head and chugged the Coke, graceful throat working, set the bottle on Phelan's desk, and drew the purse over again. Rummaged one-handed. Plunked a wallet on the desk, stifling a burp. "Take out some hundreds."

"Wait. Gotta fix some terms here, Cheryl. About intimidation, you know that old horse saying. Your mother's cousin Caroleen wanted me to shake her son out of a frying pan, you know how that went."

"Yeah. But Caroleen wanted you to find him and what he was doing, and you did. You found him that same day. What horse saying?"

"Lead a horse to water. Your husband's a grown man. I can pour him out a shot of You're-Screwing-Up, but I can't make him drink it. I'm a private investigator, not a bouncer or a preacher."

"Take the money, Tom. I can make him drink it."

With that proclamation ringing in the warm air of Phelan's office, the AC belched a delicate aroma of fire and died.

Cheryl flicked her eyes over to it and back to Phelan. "Well, gotta run," she said, seizing his hand to shake it.

While they waited for the whizzing molecules in Cheryl Sweeney's wake to settle, Phelan went downstairs and reported to Milton-the-dentist's receptionist that his AC needed a new compressor. If she could make a call, that'd be ace.

Then he leaned against his office doorjamb, wiggled his shoulders a little to massage a hurting spot between them, and lit a cigarette. He suggested to Delpha that they hold off on Cheryl for the moment and update each other on Xavier Bell.

Because he had this to say: of all the homeowners he'd met on his long Friday, he was pretty sure none of them was Rodney. Several of the men were old enough, but definitely not Rodney. He had two left to see. How about her?

"Finished the babies."

His eyebrows rose. "Wonder Woman."

Delpha smiled. "Always did like her magic lasso. Bell called Friday night."

"What?"

"Yeah, I stayed late, and when the phone rang I answered it."

Phelan's head fell forward, and he scrubbed a hand over his face.

"I know, I know. I won't do that again, OK? Just got kinda carried away with the babies. Couldn't stop till I finished, then, well...I was here. I locked the door."

"At the very least," Phelan muttered.

She shared Bell's message, emphasizing the more interesting part about Rodney's friend.

Phelan wheeled, went to his desk, came back with some stapled carbons of homeowners' addresses and an ashtray, tapped ash into it. Eyes on the paper, he sat down on the edge of an aqua chair, sank, and grimaced.

His finger traced the names as he read and thought. Finally, he looked up. "Still fairly convinced I didn't find Rodney. Friend or not." He wiped sweat from his upper lip. "I need to get a map from the car and start on some Cheryl-related calls. Then let's rendezvous again, OK?"

"One more thing."

"What?"

Delpha told him about her Saturday and the page labeled *Merchants*.

Her tone caused Phelan to cast an eye backward. Delpha was smiling in a pointed way. Woman knew something. He took hold of the typed list *Merchants* that she must have been banging out while he and Cheryl had their interview. Decades of names of the people who had run the right kind of shop in New Orleans.

"Son of a bitch," he murmured. He walked the paper over to Delpha's desk and back, reading it again. Xavier Bell's name had still not appeared on it.

"Son. Of a bitch. What is he up to? Would you get me his phone number?"

Delpha provided it, and Phelan called, let the phone ring a dozen times. He set down the receiver. "Goddamnit, why? Now we don't know either brother's real name."

"Asked myself that."

"What was your answer?"

"We still got his money. We'll find out." Her face was neutral, looking at him.

"You wanna quit?"

"Noooo. I'm continuing this game pissed. And it's

hotter'n fire in here." Phelan went over and wrestled with the secretary office's window. Pulled out a pocket knife, chipped at the paint seal till he got the window raised. Sultry September opened its square mouth and breathed.

XXIV

YOU FUCKING LIAR, Phelan cursed Xavier Bell as he went downstairs to his car, snagged a regional map from the trunk, and *You mealy-mouth sunglass-wearing lying old con-man* trudged back up. He added six or eight variations until he was chill enough to switch his brain over to Cheryl Sweeney's request. Wasn't easy. He was still simmering, and so was the office.

OK. The shrimp her husband had brought her said "boat," but the guy could've bought shrimp at the grocery store. Best bet, though, was that the case would involve watery, out-of-the-way channels that could accommodate a boat. In addition to the geography of the operation, Phelan'd need to go kick the can, bullshit with people, see what he picked up. He called the Marine Safety Unit's office and asked a chipper lady if they had a publicly available map of local waterways.

They did, but it didn't have every little podunk bayou and stream on it. Texas Parks and Wildlife had those. Whyn't he call a game warden down at the Sheriff's office.

"Yeah? How podunk do they get?"

"They're Wildlife, son. We're Law Enforcement. Our boats don't run in holes and ditches."

"Thank you, ma'am. The one you got'll be fine." He'd run over there in a minute, but next he dialed his friend Joe Ford the parole officer and asked him if he'd say he had his finger on the pulse of the crime community.

"Might say that to you. Nobody intelligent would believe me."

Phelan described Cheryl's husband's job behavior. Did Joe have any guys on his roster who'd been employed in a similar manner?

"Shit, yeah," Joe said, "hijackers, transporters, petty merchants. But not pirates. Not in my file cabinet. Yet."

"Pirates."

"Smugglers, dope-runners, whatever. My clients are getting out, not going in, and they're landlubbers. They sold outa apartments, on the streets. 'Round the racetracks, bars. That who you're looking for?"

"Maybe. Not sure."

"Even had some college action, kinda rinky-dink, far as I can tell. I had a higher-dollar guy when I first started here, jocks' agent, did seven years for marijuana. But if you're looking for good buddies of your guy and he's a sea-faring man, can't help you."

Phelan set down the receiver. The Cheryl case rolled out in front of him. Possibly labor-intensive.

He called the telephone number on Bell's contract, listened to it ring fifteen times, damn him. Phelan's blood pressure hopped a notch as he hung up.

If Rodney was dangerous, what was his friend like? Phelan picked up the list and reviewed each homebuyer for the third time. One of the younger guys could have been Rodney's friend, and old Rodney hiding behind the door.

When he'd come back up from his cursing mission, Delpha met him at the door, hand out for the list of homebuyers he'd seen last Friday. Digging it from a pocket, he gave it to her. Did he write notes on it? Yeah, he did. See. He'd jotted the reasons he crossed off each name. He wiped his hairline with the back of his hand and went off to spread out a map of wavy blue fingers that designated waterways.

The night Bell had called, when she'd spun around in the headlights of a motorcycle and run back to the office, Delpha'd got chills reading Mrs. Guidry's list. Two names Mrs. Guidry remembered, Smith and Hebert, these were also on her *Homebuyers*—and now *Merchants* lists. Her net was working, seining out names. Mrs. Guidry had recalled three more shopkeepers: Sparrow, forgot Christian name, soldier son; Athene, Georges, chased married ladies, cold-shouldered single ones; and Solomon Wertman, passed a few years after the war, nice kids that moved west, Beaumont or Houston.

These names were confirmed by *Merchants* as well.

But now...no no no. As she read Phelan's *Homebuyer* notes, she crumpled bitterly into her chair. Mitchell Smith, a black man in his thirties, could not be Rodney. Barton Hebert, late thirties, white, bereaved, was not Rodney, either. Sweat dribbled to her waist.

After a while, she lifted up again. She blotted under her chin with Kleenex as she scribbled over names Phelan had already crossed off. She lined up the piles of paper on her desk. All right, here they were, the uncrossed-off names, ones that had appeared on at least two lists.

1. Wertman
2. Sparrow
3. Davies
4. Anderson

She swept her hair back from her sticky face, brushed off the stacks of papers for no reason at all. Then she reread aloud the notation beside Solomon Wertman on Mrs. Guidry's list: "Passed a few years after the war, nice kids that moved west, Beaumont or Houston."

Delpha slid over her own book of Beaumont Yellow Pages, expecting nothing, and traced her finger through different columns of bold print. Antiques, Firearms, Gold, Coins. How had she not done this before? Probably because she was hell-or-high-water bent on arriving at this shortlist of final names. Now her finger was pressed directly on one Yellow Page name lest the print wriggle off the page.

Wertman.

Not Solomon, as on Mrs. Guidry's list, but Herschel and Ruth. Not a common surname. Disappeared from New Orleans records in 1955. Xavier Bell claimed he had worked longer than that. Yeah, and why would they believe what he said?

She touched her stomach: a new sizzle had begun.

Would there be anything like finding something she'd gone cross-eyed looking for? Be every bit as fine as locating the size of Orleans Parish—or calculating costs on a tenderloin dinner. Provided she could ever pinpoint the right man.

The door knocked. Delpha set down her pen and went to answer it, Phelan striding in from his office. "You don't have to," she said under her breath as she passed him.

Phelan looked at his secretary then at the big, soaked handyman with the steel toolbox.

"Calvin," he said. "AC conked out."

Calvin tamped his whiskery upper lip and neck, stuffed a red rag back in his pocket, and stepped in, surrounded by a bold scent of vintage perspiration. He turned his head and nodded at Delpha. "Ma'am."

She opened the door wider, and Phelan followed the handyman's wake into his office.

"Hep me move your desk, Tom. Need some room to work."

"And we're gonna give it to you." Phelan took hold of the desk's far end, and they walked it back to the wall.

"Delpha, I got to go stir the bushes. I'm thinking you could run down the last two homebuyers. That OK? Good.

Calvin, we're outa here. Just close the door when you go. It'll lock."

"Hell, I know that. I installed that lockset."

Phelan tipped his finger to Calvin, who had set down the toolbox and was pretending not to be looking toward Delpha.

"But what about the phone?" she asked. Like it was a child they shouldn't leave alone.

Want us bad enough, they call back. That's what Phelan thought—that's what he wanted to think anyway—his business in demand, this business in demand—then he thought better. Might jinx it. From the day he'd had the door painted with his name, he'd eaten plenty of pintos. He shrugged at her question about the phone, tilted his head toward the door. Delpha swabbed her forehead with a Kleenex and got her purse.

"Whew," he said on the stairs, out of Calvin-range, waving his hand in front of his wrinkled-up nose. "Forgiveness is the fragrance of a violet on the heel of the one who crushed it."

Delpha turned sharply to him. "Who said that?"

"Dear Abby."

They split up in the parking lot.

XXV

GOING ON DETAILS mentioned by Cheryl Sweeney, Phelan
dedicated the afternoon to tourism. He viewed back roads
bordered by reeds and seeping water, an eye out for a spot
a boat might pull in, site near a highway. Some dock-like
construction or posts to tie up to or even a shack or a trailer
that'd hold supplies—and plenty of tire tracks.

He roved the shores with a large cooler in the back seat.
Stopped at fish markets, food stands, fresh-catch tents near the
water where pelicans lurked like hopeful hoodlums and men with
few teeth and bloody hands chopped and gutted with expertise.
Phelan sweated in the eighty-eight degree sunshine, blotted his
forehead and let the breeze cool it. He feasted his eyes on the plenty.

Mind-blowing plenty: fresh oysters in their rocky shells,
blue live crabs and red cooked ones, mountains of beady-
eyed crawdads, wide-mouthed catfish with their feeler-
like mustaches, speckledy red-fish, red snappers that were
sunset pink. Piles of ice and staring eyes and the glistening
masterwork that was scales.

Everybody stocked filé gumbo mix. Even fairly small
outfits stocked a shelf of breadcrumbs, marinades, hot sauces,
cocktail sauces. One big market featured a still life platter
pretty as any bouquet: dollops of oysters, dollops of shells,
disk of salmon topped by a fat little snapper, trailing stems of
bright orange crab legs.

But the star, what Phelan had come for, was shrimp:

brown Gulf shrimp, jumbo Gulf shrimp, super jumbo Gulf shrimp, colossal Gulf shrimp. That was what Frank Sweeney had smelled like the last time he came home. Shrimp were connected to shrimp boats, which were connected to bodies of water, which connected land masses. If you didn't yaw off into Cuba, it was a straight shot across the Gulf of Mexico and Caribbean Sea to Colombia. That was how Phelan had parsed the matter of Frank Sweeney. When he himself had come off an offshore rig, he did not smell like shrimp, he smelled like whatever he'd scrubbed with—Lava soap or Gent-L-Kleen. Besides, Cheryl had said her husband wasn't working a rig.

Phelan bantered wherever somebody would take the time to talk. Prompted people by bringing up *boats, loads, making money*. Listened. Bought shrimp. The cooler stacked up.

Late in the afternoon, after some possibles—eye contact held too long or evaded altogether, a sour remark about some people being richer than Croesus—he'd stopped at an isolated roadside tent near High Island. The tent was set up on a road with a peeling sign that featured a flying red horse. Could have been less quick-draw with his wallet at the beginning of this trip—saved himself some bucks. Now he'd have to buy more shrimp.

Why is it you can't just think the right stuff up in the first damn place, 'stead of having to stumble onto it? Jeez. Shirt's soaked through to your waist.

Phelan hailed a guy splayed in a lawn chair, eyelids at half-mast, jumble of empties behind him from the old over-the-shoulder toss. The tent read PHIL'S, but according to this fish-seller, he worked for Phil on the boat and was only here today as a favor because the usual guy, Terrence Dumbass, had shot himself in the knee with a nail gun. He was Ticker. Could give Phelan an end-of-the-day deal buster, sure enough.

Phelan considered the six pounds of shrimp in his cooler, said, "Why not," and bought one more. Ticker hoisted himself up, fumbled half the shrimp onto the ground, had to get down like a dog and gather them up, slosh some water from a bucket over them. The altitude changes compelled him to establish a firmer footing. Once his flip flops were planted, Ticker seized his brown ponytail and wrenched it two-handed, tightening up the rubber band and getting hair cooties on his soiled hands. Then he wrapped up Phelan's shrimp in newspaper. His smile was so loose it almost fell off his face.

Phelan aimed the conversation once, then again. Acted spellbound at a story the guy told until he raised an eyebrow and tweaked out a joint from the breast pocket of his Captain Beefheart t-shirt. When Phelan rumbled, "Now you're talkin'," Ticker indicated a lawn chair next to his that Phelan could use to take a load off. If he'd pull it over because Ticker was good where he was. Phelan parked himself. They high-fived and passed the joint.

"So how'd you get the name Ticker?" Phelan asked him.

"Boo-boo. Quang Tin. '71." The guy grinned crookedly and jerked up Captain Beefheart, flashing a ropey foot-long scar that meandered down his breastbone. And, partially peeking from the back of his jeans, a walnut pistol butt.

Phelan recalculated his first impressions of Ticker. Made another, more careful sweep of Phil's shrimp stand: table with coolers on and under it, a scale, box of newspapers and trash, the tumble of empty beer cans on a sandy dirt floor. Few more folded lawn chairs piled against the tent's back wall. There, behind the green and white webbing and aluminum legs, a vertical shape like the stock of a shotgun.

Phelan didn't show anything. Finally he offered, "Dak To. '67."

Ticker made a fist, stretched out toward Phelan, who

formed his own fist, let Ticker tag it. "Funny. Couldn't wait to ride that freedom bird home, right? Then ain't nothing been like that since, like all your boys together. Thought maybe it'd be like that on the boat. Naw." He waved away the boat.

"You work on a boat?"

Ticker's eyes, on Phelan, glazed. He shook his head and they cleared. "These stateside boys—they just Jody."

Surprised, Phelan grunted. Hadn't thought about that name in a dozen blue moons. But his brain chanted *Ain't no use in lookin back, Jody's got your Cadillac. Ain't no use in going home, Jody's got your girl and gone.*

Ticker rambled through a couple anecdotes: his uncle's landing at Pelelieu, its dark-green and blue lit up by twinkles from the machine guns. His own entry in-country, when a corporal riding ahead on a tank unloaded on a water buffalo in a field. For the fun of it. Thing wasn't no more than a black, gentle old cow, and it sank down on its knees in the shallow water. Ticker did not go for that, no sir. No how, no way.

"For sure," Phelan said.

Conversation bobbed along. Not even trying, Phelan collected a string of innuendos. He was about to let slip a name, Frank Sweeney, until he saw that his party partner's pinkened eyes had gone soft and moist. The temperature had slacked off, and cars whizzed by melodiously. The sun was headed for the water.

"Look at that, man, like a, you know, look at…look at the clouds. You know? I swear, ain't it the…the end? Know what I mean?"

Phelan did not. But he hung on.

"Who wants fucking streets of gold—gimme sand. You know, all we're doin, me and Phil and Ding-ding, is…we're just makin it so more people'll sit their foolish asses down and see all this."

The end of the day washed around them, and Phelan, prodded into contemplation, let it. He craned around to watch the gray underside of clouds enflame, above them blue sky. The scrubby trees tossing their branches had begun dimming to silhouettes. Birds bumped up their calling, insects chirred. Two men and a tall egret over a ways in a ditch maintained holy silence while the ball stained the horizon and slipped away.

Took some maneuvering to regain the jokey camaraderie after the sun's rite. Phelan managed to work in a mention of Frank Sweeney, friend of his really good on boats.

Ticker blew out a mouthful of beer. "The cheese weasel?" He scraped together a straight face, then gravity imploded and he cracked up. Eventually, he locked in a middle-of-the-road expression. "Tall guy, mustache, movie hair?"

Phelan remembered Cheryl saying her husband was good-looking, so he nodded.

"Hey, look, man, stir around in the cooler, that one with the blue top, and fish you another beer. Don't take the last one, OK?" Ticker sat back, chuckling under his breath, brushed a strand of escaped brown hair off his forehead. Waved away the offer of a cigarette from Phelan, produced another joint with the same flourish as the first one, and clamped his lips around it. Phelan tossed over his lighter.

Cheese was a hand on one of the boats, same as Waffle and St. Peter and Ding-ding, same as Ticker, but Ticker was Numba One sailor. He knew his shit. The cheese weasel knew no shit, he was Numba One Jody. Guys only tolerated him because he busted his ass—Ticker would give the fucker that, he hustled—and on land The Cheese drew women like blue fin drew kitty-cats.

Phelan's nose tickled pleasantly. "Land? You mean when you get back here?"

"Naw, man, land on the other end." Ticker expelled

a slow load of smoke and handed over the roach. Brought up a dirty pointer finger and shhh'd on it. "Man, they got squeezeboxes, you know, just like the Cajuns, horns, cor-coronets, bongo drums." He wiggled his fists in the air, shimmied his shoulders. "You know, rattles." Not that bars or music happened much. Usually was load 'em up, move 'em out, rawhide.

Phelan waited a bit, went for it. "How much reefer y'all floatin'?"

Ticker's eyes shifted one way then the other. He extended his neck and hauled Phelan into focus. Then rared back and brushing aside the t-shirt, drew the gun from his waist band. Pointed an old S&W semi-automatic toward Phelan's nose.

"Man, shut up. I never said nothing about reefer. What's wrong with you?"

Phelan's hands, holding the beer can, had slammed into the air. He had the can gripped and poised to heave at Ticker, but he was going with patter first. "Sure, man, OK," he said, "sorry, my mistake, no problem—" He stumbled on humbly until the semi-automatic was stuffed back into the jeans and Ticker himself was reinserted into the groove. After twenty more minutes of racheting the subject far, far away from boats, shrimp, or Frank Sweeney, he laid down two bucks for another six-pack to polish the evening and said sayonara.

That word wasn't Ticker's idea of a proper sign-off. He blundered out of the lawn chair and, wobbling in his flip flops, muttered, "Hey, sorry about the piece, hoss. Just playin'. I wouldn't pop a brother." He hooked Phelan's fingers with his fingers and pulled him into his chest. Phelan hadn't seen many white soldiers dap like that, but he went along. Bumped Ticker's shoulder.

Walked away, his hair blowing crazy in the warm wind.

XXVI

WITH A BAD conscience, Delpha deserted the phone again in order to check out the last two homebuyers. She drove west on I-10 and gradually began to notice an unwillingness in the rumbling Dart. A gimp that felt unsteady on the freeway. She took an off ramp and drove, limp increasing, until she found a gas station with a line of cars waiting to pump gas. She skirted the line and pulled up to the bay. Delpha got out, flat-handed the car door shut, walked around it, and spotted the problem on the passenger side front. She stuck in the trunk key and unlocked it, checking to see if the jack and tire iron were there. They were. A uniformed young man with a Cab Calloway complexion and a junior mustache approached her.

His nametag read Wesley, and he was probably about eighteen, but he did not have a bandleader personality. He was sober, silent. As Delpha assessed this stranger, it briefly occurred to her that no one in her thirty-two years had ever called her a chatterbox, either. Then it occurred to her she was measuring herself against other people out here in the free world. How long had she been doing that—ever since she got out? Sure she had. But till she'd got a job and a place to live, she'd had no inclination to note what she'd been noticing, at least about herself. So now she had to? It jarred her.

She stood there with her head bent like the gas station attendant's. Both of them considering the sagging tire, which did all the talking, anyway. The young man loosened the lugs, jacked the car and spun them off, he had the tire lifted and up on his tub in no time. Delpha peered intently as he sprayed it with soapy water. When the bubbles began to blow, neither one of them remarked, *There it is.*

Wesley pointed at the leak with an eyebrow.

Delpha asked, "How much?"

"Three dollar."

Nod of agreement. "Check the oil?"

Raised thumb.

She went into an office with candy bars, cigarettes and chew, Pennzoil cans. A rotating fan ruffled her hair, then relocated the office air, then blew on the fifty-ish white woman smoking on the stool behind the counter. The top of her long blond hair was cut in swoops lifting every few seconds, like she was flapping away. "What can I help you with, honey?" she said.

"He's fixing a flat for me."

Ka-ching. Delpha handed over three dollars and sat down in a folding chair. An outside bell clinked. She studied the assortment of calendars on the far wall: a naughty Mexican señorita, some preening cars, a locomotive snaking around a snowy mountain track, and a cartoon character, a giant-size, bottom-heavy yellow bird with orange legs. The message by the bird said *Today is brought to you by the letter U for Unemployed.*

"He's such a hoot," the woman at the counter said.

She couldn't mean the yellow bird or even young Mr. Calloway repairing her tire. Delpha turned to look.

A car had reached its turn at the pump. A brownish-faced man got out, middle-aged or older, rumpled hair and sunglasses, and stuck the nozzle into his tank, turned his back to watch the numbers roll. Had an arm up, shading his eyes from the sun. The passenger side window was hiked down, and a big kid in a baseball cap was smiling and waving.

The woman behind the cash register waved back with her cigarette, saying, in a squeaky voice not meant to make it outside, "Hi, there, Hi there!" She brought her waving hand back to take a drag. "I swear, wouldn't you like to live your life that way? All the time, happy as a clam."

"Friend of yours?"

"Customers. I have never once seen him in a bad mood. Even with this gas crisis and all the waiting in a line just to fill up your tank." She exhaled a smoke-stream and cranked up her waving.

The door to the office opened, and the attendant came in and handed Delpha her keys. "Oil good," he said. It seemed to her he looked at her curiously. She thanked the back of his shirt.

She slid into her car, reversed, and drove slowly past the pump. Silent Wesley was high-fiving the cheerful kid on the passenger side. The kid kept throwing out his hand so that Wesley could high-five him a bunch of times. Damn if it didn't look like Wesley was talking to him.

This was the free world. There was no explaining it. Here she was, out in the town with *My god* streets going ever which way, stores, buses, and she was driving a car, not in a box wearing coarse white clothes. Like a kind of hard-edged dream that she could walk to her car without running up against some barrier. That nobody stopped her. That she wasn't dragging tangles of wet sheets from an industrial-size washer or burning her fingers through a worn-out oven mitt on a tray of three-dozen rolls or holding a bedpan under a woman's bony butt. Instead, out here in the world she was searching for a man who didn't know he was lost. Teenagers pointed out ghosts, and tight-lipped people talked. Tall birds needed jobs. She felt relief at having one because for sense in the short-term, at least you could count on work.

Delpha had two last *Homebuyer* names to scope out: Davies and Anderson. J.T. Davies lived in a powder blue box with white shutters, a bed of purple-pink hydrangeas, and a metal awning over the front door. She pushed the bell then stood back on the small concrete landing, one foot on the step below.

No one answered.

Phelan hadn't got any answer, either. She rang again and waited.

Rang, stood, rang again. Nothing. But there was a Chrysler in the driveway and damned if she was going to give up. She knocked, calling out "Mr. Davies?"

A man cracked the door. J.T. Davies was white, stubble-faced, pouchy-eyed. Seventy if he was a day. Delpha fetched him a friendly smile and offered him the phone book Ma Bell had forgotten to leave him.

He had to stick out an arm to grasp it. Pulled the book in. Quickly she asked if he was enjoying his new home.

Davies craned around as though the house were a frame that had just set down around him. Too many flowers on the wallpaper. His sister had given him a deal, though.

Delpha seized on "sister." She asked casually if it was just him and his sister in their family, adding, "I got six brothers. Boy, was our house crowded."

In the lifeless tone that the head of a parole board would announce *No release*, Davies said, "We have a brother." A knuckle brushed his chin as he frowned. He gave the impression of having reviewed some regrettable memory and judged it, but Delpha didn't see his head move. J. T. Davies was not an easy man to talk to.

He did, however, have a brother who was still alive and did not inspire happy feelings. They had a candidate here. This could be Rodney. Out, she decided. There could be a friend, and that friend could be out. Maybe the friend still had a job. OK then. She wouldn't cross off Davies. Though he didn't strike her as dangerous. He struck her as gloomy.

Doubtfully, Delpha wished the man a nice day and drove back in the direction she'd come. She located the Anderson house—Phelan's 'Not Home' note in the margin—only because its street number was stenciled on the curb. In between the stout trunks of loblollies, whose evergreen branches began high up, stood a lot-sized, haphazard forest of spruces and junipers, a few dogwood and redbud, a raggledy magnolia. A rug of rust-colored pine needles lay beneath the trees. She spied the end of a weathered gray ramp and walked it around to the door, which was, like the windows, cast in shadow. She knocked, then just in case, stepped back a good arm's-length from the screen door.

Which was lucky because it banged open.

To a surprise.

The teenager holding the door was the smiling passenger at the filling station. He was tall, tilted a little to one side, and appeared overjoyed to see her. He stood, unsteadily upright, like a skinny bear, feet wide apart, knees bent, hands drooping from his wrists. Behind him was a sparsely furnished living room: an upholstered couch and brown armchairs and footstool, a wheelchair next to a dinette table with two vinyl-seat chairs. On the dinette, a smallish black case with a trailing strap and a scattering of small, spiral-bound tablets.

And birds. To the left of the door where she stood: two huge cages, across from the dinette. The first, floor to ceiling, held a three-ring circus of blue, yellow, and green parakeets and even smaller, stripey-black birds. Through it she could see another cage, not as large, with one grand gray bird weaving on a perch.

Delpha swallowed her surprise—at seeing the same boy who'd been high-fiving Wesley and also at this boy looking wildly glad to see her.

"How you doing, Mr. Anderson? My name is Delpha Wade, and I'm from the phone company. I'm bringing you this book they shoulda give you when they installed your phone." She held up the new phone book, smiling back, but her smile strained as she examined him.

She'd placed him as young, but up close the fine lines around his eyes and across his forehead were much more pronounced. He wasn't a teenager. The hair that fell on his forehead in boyish bangs, that had appeared fair, was mainly gray, laced with pale brown. His age might be forty, even closer to fifty. He looked like…a happy, withered child.

"Raffie," someone called from the back of the house. "Bring your bag back here, and get your towels."

The man grinned, showing small, widely-spaced teeth. "Bitch," he said excitedly.

Delpha startled. Then felt irritated because she'd let this unusual person's high spirits disarm her.

He turned and lunged past the table and a galley kitchen to the hall, dragging a canvas duffel bag by its strap. In a minute he came stumbling back, the bag fuller. He grabbed her hand, saying *Bitch bitch* and yanked her around, laughing.

Delpha cast back through her experience but did not find a cue to guide her here. Moving slowly, she caught their joined hands, patted his, and gently extracted hers.

An old man tanned to the shade of a football except for a white band of upper forehead skin, entered the room with some folded clothing. Seeing her, he dropped the clothes on the dinette table and strode across the living room to guide the other man away from Delpha. He inserted himself between them.

"If you're selling somethin', we're not buyin' today," he said, pleasantly, matter of factly. His gaze, though, slid around her, verifying she was the sole person at the door. He bent over to cough.

"No, sir, I'm not a peddler," Delpha said. "Bringing you your phone book. You Mr. Anderson?"

"That's me, and I got one. You'll have to 'scuse us, but we're packin' to go to the beach." He took hold of the doorknob.

"Oh, sure. They musta made a mistake down the office. Sorry to bother you."

The door shut on Delpha's sociable wave.

…on the songs of birds. So many birds.

J.T. Davies sank. Jim Anderson bobbed to the top of her final list. He had a friend. And the birds. Could be a coincidence. People did have friends and pets. But then there was his reaction—the man'd creased forward from the breastbone, and when he straightened, it was with a cough, and his tanned face was longer.

Delpha's head was yellow and green and hopping and flying. She was dying to tell Phelan she'd found Rodney.

Well, she was 98 percent sure she'd found him, but Mr. Wally, the business teacher at Gatesville, always cautioned them not to rush: "Think slow, act fast." So maybe it was best her boss was off scouting in the waterlands today. There might be a way to nail down that last 2 percent. She'd visit the Wertman's shop. Check out the proprietors, and see if they'd known an Anderson back in New Orleans.

Or as they kindly said out here in the free world: two birds, one stone.

XXVII

DELPHA WAS SWEATING at her desk in the morning when Phelan walked in and sniffed at the office's roasting air, underlaid with an element of mildew. He spread his hands out in front of him, saying, "What the hell, Calvin?"

"Well, good morning to you," she said. "Calvin called. Said he had to drive over to Orange and pick up a part there 'cause the one he brought didn't work. Be back soon as he can."

"I hope that's five minutes." Phelan shook loose the knot in his tie, slid it off, and unbuttoned his collar. "Gotta make a call. Then let's catch up on our business."

"Got somebody to see. Maybe I could do that now, then we could catch up?"

Pretty sparkly smile, Phelan noted as he nodded. Delpha, already holding her purse, headed for the door. Something going on.

Well, he'd find out soon enough. Phelan held the line, waiting for his uncle to answer, grimacing at the defunct AC unit. Least E.E. wasn't mad anymore, he didn't think. Having his uncle mad at him had been like a slow-mo heart attack.

"Guidry."

"Mornin', E.E."

"You again."

Like a beekeeper gingerly removing a tray from the hive, Phelan set aside this ambiguous greeting. "Callin' cause I got something for you. Give me three of your precious minutes if you will."

"Throw me somethin'."

"You might send a couple guys out, watch for a boat docking in the middle of the night, carrying more than shrimp."

"*Merci beaucoup*, Tom. Now you gonna tell me how you come to make that suggestion."

Phelan was quiet. "Not news to you, is it?"

"Less say, there are certain operations at work, yes. And recently, very recently, so I wanna know how'd you hear about it. What's your interest here, Mr. P.I.?"

"Simple business. A wife that wants to keep her man at home. He's making monopoly money, and she doesn't know how. Doesn't know what he's doing, but she knows he needs to be stopped from doing it."

"That is one smart wife."

"Yeah, she is."

"Think he's running dope?"

"Think he was, she said he used to stay gone a while on trips. Now just overnight."

"You don't know anything else? 'Cause if you do, you betta say so yesterday."

"Few names like Phil and Waffle and Ding-ding, sound like clowns for kiddies. But listen, my guy's an upholsterer. Strictly amateur. My source called him a cheese weasel."

"Source." E.E. laughed *huh*. "You takin' this serious, Tom."

"It's my business. I don't, who will."

"My crystal ball tells me you 'bout to aks me for somethin', and I'm gettin' a picture of what it is."

"'Magine you are. The wife tells me when he's going out, I tell you, and you let me take my upholsterer home. You get the rest of the operation. The crew, the load, boat or trucks—whatever it is."

This was a first-rate trade, and Phelan knew not to say

so to the Chief of Police. He knew to pile on. "'Course I'll tell you when it's going down anyway, you know that."

"Yeah you betta. 'Specially now I know you know."

"There's that. You agree?"

"You can have the upholsterer. Call me the minute the wife calls you."

"You bet." Phelan tossed up his ballpoint and caught it. Didn't say another word. He'd heard steam building, and he was not about to step into it. Again.

There was a clangy crash from the other end of the phone line.

"I'll be god*damn*," E.E. burst out, "if this ain't some Key West shit come to Texas. Oh, I can see it." *Clang*. "These Texas boys, their granddaddies cooked shine, their daddies ran shine, they heard the stories 'bout outrunning and outgunning the revenuers, they heard the rock n roll songs, they gonna get in on it. They all swashin' and bucklin' on the high seas. Dodging the law, fanning wads of cash in the mirror. You smoke that stuff in Vietnam?"

Wiping off the sweat at his temple, Phelan recalled: *With booze you lose, with dope there's hope. Always ripped or always stoned made it a year I'm going home.*

He told the sort-of truth. "Once or twice."

"Well, now you on civilized land. Now you back in the U.S. of A. Nixon's got him a whole chart. Marijuana's not Fritos, cher, it's a Schedule 1 drug. Schedule 1. You want the skinny, come by the station and read the reams of info they sending us. Lemme tell you, Tom. When those trucks roll in or the pirate ships sail in, however they're hauling it, maybe we can't get 'em all, but we'll get some of 'em. They gonna find out it's not Tinkerbelle waitin for 'em at the dock."

Clang. "Fuck Florida."

The phone flat-lined.

Ear ringing, Phelan came and stood in his doorway, ready to report yesterday's work to Delpha. Nobody behind her desk. It had skipped his mind that she was gone.

A knock on the door interrupted his disappointment.

Ben's hesitant entrance was trailed by an odor of chemistry lab. He stepped in wearing a weathered blue work shirt, holey jeans, and a spooked expression. Hair looked like it hadn't been combed since his last visit. He was carrying an oversize manila packet and the black folio.

Ben nodded. It was an agreeable nod, but he also looked like he might throw up.

"So—" Phelan tipped his head—"what you got?"

"The blow-ups. Plus something else. But here, look." Ben whipped the photos out of the manila packet and slapped two onto the desk. The first seemed to show a gray slab that featured protrusions and indentations; it met a haze of gray and darker shapes. The second had the same protrusion, but its angles were marked by a pencil applied with force.

"Look, nine centimeters to the tip, almost four around the curve, see?"

"See those numbers. But that's close to double life-size, isn't it?" Phelan had figured out the main object was a nose.

"Right. I got ears and jaw on another sheet." Ben flicked down another weird photo beside the first. This one was color, pinks and grays, connected to a complicated black structure. A nose, glasses.

"Not as fuzzy as I thought they'd be. This one's the closest angle to mine. OK, now look." The next photograph was another print of the color photo, only measured and marked. "Tip's a little bit longer or fatter, one, because the measurement's off a little, but, man, they're close. See, check out the shapes. If you can't see it, Tom, think of geography, like these are hills or something."

"No, no, man, I'm seeing it." Phelan put his finger on the color one. "This is my client." Then he tapped Ben's black and white. "And this, this is yours. Who is he?"

Ben flipped out a black and white eight by ten—a man in a bucket hat. With a tripod for his camera. He was standing back from the instrument, back of his hand to his forehead, as though he'd just wiped sweat off. The hat was tipped up. He had hair.

"Him. Probably your man's brother. Or the closest one to your color shots anyway. Figure the odds."

"Done that. So my client told us the truth about his brother's bird-watching habit. Here's the brother with a family resemblance." Phelan cheered, clapped the boy on the shoulder. "I'll find him out there, track him home, and end of case. What he does next is his own call. All right, Ben. A plus for this class."

Ben's shoulder had no give, and his face had no A-plus joy, but Phelan charged on, "I've got your picture, I'll find him. You're off the clock, kid. Go home, write out your bill, and pat your own back. Got it?"

"Tom…"

"What's the problem?"

"No problem. No, I mean, problem, but…" Ben licked his lips.

"Spit it out."

"Don't know if this is the man you're looking for, but… hot in here, isn't it?" Seemed the boy became aware of and simultaneously forgot this fact about the office. "Last evening I drove over to the wetlands at Anahuac. Thought I might spot your guy. Wasn't there, but I hung around. Before sunset is when all the birds fly in—and early in the morning. Tons of birds, and there'll be lots more next month. The light, the water quality. It's incredible. You know."

"Not really. But go on. Excuse my manners. Take a seat over in the blue chair, you want."

"No, I'd get something on it. I need to show you these." He offered the black folio to Phelan.

Phelan took it and sat down behind Delpha's desk. He pushed aside her paper piles and unlatched the folio. Eight by ten photograph of gray reeds, above their straight edge, a blur, a thick litter of salt and pepper against the pale gray sky. Next, a shot of low ponds ringed with white birds, in between, patches of field where black birds and white birds stood or flapped in the grass.

"Ground's mushy. I laid down a tarp and lay out flat. So I wouldn't scare 'em off. Still got wet."

Water, land, birds descending, far bank of clouds.

Birds, feet out, wings back-stretched for a water-landing, behind them reeds, grasses on the land, far to the left side of the scene a low white sun stippled with black flecks. Other birds coming in.

"What? These're pretty, I can see that. But—"

"Look at the next one, Tom."

The birds that had been landing now navigated the water, and the focus was raised to the bank, where more birds milled, facing every-which direction. The reeds were darker than gray now. "Look at that," Phelan said. At the far left of the picture, in a break in the reeds, stood a sunlit doe, her hooves at the waterline and her head lifted and turned toward the rest of the shot, ears flaring. She looked ready to run.

"No. Over there."

Phelan transferred his gaze to the picture's right side. One tall fattish bird with a long bill stood by itself, facing back toward the deer, though too far away to see it. Behind the bird was a hump from which extended a thick branch that grew long and then…

"What's that darker thing?"

"Keep going," Ben said. His hands were now tucked in his armpits.

In the next shot, the long-billed bird stood as before, except now it more nearly faced the camera, and Phelan could just make out the paddle-shape of the end of its bill that rested on its feathers. The hump was taller and the branch raised into the sky. But blurred. Phelan snatched up the next one, pretty sure what he'd see.

The photographer had caught the branch—some kind of sword—just as it fell onto the bird, and the upper part of the branch was bifurcated—two arms. The dark hump, which had to be a man, was compressed again.

Ben had captured a few frames of a man in the wetlands murdering a bird.

"Chopped the everlivin' shit out of him, didn't he?"

"Little pieces. I think. I didn't go look."

"Machete?"

"Maybe. You tell me."

Phelan squinted. "Blade's straight. Bayonet. Christ." In the following photo, some few features of the hump could be discerned. Two lighter specks in the black. Eyes. Below them, a white glint…teeth.

"Why in hell didn't you take him close-up," Phelan said softly.

"I know, I know!" Ben's face was anguished. "My friend was using his zoom for class. If you're mad, I understand. Man, *do I*."

The boy dug the heels of his hands into his temples and clamped his head. "And I didn't even shoot him leaving."

"See him well enough to describe him? Concentrate."

"I don't know, old? I didn't budge, Tom. Just a big fat chicken. You probably want to fire me now. Go ahead."

A cloud of mortification and vinegar sulfide wafted toward Phelan, who drummed his fingers soundlessly, absorbing, calculating. Finally said, "You stayed up late to develop these. Didn't you?"

Ben's arms dropped. "Pretty near all night."

"OK then. There's chicken, and then there's stupid. Might be, just might be, I don't know—you're not either. Best thing you could a done was not move a fuckin' inch. I'm not gonna fire you. Next job you do for us, I'mon buy you a movie camera."

Ben's head whipped up so fast he had to steady his wire rims, and his mouth flew open. He practically bowed at the door.

XXVIII

THE DOOR TINKLED as she entered Wertman's. Toward the back, sitting on a tall stool, was a trim white woman in a navy blue suit that could have been tailored in 1950. White lapels. Double-stranded pearl choker. She tipped her gray head, and Delpha nodded back.

She hoped to pick up information that could airtight-prove Anderson was the Rodney they were looking for. Before she talked to the proprietor, though, Delpha wanted to examine the shop, ringed with glass cases. Like Xavier Bell's world, this shop. Or so he'd claimed.

Nothing on the counters that might be slipped into a pocket, a purse. The walls were hung—up high, beyond grabbing distance—with swords, muskets, rifles, paintings, and maps. The sword nearest Delpha had a hilt carved from yellowing ivory in a spiral pattern. Its scabbard hung below, two thick rings on it. So it could be attached to a horse? A belt? Its blade was straight, but the next two swords were curved. She leaned in to read the cards beneath—an artillery saber, leather and wire hilt, Civil War. An older—1818—and less graceful saber, next. Then a very long rifle, French. A Civil War carbine and one from before the war, with fancy brass in its stock. Each gleamed softly, dustless.

The cases guarded pistols, labeled and priced coins of all kinds from Greek to Indian Head nickels, and jewelry in fussy, old-fashioned settings.

The walls nearer to the saleswoman featured framed

maps. One seemed to be a map of a lake with low, pointy hills surrounding, but Delpha wasn't sure. Its writing was not in English. Funny faces formed its margins, fat-cheeked men spitting. A map of Africa, brave little sailing ships blowing toward its pink coasts.

"May I help you?"

"Oh, I'm just looking." Delpha craned her head. "Your shop is kept so nice. You must use one of those dust mops on a long stick."

The lady's lips twitched. Close-up her pretty white lapels were ivoried with age. One was adorned with a small pin in the shape of a butterfly made from ice and frost.

"Oh, yes. My brother is very particular."

"That would be Mr. Wertman? Who used to do business in New Orleans?"

"Yes, our parents did. Now. What may I show you? Not, I think, a sabre."

Delpha shook her head. "Who buys those?"

"Collectors. Long-time customers. Also now, home decorators. But you, Miss—a pair of pearl earrings, you'd like to see maybe?" She tapped the case in front of her, where two fat pearls nestled in midnight black velvet. Not white, not quite pink. Delpha didn't intend to even look at them.

"Oh, no...I—"

"Try." Smoothly, the woman set the box on the counter, followed by an upright mirror. One second the earrings were in the case, the next they were before Delpha's eyes. The woman held up one of the pearls, and Delpha saw that it dangled from a short gold chain.

"I couldn't. I never pierced my ears."

"Ears..." The woman waved away ears. "Anyone can pierce. Hold them and—see."

Her voice was warm. She must not get many customers,

Delpha thought with sympathy, and then, as ridiculous a thing as she had ever done, she hooked her hair behind her ear and held one of the glossy pearls to her left lobe. It felt cool. So close, she saw that the pearl was one of those shades of dawn before the sun hikes into the sky. First out of jail, she'd memorized those shades from the backyard of a halfway-house, and later, out in front of the New Rosemont. She let the pearl drop on its fine chain. It swung merrily, a tiny, lighted globe.

Delpha had wanted a lot and daily: to be free, to have a room that belonged only to her, not to be told what to do, not to hear other people—to disappear them, to pick her own food to eat, to walk near water and under the sky, see spring coming by the change in the light, have a beloved arm enclose her waist. In prison, a section of her brain was watching, one was judging, and another, a big, hard-working section, was withstanding. Though she didn't have command of it, there was a dead section she tried not to add to. Most all sections knew how to yearn. A pearl, she had never yearned for. Not even in the top hundred things. But yearning, she knew, lay coiled in a lidless case, so it could spring out at any time.

She put the second pearl to her right ear. Its luster touched her like a voice. "Are they from the ocean?"

"I'm afraid I didn't hear you." The lady leaned toward her.

Delpha cleared her throat. "Real pearls?"

"You are in Wertman's, young lady. Only real, we sell."

Delpha's chin slanted. An adjustment had just occurred, a shift in perspective, as she understood she had not been in a store like this before. This lady with the frost pin was a different deal than most people that ran a cash register: she had a connection with the items she sold, and she enjoyed handling them.

"How much would these cost?"

"Genuine freshwater pearls. Not treated in any way, their color will not fade. Eighteen carat, the gold. Forty dollars. And—for three more, a deposit, these studs you can take." Her palm appeared with two ball-and-post earrings. "These are stainless steel. Use them for six weeks after your ears are pierced. Return them, we refund the three dollars. A very fair price."

Delpha's salary was sixty-four dollars a week, room and board fifty-five. "Do you take layaway?"

"What is your name?"

"It's Wade. Delpha Wade."

"Mrs. Singer." The lady's glancing handshake was a pantomime. "Yes, Miss Wade, we offer a layaway plan." She reached into a drawer behind the counter and came out with a pad of forms. "Now, each week, how much will be your payment?"

Delpha pressed her lips together. Then said, "I'm sorry, ma'am, I can't. Pretty as they are." The reluctance in her own voice sounded false. But she wasn't acting. She'd run out of breath at the end of that sentence.

Mrs. Singer continued to study her a second longer. The trace of a smile on her narrow face did not signify offense, possibly calculation. "Today, it's not necessary you decide. Come back anytime. Seventeen years, Wertman's is here." She placed the pearls in their velvet box and set the little box back into the display case, where they gleamed from behind the glass. "Everyone should have something that is lovely forever."

She wrote down Delpha's full name on the form and then tucked the form tablet away. By the time the shopkeeper looked up at her again, the roundabout speech Delpha had planned in order to extract information had somehow dispersed. Her head was dizzied from considering such an outlandish purchase.

She asked Mrs. Singer directly about other shops of this kind in New Orleans. Years ago. Told her, straight-out, that she was searching for someone for her employer, who was a private investigator. It was a matter of two brothers and a business. Delpha had thought there might be resistance to questions some would consider prying or time-wasting, but she found none.

"On behalf of this family, you are searching. I see." The woman swiveled on the stool and called, "Herschel, come here. Help me remember the stores in New Orleans."

A thin man older than Mrs. Singer appeared in an open doorway holding a cloth, his eyebrows raised in anticipation of helping his sister.

On hearing the name Delpha was interested in, *Anderson*, Mr. Wertman exclaimed, "How old do you think we are?"

"And how wicked?" asked his sister.

XXIX

EXITING PHELAN INVESTIGATIONS, Ben almost ran
down Delpha. He excused himself three or four times and was
gone. She entered, her blue-gray eyes snapping.

She and Phelan were looking straight at each other, and
funny, for a second his view rippled like there was no office
but a walless, placeless distance they were looking across. He
shook his head. *Heat mirage? TV commercial? What kinda mind-
slipping shit was this?*

As Delpha passed him, he closed his hand around her
upper arm. Damn, meant not to do that again, just couldn't
help it. "Listen, I've got some news on Cheryl's case. But
Ben's was even better. Ten'll get you twenty, the kid's found
Rodney."

Delpha looked at his hand on her arm. "Been longin' to
tell you. So've I."

"Well, hell," Phelan said, grinning, "this calls for a road
trip." He suggested a conference—somewhere out of this oven
of an office.

They took highway 69 and then 96 South toward Port
Arthur. He thought of a remark to say, but he didn't say
it, and she didn't talk either. Quiet was nice. Tires singing
on the road. Rushing air. The AC was running on high and
car window was down, too, wind whipping Delpha's hair.
When they got into town they cruised through a couple
neighborhoods of small houses, nothing tall, like a big hand
had evened every house down to the same low height. Some

well-used boats in the yards, some camper trailers edged with rust. They curved around, took the avenue that led only to the refinery, broad as the brown road to industrial Oz. Phelan pulled off on the shoulder, giving them both a full-on, full-on view. The oil pumped by the deep-sea rigs Phelan had worked—this was its destination.

The refinery rose behind its wide-opened gates, the metal skeleton of a majestic smoking city. Connected by a network of gray pipe as concentrated and looping and linking as a body's exposed blood vessels. Square, woven formations like unfaced, unwindowed apartment buildings. Gray towers ringed by successive platforms only wide enough to hold a man or two, rows of squat round tanks, close to the ground, higher tanks oranged with rust, derricks, towering cranes, flares flagging out flame and black smoke.

Without the refinery, Port Arthur might be a village with a little fishing, people selling to day-trippers down to dabble in the water or serving the bankers whose sailboats snugged into the marina. Refinery gave you hamburger and chicken five nights a week instead of macaroni or collards and cornbread, gave your family a pickup truck and a sedan, sent your girl to nursing school and your boy to college with a slipstick in a case.

Phelan U-turned and drove, stopped the car by a grand old house not far from the seawall. All white like a wedding cake left in the freezer for fifty years, its pillars and wraparound porch salt-air-peeled, chipped, wind-whipped, lonely. "Rose Hill Manor," he said as they got out of the car. He lifted his chin at the old mansion's second-story veranda that would have hosted a hundred guests hoisting bourbon or lemonade. The water was just out of sight over the hill.

"I'm glad and proud to have my own office," he said suddenly. "My own business." His dark hair, glinting auburn in the sun, blew around his face. "But out here…I'm somebody else." His face worked, and he turned his back on her, starting toward the water. "Thinking you might know what I mean."

Saying this, he didn't look her in the face. Delpha appreciated that. And she knew what he meant. Fourteen years locked in cinderblock and steel? Hell yes, she knew. Out here the salt wind blew. Sunshine poured down, not summer-roasting right now, but hot enough to burn your nose. Up over the rise was about to stretch an expanse of water, and she was about to see and feel it. She followed him up, her arms rising lightly from her sides. She couldn't keep them down. Riding on the wind, coming off the old white-on-white mansion, the smell of roses drifted to her nose. She scanned for the rose bushes to see what color was blooming so late in the season, but didn't see any bushes. Just some honeysuckle vine over by the house.

They walked up to the sea wall, the barrier of granite chunks lined far as you could see.

Phelan'd been heartened when, in the beginning, Delpha Wade had said "we" about the business. Felt like he wasn't alone in this flyer he was taking, someone was on his side. Someone who fit with how he saw stuff. Her getting grievously hurt had added another layer of complicated, job-related feelings. Now he gazed out at Sabine Lake, glittering fiercely under the sun, past it to the far shore, which belonged to Louisiana, trees and green scrub. Sun, air, water, the view free and wide. He took a deep, windy breath and examined his proprietary attitudes toward Phelan Investigations. He poked at them, found them surprisingly elastic. Possibly because she was a woman, it seemed more like she was helping and less like she was horning in. Was that right? Or not?

"This conference is a fine idea," Delpha said. Her arms were out, the wind ruffling her sleeves.

Phelan got to it. "Our first cases, it worked out I could do most of the footwork, and you were in the office. Isn't working out that way now."

"Noticed that." She angled to face him, wind streaming her hair backward.

"Listen, Delpha, you're gonna help out on jobs, I should pay you more, but it's only right to ask if you wanna do that. I know you like keeping the files and stuff and you know how to lay out bills and you sure as hell know how to talk to clients but—"

"No, I do."

"Do what?"

"Like working on the jobs, too." She stayed looking out at the sparkles popping on the water, not at him.

"Driving around to the realtors, maybe even the homebuyers, that's OK with you?"

"You mean, do I get homesick for my desk? I like finding things out, Tom. Like I look at those names, and I wonder what these two old men playin hide n' seek want with each other."

Phelan nodded. "Yeah, me too. OK then, guess we agree, so gimme the big news. Tell me about finding Rodney yesterday."

"Tell me your Frank news first."

Phelan shot her a look. "Oh, man, yours must be good." He ran down his coastal-reconnaissance/shrimp-buying trip, the odd envious comment about other people's riches or smug stare—and his talk with Ticker, who most certainly was an ocean-going man. One who carried a Smith & Wesson backed up by a shotgun while he was doling out shrimp at a roadside stand.

Delpha's eyebrows raised. "That's sure something. So you'll just wait to get a call from Cheryl, that the plan? She'll tell you where Frank's going. Think Frank tells her the truth?"

"No. She might come up with some trick that makes him, I don't know. I do know that I'll follow him." A private investigator with years instead of months' worth of experience might have all sorts of tricks for tailing, but until he had those experienced years, Phelan's Operating Procedures were Common Sense and Winging It.

They stayed out there in the windy open a while, strolling the cement path, watching the lake ripple and gleam. Then they drove back in the direction of Pleasure Island. "Used to be a park over there on the island," Phelan said, "golf course, biggest roller coaster in Texas. They had a ballroom three thousand people could dance in."

"Really. Ever dance there?"

"Nah. Heard it was big during the war."

"Guess it would be. All those girls in homemade sundresses."

"All those sailor boys and Guadalcanal waiting for 'em."

Delpha pointed. They checked out a couple shrimpers at the marina, just floating there unmanned. Docked and docile. They drove up and down by the channel, checking out spots a boat could berth. Not here, too public. Their boat, Phelan thought, would slip into the wetlands, some dirt road siding a channel, like the ones he drove the other day. Somewhere not so far from here, makeshift landing pier maybe, channel dredged so the boat could come in, somewhere middle of the night. Close to a highway. Maybe they'd have a lookout, maybe just a bunch of offloaders, working fast.

Farther on, a pick-up-sticks jumble of white masts attached to a bunch of sailboats, their slender hulls painted candy colors. "Pretty," Delpha said. "So here's what I found out yesterday."

"You don't mind, let's talk about Bell at the right place." Phelan grinned. "This conference's a field trip. Smugglers and birdlands."

"Where's that?"

"Aw, there's a few of them. Let's drive."

They wove around through a patch of slash pine that looked like a pencil plantation and on into the tangled piney woods. House tucked here, one there, back seats and flower pots on the porches, girl in one yard lolling in a tire swing. Round and round to a sharp right turn onto a gravel road the car crunched down. After a while screens sprang up both sides of the road: six-foot reeds bearing white flowers. Phelan rolled his window all the way down. The tall reeds blowing and brushing in the wet wind made the sound of cloth ripping. Moist wind again as they rolled down this green, swaying tunnel to a ranger hut. No ranger. The wooden booth was empty but had a rack with saggy pamphlets you could take.

"Shows how the road goes," Delpha said, her finger tracing, "this line. Lookit all the birds. They got a list of ones stop here." She ran her finger the length of the pamphlet. "Look at all the kinds of egrets. Great egrets, little egrets, middle-size egrets. Like Goldilocks in the bears' house. There's even a red one. And a Chinese one."

They rolled on down the narrow, shell road, leaving behind, after a while, the reed walls. Grasses green and dried-tan, grasses with bayonet edges faced the full ditches that ran each side of the road. When the road rose, they could see past this dense border to marsh islands beyond: curly green islands dotted throughout brownish water. Then the road descended again, even with the ditches. Birds were calling. Phelan slowed further.

"Turtle," Delpha said, twisted to peer out her window, "swimming over here. Dragonflies! See 'em? Big brass ones." She turned back to him, hair flying, her face alight.

His breath skipped. Hadn't seen that expression since…

when? Back in May, the evening he handed over the duplicate key to the office of Phelan Investigations. Or August, at the wake of an old woman she'd been hired to care for, when she'd helped load the Rosemont table with pies, pralines, ham and barbecue, and lilies.

Up ahead a great egret coasted down to the ditchwater, back-flapping so he could land. "Wingspread of a B-52," Phelan said.

"Lookit them."

He turned from watching the huge white bird plunge its stick legs into the water to see that farther down the road seven or eight smaller egrets had self-assembled. Every one stared seriously into the wind, intent as remnants of a squad, scanning the field after the fight is over. Their staggered line, produced when each landed separately to join its fellows, their still attention, gave him this image. The egrets didn't stir until the car came within ten feet of them, and then only reluctantly, a little one hopping into the air, the others flapping a short distance to the ditch, reclaiming their road after the car had passed.

Delpha whispered, "Lookathere." Visible, through the wild greenery, a long flat head and jaws, part of a mud-colored barrel on the mud bank. Ridged tail, short, fat-clawed legs camouflaged by ferns and reeds. Maybe hunting, maybe just hunkered there soothed in his mud-water world as the poor, unbounded air creatures cried above him.

"OK," Phelan said quietly because this place made him quiet, "let's have it."

She turned away from the gator, back to Phelan.

"I b'lieve Rodney's name's Jim Anderson. His fake name. He's a homebuyer. You went to his house, but he wasn't there."

"Anderson. Right, the house with the Christmas tree farm in front. How do you figure it's him?"

"Bunch of reasons. Right age, giant cage of parakeets,

a younger man with him that's…sweet and not right in the head. I talked to some Beaumont shopkeepers used to do business in New Orleans, and they told me Anderson was a big name there, back at the turn of the century. You're picking a fake name, maybe a familiar one comes to mind quicker. He's outside a lot because his face is real tanned 'cept at the top. Like a farmer's. But he's not a farmer. There was a little black case with a strap on his dinette table. Right size to be a case for binoculars. Like somebody watching birds would carry."

Phelan stared at this news. "Stellar work, Delpha."

They looked at each other, sitting there with the warm wind running through the car windows, bending and rustling the reeds.

Delpha pointed. Large bird, wings outspread, canted a few degrees in the wind. Phelan leaned into the windshield. "Hawk. Can't tell if it's redtail or white."

"Doesn't matter if you don't belong in this place. Nobody does. It belongs to them."

"Who?"

Delpha spread her arms wide, the left one grazing Phelan's shoulder. The right one arced out the window, taking in the hawk wafting the currents, uneven line of egrets reading the wind behind them, the gator bellied in the reeds.

"Them. They'd bite you if they had to. But not for fun."

Phelan smiled at her, and, instead of running his hand through her hair, he proposed they get hamburgers in Winnie.

On their way back down the road, they passed a weathered middle-aged couple squatting by the ditch at a juncture where the road split, a cooler and a bucket beside them. The woman quickly lowered a wire contraption back into the water, and they both turned to watch the car go by.

Trapping themselves some free, live bait. Minnows.

Phelan waved. Then he braked and put it in reverse. When he reached the spot where the couple was, the bucket was not in sight.

"Hey."

"Hey," the man said, standing up.

"This is gonna sound funny, but y'all seen a guy with a bayonet wandering around out here?"

They stared. The woman looked at the man and away. The man said, "In my dreams, mister."

Phelan Investigations smelled like Aqua Velva and cigarettes and felt like autumn in Anchorage.

Calvin stood up from Phelan's desk chair and strode forward, craning to see past Phelan. "I fixed it for you," he said. The handyman had shaved, anointed himself with oils, and dressed in clean khakis and a t-shirt with an R-rated Harley decal that read—Phelan peered at the dumb cluck—*Put Something Exciting Between Your Legs.*

Delpha entered, glanced at the decal first, screwed up her eyes at the handyman, then passed him to drop her purse in her bottom drawer. In vain Calvin smiled his way out.

Phelan adjusted the AC down to normal. He'd go see Jim Anderson tonight, tomorrow at the latest. He felt good about having toured some waterway geography, though he planned on memorizing specific, likely locations from the map he'd picked up. Just because you dropped out of Boy Scouts didn't mean you couldn't be prepared.

Because: what if he lost Frank? That scenario made Phelan's ego shudder, which reaction he kept to himself. Instead asked, "How's that Dodge running for you?"

"Loud. OK I do an errand in the morning? Won't be too late coming in."

"You don't have to ask," he said.

XXX

DELPHA HAD FINAGLED an advance from Oscar. Along
with prior savings, she had $211 unspent, tucked inside a sheet
corner. Up in her room in the Rosemont, dim morning light
from the alley slanting in, she took out two hundred. Left the
eleven and ran across the street to the Dodge.

In five minutes she was sitting on a soft leather couch
by a receptionist's desk, which was arranged on an area rug
decorated with brown circles and gold squares. On the walls
hung framed pictures of clean hunting dogs, a vase of cattails
on a side table. Cattails stiff in a vase, that was kind of funny
because the last thing they'd been decorating was a ditch.

The receptionist smiled. Her plaid dress, hiked up to
her thighs as she sat in the steno chair, was trimmed with
a large white collar and white cuffs. She rolled her chair to
the phone, punched a button, and held up a finger. "Just a
minute," she mouthed at Delpha.

Who nodded. She was thinking about Mr. Wertman
and Mrs. Singer and asking them about shopkeepers named
Anderson. They'd laughed when they explained that Anderson
had been an important name in New Orleans, but before they
were born. They were far too young to have known him, but
who didn't know of him? Tom Anderson was New Orleans
history, the unofficial mayor of Storyville. Big restaurant,
saloon, and all the—did she know what was Storyville?

Delpha knew. An old inmate had entertained a chow-hall

table once, gabbing about a frolicsome district devoted to the sporting life.

"It was a place," Delpha said, not adding: where whores lived.

The brother and sister painted Storyville in proper names: Iberville and Basin Streets, the houses called Mahogany Hall and the Phoenix, madams Minnie White and Jessie Brown. Tom Anderson with the reach of it all. Mardi Gras krewes and Buddy Bolden's cornet. The brother and sister seemed to enjoy themselves, scattering this history before Delpha. *Yes*, Mrs. Singer had said, *it was a place. Quite a place. And then it wasn't anymore.*

Delpha shifted herself on the couch. Why hadn't she gotten a cashier's check at the bank? She could've just left it for this smiling receptionist to pass on to Miles Blankenship. Delpha compared her white blouse and ironed black skirt, her well-worn black flats, to the short plaid dress with the oversize white collar, the style she'd glimpsed on magazine covers where models kicked out their legs at party angles. She felt like a drawing for ladies' goods in a farm catalog.

Shut up, she told that thought. She was out on a work day doing a personal errand. She had a car to drive. Sometime very soon she'd buy a *Mounds* in the red wrapper, dark chocolate over coconut and an almond in each half, and eat it outside as it melted. But right now she was waiting here with her dishwashing savings in a non-indigent-sized envelope, paying her own way, and that was the name of that tune.

"Mr. Blankenship?" the woman said into the phone. "I have a Miss Wade out here wanting to pay an invoice—" She listened for a minute. "Oh, yes sir, I'll check." The receptionist put down the phone and told her Mr. Blankenship would like a word, then asked her if she had brought the invoice with her.

Delpha pushed it over. Then she opened her envelope and counted out $180 into the woman's hastily offered hand. As the receptionist began to write something, Miles Blankenship strode out into the reception area. Another handsome suit and a faint pink on his cheeks. "Miss Wade," he said, reaching for her hand. "I wanted to say hello. I hope you've recovered from your hospital stay."

"Sure have." She stood up and shook hands. "And I thank you again for what you did for me."

"Just ran defense. You carried the ball. Attorney meetings tend to be forgettable, but not that one."

Delpha had nothing to say to that, and she became aware of an awkward attention from the receptionist. Mr. Blankenship said, "I wanted to ask you, too, about the first trial you had, in 1959. You didn't have an attorney?"

Her face closed. "No, sir. Not really."

Mr. Blankenship looked pained. "After the Gideon case, I mean, after the law changed in '63, you should have been released."

"I know who Gideon was. He didn't play his trumpet for me, Mr. Blankenship."

"I see. Well. Someday I'd like to hear about your trial."

Delpha pressed her lips together, nodding once.

He told her not to hesitate to call if he could ever be of service. "Sincere offer, Miss Wade. Nice to see you again." He walked back the way he'd come. The receptionist's curious gaze lasted a couple seconds longer then gave way to a smile. What a happy employee she was.

"That the receipt?" Delpha asked.

"Yes, ma'am. I wrote your payment down right there for your records and the date," the receptionist said. "Covered all the bases. Can I help you with anything else? No? Then you have a nice day."

Delpha walked out mindful of the power of her own two feet, climbed behind the wheel of the Dart, and creaked its balky door closed. In the rearview mirror, she made the Griffin & Kretchmer smile. She didn't like how she looked in it.

OK, she'd put the $20 left in the envelope into her purse, and later she would insert the lightly-used business envelope back in its box with the others. That would do it.

She pulled into the bumpy parking lot, walked up the stairs and greeted her boss, who was stewing over a phone line that was not reaching Xavier Bell, wherever he was. Phelan strode out to reconnoiter the address Bell had given them on the Phelan Investigations contract and returned steaming. Turned out to be a liquor store. All right, their client would remain ignorant of his brother's location for another day. Phelan needed to go talk to Anderson, anyway, confirm his relation to Bell. But Cheryl's job nagged at him. He and Delpha spent a concentrated two hours on maps with meandering blue lines and blobs, identifying spots a boat might venture in to unload its grassy booty.

Phelan was still at it when Delpha realized she had left a base uncovered.

Delpha met Mrs. Singer at the shop's door, where she was in the middle of turning the sign around to close. The bell tinkled as the shopkeeper let Delpha step in. Sun slanting through the wide windows lit the woman's lined face. Delpha thought how when you had the right bones, a beautiful face stayed a beautiful face.

"Good afternoon. We're closing a little early for the holiday, Miss …?"

"Wade." Delpha didn't know what holiday she could mean.

"Miss Wade. I remember. For the pearls you came back?"

"No, 'fraid not, ma'am. I just have one more question. About somebody else. I'll be quick."

"Why not? We've just had a very nice sale, and as of two hours ago"—Mrs. Singer's smile broadened—"we have a new grandchild in the family. Come up front. We can stay a short while." She raised her voice. "Hershel, bring another glass. We have here a future customer."

Delpha followed her past the display cases to the counter. The shawl collar of her pale gray suit had black piping, and her waist a narrow black belt. Her brother, Mr. Wertman, free of his apron, was bringing out a green bottle. He set down three tiny glasses and filled them with a clear, pale brown liquor.

"You like sherry? Surely you do." He lifted his small glass of crystal, swept with images of ghost-white flowers.

Sherry was a girl's name. Sherry was a song. Delpha was dying to ask the Wertman's her question but found herself saying nothing, only touching her glass to theirs, taking care to be light about it.

"Whose grandchild is it?"

Mrs. Singer said, "Herschel's youngest son has a son." Sister and brother beamed at each other, privately somehow, though they were standing right in front of her.

Delpha still held up her glass, casting around for a right thing to say. "Well, I hope…I hope the little one has a happy life." Then, with relief, she added, "Congratulations to you." Hadn't ever used this expression before that she could remember. She repeated it in her mind, *Congratulations to you*.

Mr. Wertman said, "Thank you, young lady. L'chaim."

Delpha tilted her head at the unknown word then blinked at the taste of the cold, nutty liquid, a light but sharp alcohol the color of honey. The Wertmans smiled a different smile than the receptionist at the law office. The three of them sipped. Her urgent purpose sidetracked, Delpha felt gladly surprised to be in this place, right now, saying a new thing to friendly people, drinking from a fragile glass.

Relinquishing the privacy between themselves, Mrs. Singer said, "Today we sold a map, a fortunate acquisition from the sale of an estate…two years ago? It was drawn in the last years of the 16th century, and it shows the southern coast of the United States. Of course not then the United States."

"Not a fortunate acquisition. My sister has a keen eye. She knew at once that—"

"Herschel," she stopped him. "Trade secrets, Miss Wade. Also called experience. And what did you want to know?" She leaned toward her brother. "She is considering pearls."

"Pearls, every woman should have," said Mr. Wertman. His gaze flicked over her plain clothes, but his polite expression didn't sour. "Single strand?"

"Earrings," said his sister, and the small black box materialized on the counter, its lid—embossed in gold with *Wertman's*—popping open, its contents stealing Delpha's gaze. Her lips parted slightly. How could it be that the gleam on white pearls consisted of the palest pink mixed with the palest gold? She raised her head, her eyebrows. Something—she didn't know what—made this sister and brother laugh.

"My boss, well, we'd like to ask about another shop you might have known in New Orleans. Long shot, but was there a store that had birds, do you know?"

Mr. Wertman was nodding. "The birds brought in customers. Customers liked them. A clever gimmick, our father thought—but imagine the cleaning they had to do."

"When we were small," his sister said, "one of the sons invited us in to see the birds. Gold cages hanging in the store, cages painted pink and green. It was like colors were singing."

Delpha's eyes went from one to the other. "Their name was…"

"Sparrow." They said the name together, but neither laughed at the coincidence.

"So there were Sparrow brothers?"

Mr. Wertman said that the Sparrows had two sons, mostly grown by the time he and his sister knew the neighborhood.

"We did business within a block of one another," Mrs. Singer said. "We never…associated. The Sparrows would not have approved of that anyway, if you understand me." She angled toward her brother. "Which son won a medal in the war?"

Mr. Wertman's brow creased. "I don't remember which was which. The Great War was before we were born, Miss."

They stared at each other, and Mr. Wertman finally shrugged. "One of them won a medal. And didn't…was it one of them who had a child that was put away?"

"Yes, it was, yes. Though again, which one…" Mrs. Singer's hands opened. "Neighbors talked about that. Something not right, so one of them put his child away in an institution. Imagine."

Delpha did not have to imagine "institution." Did your parents know the boys' parents?"

"Not after Kristallnacht. In Germany. You must know of that? WSMB—that was the radio station—and the papers reported that smashing of Jewish shops and synagogues, and …everything else. Not long after, someone threw a large stone through our window. A shopkeeper across the street saw one of the Sparrow men, one of the sons. Our father went and spoke to old Mr. Sparrow. He turned his back. After that, our parents stopped knowing them. For us, the Sparrows weren't there. For them, no Wertmans."

For a second the Wertmans' lively faces appeared to be shaded in curves of charcoal. The cheer in the shop had drained. Delpha understood that she'd done that, as surely as if she'd dropped the delicate glass.

"The proprietor of a nearby restaurant helped my father

glaze the new window. There were others like that. Later when Herschel went to the Army, our mother hung the blue star in the window."

"Would you like more sherry?" Mr. Wertman's finger left a damp print on the cold bottle.

Alcohol was a parole violation, but Delpha said yes. She had her information, but she found she longed for the mood to return, the light mood between the Wertmans that had spilled over onto her. It too was a discovery, and she realized that she was even more curious about that. She prolonged the conversation.

"Your client come and get his map yet?"

"Oh no, we'll ship it to him in Miami. For his law office, he bought it. Would you like to see?"

"I would."

Mr. Wertman produced from the other room a drab drawing only about a foot wide and not even as tall, expanded by a mat and a plain black frame. Delpha was disappointed. She'd expected something bright, maybe with gold on it, and much larger, say, the size of the U.S. maps of multi-colored states like the one that had hung on the wall of Gatesville's day room. In that one, Texas was green, and Louisiana and Oklahoma were yellow.

How neat the design on the browned old paper was, though, with its edges marked off by squares and numbers. Its maker had labeled the country *Flo ri da*. He had included a chopped-short Florida, a southern coastline with inlets of water, and far up above, groups of pointy hills, the stray tree here and there.

Delpha looked up. "But…it's worth a lot of money even if …if Florida isn't shaped like that?"

"In 1597, Miss Wade—"

"Please, call me Delpha."

Mrs. Singer inclined her head, her palm hovering over the map. It was clear she enjoyed gazing at it. "In 1597, Delpha, it was the height of knowledge that this cartographer showed the world. This is what they knew."

This is what they knew. Cartographer. Delpha took in the unfamiliar word. The idea was not unfamiliar. He'd drawn what he knew. That was not much more than the shape of a coastline. Other people would draw different pictures, later, when more territory was known, all the way up to the colored map in the Gatesville day room. Which was correctly drawn. But nobody would pay a lot of money for that map, while they were paying it for this old one.

So, discoveries mattered. Even the beginnings of discoveries. They mattered in the world and to Delpha personally, and this idea struck her as a form of advancement. To know that about herself.

She sipped the cold wine, lifted back again into Mrs. Singer's and her brother's almost-restored mood, which was, she understood, held aloft by the grandson. The mood was a picture into a possible place where some people lived, as remarkable to Delpha at first sight as the old map had been to Mrs. Singer. As near as she could tell, this mood was a family place. They were long used to friendliness, this brother and sister, at ease. A searing feeling passed from her stomach into her chest. There could sometimes be friendliness in prison. Not ease. To make a mood like this took time and habit.

Delpha coveted it, this calm and friendly place she had just glimpsed. Yes, she did. Not so long ago, someone had asked her what she wanted. Here was something. How many years to make a thing like this? And with who?

Mrs. Singer added, "Cornelius Van Wytfliet was one of the first to map the New World. This is only one page of his atlas."

"One page," Delpha repeated. Oh. Like a road atlas for

a territory without roads, this drawing was one page from a book of maps. That explained its size. It had been in a book. At the bottom, flowing from its boxed border upward to the curved coastline, Cornelius had drawn a broad field of wavy lines that meant water.

An idea lapped onto the shore of Delpha's mind.

"I'll go," she said. "Thank you." She would not say congratulations again, but she searched for something. "You said it was a holiday?"

Mr. Wertman capped the green bottle. "A Jewish holiday. Today is—"

"—the birthday of the universe," Mrs. Singer finished. Keys jingled. "I'll walk you to the door."

XXXI

SHE WAS CLOSE to whispering, but Phelan recognized her voice when she said his name because he'd been waiting to recognize it.

"It's Cheryl. Frank's going out tonight."

"When?"

"Round ten."

"Know where?"

"Hell, no. The king doesn't tell the peons where the ball's gonna be."

"Try to find out, Cheryl. I'm on come over by your house. You know the UTote'M?"

"Down the end of the street, sure. Hit it twice a day."

"OK. Number of the pay phone there's 361-5709. Write that down. You call me there. Try to get it out of him. Anything else you know?"

"Yeah. It's for sure only tonight. Not going off on a trip this time. He's all bent out of shape about that."

"Like how?"

"Like he doesn't get to play with the big kids. He said to be ready to make pancakes and link sausage when I see him next. So I said, 'And when would that be, Your Royal Highness?'"

"What'd he say?"

"'Shut up.'"

"You sure you wanna keep this husband, Cheryl?"

"I wonder." The receiver set down quietly.

Phelan sadly beheld the heat-rising feast he'd just unpacked onto a dinner plate. Pile of fried catfish, crispy hushpuppies. Side of slaw, side of beans, tartar sauce in three separate containers, lemon slices, and napkins.

He dumped most of the Styrofoam container of beans into his mouth. Then the hushpuppies. Couldn't risk choking on catfish bones. Still chewing, he pissed and then stepped out of his clothes and deserted them on the bathroom floor. Yanked on dark pants and t-shirt, black low-tops, the Bellas Hess outfit. Had gear prepared: binoculars, a big flashlight and a little one, hundred dollars in twenties, his gun, and a ball cap that shadowed his face. In the glove compartment of his car was stashed a roll of dimes for the phone. In his trunk, among other equipment, a tire iron and a baseball bat. If there was something else he needed besides ESP, Gorilla Monsoon's backhand chop, and a poncho of invisibility, he was sure to find out.

He made a phone call.

"What?" E.E. barked.

"The upholsterer," Phelan said, "he's going out tonight, and I'm calling you like I said."

"Where?"

"Don't know. The wife's gonna call back. She finds out, I find out."

"We find out."

"Iffy, E.E. Put somebody sneaky on him, and we'll all caravan out to the location. Or send your guys out wherever they've been looking. Seeing as you're the police and you have guys."

Phelan coasted into a spot near the UTote'M's outside pay phone with its dangling, ripped phone book, sat, his ball cap low. If he walked out to the curb, he could sight down Figg Street to Frank's driveway and his wife's pretty Mustang.

Also a spavined pickup with new tires. Phelan had scoped out the pertinent geography soon after Cheryl's visit to his office, including the pay phone's number, which he memorized. Now, given the abused state of its directory, he hoped the phone was still in working order.

He got out and tried it. Dial tone, all right. Hung it up and leaned against the wall, waited. The breeze mild, pleasant. Clouds on the moon. The station's orange security lamp stained the leafy underside of the nearest tree an orangey-brown. Weird effect. When the pay phone rang, he went for it.

"Tom?"

"Yeah, what you got?"

"Oh God," she said in a strained voice, "High Island."

A cloud sailed past the moon, and it shone out.

"All right. Good job."

"Keep him outa jail, OK?"

Phelan hung up, dialed E. E.'s number again, but his uncle was no longer at home. He told his Aunt Maryann to get word to E.E. that it was High Island. "Okey doke," she said. She did not ask what "it" was.

Phelan cruised down Figg Street, parked on the street behind a white pickup with an over-the-cab camper, pressed himself into the door to keep an eye on Frank's house. In an hour and twenty-seven minutes, a tall man dressed in dark clothes a lot like Phelan's came out the front door, pair of gloves tucked in his belt. Dome-light hit his profile as he opened the truck's door and stopped there a second to lift a lighter to his cigarette. Whoa. Far as Phelan could tell, the guy with the layers of sun-kissed blond hair and the long mustache was the Sundance Kid.

Frank lit his smoke. Then pivoted and cast a glance back at the house. Closed the truck's door. Slid behind the wheel of the Mustang.

Really?

Well, the guy was an upholsterer, liked his leather seats. Had probably never put *asset* and *forfeiture* together. Unlike Phelan, he had not acquired and studied government information sheets disseminated to the local police. Frank had probably not paid attention to the roger-dodgers of Congress who had just signed in a new department called the Drug Enforcement Agency. Given they were the federal government, though, those guys were probably still sitting around, tipped back in their chairs, arguing over a logo.

Damn, he'd counted on tailing the slow old pickup.

Look at that. Tan car in his rearview, pulling out way back at the end of the street. Maybe a woman going out for diapers. Or it could be an unmarked car. A half-second horror movie flickered: Tom Phelan walking into the station house after having gotten lost on his way to a bust he himself had called in.

He nailed his eyes to the red of Frank's three-part taillights. If he lost this Mustang, he might as well keep on traveling down to Mexico.

XXXII

THREE A.M. AND he was not in Mexico. He was mashed down behind tall, scrubby grass and a bunch of discarded crates, observing bales of marijuana transferred from a trawler.

Every black stitch Phelan had on was sogged by his proximity to spray and lapping water, and the watery wind had blown straight through his bone marrow. Calf threatening another cramp, he had to shift position again. He lowered himself onto his butt, pulled up his legs, and rubbed one. He assumed that E.E.'s men were out there somewhere. If they'd found the right place, they were. So as far as he could tell, his plan had to be: wait till the cops swarmed in, then talk himself into possession of Frank, either here on the makeshift dock or down at the station. Wouldn't be so copacetic for Frank if his fellow smugglers were to witness that. If E.E. was here, maybe Phelan could get the nod and just siphon Frank away in the general roundup. If the cops didn't swarm in, he'd follow his man home, confront him in his driveway, and recommend retirement in the strongest possible terms.

Why wouldn't they swarm in? How would he know?

Maybe they'd just wait like a big old spider, seize the dope-packed vehicles like stupid buzzy flies, one at a time, bind up the trawler in yellow crime tape. Which, as far as he could see through the binoculars, looked to be tied by only one bowline. Occurred to Phelan that it would have been good to talk all this over with E.E. before tonight. He liked to think he'd have done that, had it not been for their recent standoff. There could have been a concerted plan, in which, of course, Tom Phelan would have been an extremely peripheral cog, but…Tom Phelan would have known what the plan was.

He frowned in the dark.

He needed to get closer if he was going to nab Frank when the time came, but there was a spotter pacing around, his post twenty yards or so past where vans were parked beside the back end of an 18-wheeler. The big truck was sticking out of an improbably large door to a portable building, just parked there, taking on dope. Phelan changed position again and watched the endless loading.

Around four a.m., the truck fired up and was backed out, driver working hard on the maneuvering on this narrow dirt road. Once the truck was out, the bare warehouse with its two huge entrances looked like a kid's out-of-scale drawing. No signs identified it, placed smack-up against the water, or the crude dock next to it. The trawler tied up to the dock had a name; he just couldn't read it in the dark, even with binoculars.

Truck driver revved and pulled off, waving from the window.

Phelan'd gotten as close as he had, maybe fifteen yards farther away, by advancing little by little whenever the spotter paced off into the opposite direction. Felt like Wile E. Coyote. If they'd hired a calmer lookout or let the guy load up on product before clocking in, the spotter might have stuck to his post, and Phelan would still be out in the boonies. In his car parked half on a reedy shoulder and smeared with mud.

He brought up the binoculars again.

Men were climbing in and out of the boat, hefting burlap-covered bales off the shrimper's deck, shoving them into two vans, a pickup with a gooseneck trailer, and some kind of delivery truck with writing on the side. Running the bale a short ways down the dock to the vehicles, trotting back to the boat for another bale. Most guys hefted a bale at a time onto their straining shoulders, one sometimes hauled two. The one that wore no hat, no bandanna over his crowning glory. What'd the bales weigh—forty pounds? Fifty? Frank was showing them, wasn't he?

Tons were coming off that boat. Couldn't judge just how many because, after the truck, the arithmetic-machine in Phelan's head had run out of tape. Didn't matter. What was the harm in pot anyway? Wasn't heroin. Wouldn't make you grab up your grandma's Motorola, pawn your sister's wedding dress off the hanger.

Pot made guys he'd known keep humping their gear, mile after mile of paddy or trailside. It minded your mind for you. Installed a sense of humor over previously un-noted trifles. Could be a time-out, a tiny party for one. Or two. It being illegal was helpful in that sense. Grunts got behind that— middle finger to the Army. Wouldn't be the same charge if you could hit up a vending machine for Marlboro MJ Filters.

Wouldn't be bad, though.

Phelan dragged the back of his hand over his wet forehead. Rubbed his cheeks and nose to warm them. The spotter had gone down to talk to somebody near the trawler.

What had he thought, as a kid, swimming out to that skyscraper ship in the turning basin? That he'd climb on, land in Italy or Spain, Greece or Africa, walk down a gangplank into a city plastered with the banners of a strange world. He'd've been screwed, blued, and tattooed, he knew now, but as a boy he'd pictured a brotherly fantasy: he'd pick up their language, eat stew with the sailors, swab the decks or tend the boilers, whatever sailors did. Be one of them. Was that how these Texas pirates were thinking, heroes of their own brotherhood & bucks movie? Or were they figuring to be businessmen with guns?

By quarter to six, the vans had sped off, and the haulers, not speedy now, were packing bales into the gooseneck trailer. Phelan felt like the Navy had used his body for knot practice. Water was still slapping the dock down there. Wind was dying. Birds were chittering in the trees, diving in the graying sky.

A hum.

Phelan sat up on his numb wet ass.

Definite hum.

The hum picked up, became an engine, became many engines. The end of the dirt road morphed into a pulsing wall of red lights, screeching brakes, and cops flying out of cars. The haulers scattered. Somebody jumped onto the boat's deck. The trawler engine coughed and caught. Down the channel bee-lined a Marine Safety speedboat with blaring white lights. *Look at those sons of guns cut the water.* Soon as they got close to the trawler, a crew member with a megaphone issued garbled commands.

Phelan knocked away bushy branches and crawled from his hideout. He thought it best not to get arrested and to that end walked stiffly to a cop who was stationed at one of the many cruisers. Police Department. Sheriff's Department. Texas Department of Public Safety. Jesus, everybody out here but the ushers at the Jefferson Theatre. Any wife-whackers, carjackers, ransackers, or safecrackers back in Beaumont that picked tonight to clock in, they'd be killing it. Phelan let himself be nabbed and frisked by an excited cop who'd been left to guard the horses. He told the officer who he was, throwing in his relation to the Chief of Police, and eventually convinced him to check his ID and let him keep his gun.

"One guy," he said, "I get one guy. The chief agreed."

"Man, if that's what happens, it happens, but don't look at me."

"Y'all get the vans?"

"Does Satan vomit pea soup? Step back and let me work here."

Phelan stayed out of the way. The back seats of cop cars began to be populated with sweat-drenched, handcuffed men whose faces he squinted at.

Nope, not Frank.

The boat police, meanwhile, were not scaling the trawler—why not? They had it needle-nosed-nailed to the dock, drowned in white light, and were bullhorn-lecturing it.

A black silhouette on the trawler's deck appeared to be lecturing back to the Boat Police.

What.

Whatever he was saying was lost under the Marine Safety Unit's superior decibels. But not his gestures. The guy had one arm over his eyes to ward off the spotlight, but with his other hand he kept pointing downward and then sweeping up his palm and pushing it at them as though he meant to say, *Stay there.* Or *Wait a minute.* Or *Stop in the Name of Love.* What was down there?

Phelan recognized a couple short patrolmen, one black and one white. They'd apparently locked up their prisoners and returned to watch this numbnuts holding off the water cops. He gave them Frank's description, but they shrugged. Phelan scanned the scene for Frank then exchanged a OK-what-are-we-seeing-here glance with the two and raised his binoculars.

The smuggler ranted into the water-cop's face and shoved a hand toward the deck. One of the Marine Safety Patrols passed off the bullhorn and jumped on, backed up by two guys who had their service revolvers aimed. Another, hefting a scoped rifle, was moving up beside them. The man aboard the trawler held up both his hands. High.

The water-cop thundered at the pirate and pointed his gun straight down.

The pirate's "Noooo" could have been heard by cruisers already on their way to the station. The man straight-armed the cop backward, causing him to drop his gun and then scramble after it.

A few weak rays of pre-dawn caught the smuggler, man with a ponytail. He'd bent down and now rose back up hugging a colossal, fat, whitish shield with speckled protrusions, flaps of some kind. He staggered toward the stern. The cop had caught up to the pirate and was hollering, smacking him on the back of the neck. The pirate hunched his shoulders and tucked his head down, managed to keep waddling forward. Whatever booty he was lugging, it exceeded his own personal maximum.

The cop kneed the guy in the tailbone, knocking him farther along, and the guy screamed back.

The shield's flaps paddled.

The Marine Safety Unit might have had a clear target if their compadre hadn't been dead-set on thumping the shit out of the pirate. Thanks to that, the pirate reached the stern and twisted himself and his leaden load. He contracted then heaved the shield out from himself, giving a mighty grunt that turned into a roar from the bottom of his belly. The shield flipped and flew, momentarily, above the water. Its wings, four of them—two long and two short—were speckled like a giraffe, as was its…head. A head. As it descended, dawn light lit up the shell, a mound of brown and verdigris green.

Phelan had been alternately watching for Frank and following the drama on the trawler. Now he stared. He'd never seen a turtle that size, nor seen a sea turtle fly, and he was dumbstruck watching it take to the air. The turtle splashed then rose for a micro-second, a darker shadow within the water. The tops of both curved flippers spread like hawk-wings before they plunged the great animal below the surface.

Spinning around, Phelan looked toward the trawler. The smuggler—*goddamn, Ticker, it was him*—thrust both arms into the victorious dawn. Then two water cops smashed into him and all three men fell, disappearing from sight. For good measure, the sniper on the speedboat let loose, firing high. The M-16 rounds were galvanizing to Phelan, home-sickening.

He turned away. Peered then lunged forward and intercepted a cop dragging along an offloader who looked like a tall, dirty, handsome, miserable bale of hay. Phelan hustled the cop aside, flashed his P.I. license, and started to confirm the deal he'd made with his uncle.

"Keep on steppin'," the cop said, waving him off. He whacked Frank on the back, barked, "Mine."

Frank's jaw was clenched but trembling. "Who the hell are you?" he asked.

Phelan told him to shut the fuck up and offered a face-saver to the cop. "Lotta noise out here," he said and finished telling the man who his uncle was. To Frank he said, "Private investigator. You led us to the party. In exchange for that, I get you."

Frank's captor lifted up his hands, made an irked face at Phelan, and salaamed. Phelan took possession.

The Marine Safety Unit guys led their prisoner off the shrimper, zigzagging around bales, coolers, crates, somebody's guitar case, and turned him over. Phelan, with a handcuffed Frank clamped by the elbow, stood back on a muddy strip of road as Ticker was escorted by without a sideways glance. He'd be looking at drug trafficking, possession with intent to distribute, resisting arrest. No credit for rescuing a sea turtle. Phelan told himself he could've been watching a body bag pass by, but that didn't help a lot.

Ticker bellowed *Wait, Cocksuckers* as they reached a cruiser. His pony-tailed head angled upward at the morning sky's white-gold spokes shining up the water world. He gazed until they mashed him into the car.

Phelan tugged his client's husband toward his Chevelle, parked ahead off the road.

Frank's fair hair was plastered with sweat. Straws of weed stuck to his neck and t-shirt.

"Wait, I gotta get my Mustang. Could you, you know, take off these cuffs so I can drive? So it'll be there when I get—"

"You don't have a Mustang." Frank smelled like a six-foot two-inch joint with end-stage B.O.

"Sure do. I'm parked right—"

"Yeah. See it anywhere around here?"

Phelan let go of him, so he could flail one direction, then the other, then all the way around.

"C'mon." Phelan walked him farther, put him in the Chevelle's back seat.

Frank leaned to the window, turning his head right then left, his forehead bumping the glass as they rolled over some ruts. "Where is it?" His voice was now higher.

"Impounded for eternity. Ever so often the police have these auctions. Ever been to one? Man, there's some bargains."

"They can't take my car! It's my wife's. I'm makin' the payments. I don't care if they're the cops, they can't just steal my car!"

Phelan explained why they could. In addition, educated Frank about the agency that would be clamping down on dope activities using methods nobody knew about yet, but Phelan was betting might be harshed-up from current penalties. Why?

Simple. Nixon had signed the order. And new uniforms, new offices, letterhead, Selectrics, badges, cars, that shit had to be paid for. People had to have shit to do. They had to reconnaissance, liaison, reconnoiter, and rendezvous. Whole shebang had to sanctify itself, the dope cops, the DC imps, Nixon. Frank should cheer up. He'd only been caught by the Beaumont Police Department, not the United States of America rolling out a brand new beef. And unless he was even dimmer than he acted, he should notice that he was headed back to his own house.

Grumbling emanated from the back seat. Every so often, Phelan checked the rearview. Frank's shoulders poked forward, the handcuffs preventing him from sitting back against the seat easily. His movie-star features squeezed or spread into different configurations as his brain processed his predicament. Only about five or six blocks to go when he spit out, "You didn't tell me why the cops picked me to follow. I didn't rat to nobody. I didn't even tell my…"

"First, clue me in, I'm curious. How much were you gonna make for the night?"

"Nine grand."

"Whoa. Tough paycheck to lose. Could be worse, though."

Phelan told him how he was picked. His freedom was courtesy of his wife, and if he wasn't grateful to Phelan Investigations, he should sure as hell be grateful to Cheryl Sweeney.

He pulled up next to the old pickup with the good tires, helped Frank out, and at the door, where Cheryl was waiting, unlocked the handcuffs and pocketed the small key. Nodded at Cheryl, who mouthed *Thank you.*

The upholsterer must've been planning his move, even as Phelan slipped the key into his pocket. Once Phelan turned away, Frank kicked him in the back of the knees. Phelan grunted loudly and collapsed, crashing down into some resistant, stickery bushes. Cheryl yelled at Frank. Phelan pushed out of the stickers and maneuvered himself up. As he hobbled menacingly toward the Sweeney's front door, Frank kicked it shut with nuclear force. There was a sharp click. From inside, soprano and tenor shouting.

Phelan finally relaxed his fists. He executed a turn and hop-limped to his car, lowered himself in. He stopped at a Fertitta's store for an Ace bandage and a bag of ice. Fantasized flattening Frank Sweeney's fine bone structure with the five-pound icebag and strangling him with the bandage. Instead, he limped into the duplex and dropped his night's wardrobe on the bathroom floor. Seeing it was a little after eight, he called Delpha at the office. Gave her a fast account of the bust and the bagging of Frank Sweeney, leaving out the parts about the turtle and the sticker bushes.

"Did it," she said. He warmed at the triumph in her voice.

"Did it. Need a few hours before I go talk to Jim Anderson. May not come in, just go over there first."

"Wait. Anderson's real name is Sparrow. That'd make Bell's name Sparrow, too. His real name, Tom."

Phelan lowered himself to his bed while he listened to some history. He swallowed four aspirin before he hung up. He wrapped ice in a towel, cuddled it to his knee. Then he pulled the covers to his ears, unthawed, and drifted away.

XXXIII

THE *BEAUMONT ENTERPRISE* ran a motor-mouthed
Spiro Agnew photo next to the Vice President's declaration
that he would *not* quit over allegations of kickbacks and
bribery, and that the Justice Department was "unprofessional,
malicious, and outrageous." A national sportswriter was
screaming that Bobby Riggs had thrown last week's hyped-up
tennis match against Billie Jean King, while a letter-to-the-
editor writer crowed that Riggs was now a "male chauvinist
rabbit." There was nothing yet on the dope bust, but had to
be some rolled-sleeve reporter over in the newsroom now
pounding the keys for an afternoon headline. Delpha had
brought a Styrofoam cup of coffee from the Rosemont, *ten
cents to Oscar, thank you*, and set it next to the lonely phone.

Tom'd be in this afternoon after he talked to Jim
Anderson—Jim Sparrow—and maybe then they'd be calling
Xavier Bell to tell him—if he ever answered his telephone—
that they'd found his brother.

One snag. Just one maddening snag. If Sparrow was his
real name…if the store full of pretty birds in New Orleans
had been run, appropriately, by a family named Sparrow with
two brothers, why weren't there two baby brother Sparrows
recorded in the original Louisiana Archive pages?

Born somewhere else was the only answer she could think
of. Xavier Bell had said he was born and bred in New Orleans.
Another lie. Delpha swept up the Archive pages, packed

them in a file folder, slotted it into the gray file cabinet, and slammed the drawer shut.

Big, big, big waste of time.

Then she spent a few minutes not caring what Bell's or Sparrow's real name was. At eight thirty-five, the phone shrilled. She put welcome into "Phelan Investigations. How may we help you?"

"Help me?" The irate speaker had called before, and she had "let it ring a hundred times." The help she wanted was for Phelan Investigations to confront her boyfriend's wife and make her let go of him. She wasn't sure where the wife lived, that was where the investigation part came in, but it was in a large house because she had five kids.

Delpha asked if the husband also lived in the house.

Yeah, he did. But he was leaving soon as he could pry the wife's claws outa him. The caller thought Phelan could handle that part, too. How much would that cost her?

Bracing for the windstorm, Delpha suggested the caller's problem was a personal matter between her and her boyfriend. She was sorry, but this was not what Phelan Investigations did.

On the other end, a wrathful breath indrew.

"Thank you for calling, ma'am, we wish you well." Delpha hung up, stood up, and wandered the office.

She did care what Xavier Bell's real name was, damn it. Maybe there was a second way to check that out.

At the Wertman's store, gazing at the old *Flo ri da* map, an idea had sidled into her mind, and here was the thing about this idea: it had a novel feature. A hidden benefit. If it didn't work, no one would lock her in solitary or assign her to the toilet-scrubbing roster or commandeer her pie or bruise her ribs with a mop handle or slap her, even, so her cheek stung or her temple throbbed, wherever the punishment landed. That's what she told herself. Out here, if she was wrong, she was just wrong, and that didn't necessarily have to leave bruises.

She was free now, and if she had to keep reminding herself every so often, she would.

Next, she repeated the advice her parole officer Joe Ford had given her on their first meeting: *Act. If you have to put on an act, do it, put one on. And ask. For what you need.* Seemed puny when he was telling it to her, but it had turned out to be sturdy advice.

It was ten a.m. in Jacksonville, Florida, nine a.m. here in Texas. The University of Houston's library would be open. Delpha dialed the number she'd gotten from Directory Assistance. When a girl said, "Library," Delpha interrupted in the friendliest tone she could conjure. "Help me out here, please. Is that Shirley Myers working the Reference desk today?" The young female voice had said uncertainly that she didn't know Mrs. Myers. It was Mrs. Powell at the desk today.

"Oh, that's right," Delpha said ruefully. "It's Monday. Mary Powell, right? Don't you hate it when you've met somebody but you can't quite remember their name?"

The soprano voice replied, more surely now, that Mrs. Powell's first name was Adelaide, but only God could call her that.

"Right. Hadn't Mrs. Powell worked at the library a long time?"

"God made Mrs. Powell then He made The Light and The Dark."

Delpha said, "That's who I'm after. Hand me on, please."

When Mrs. Powell picked up, Delpha greeted her and asked her about the statute of limitations and how it worked in Texas for the crime of murder or attempted murder.

"There is *no* time limitation for the prosecution of murder or attempted murder."

"My goodness, you didn't even have to look that up," Delpha said.

"It's common knowledge. May I help you with anything else?"

"No, that's it." Delpha thanked her and hung up. She'd known the answer to that question. What she'd wanted—and had gotten—was Mrs. Powell's tone of voice: the authoritative, matter-of-fact, no dog in the race last word. Angela was still too in love with being reference librarian to rap out an answer like that. A bored and bossy chow-line convict could do it as well, but without the correct undertone of neutral authority. Chow-line girl'd add an edge of superiority: she had the grits and you didn't.

"There is no time limitation for the prosecution of murder or attempted murder… There is *no* time limitation for the prosecution of murder or attempted murder." She sat forward in her chair, spine straight.

Then she called the Jacksonville, Florida, Police Department and asked for a detective who worked old cases. She was passed on until she heard: "John Perch."

She identified herself and her employer and told Detective Perch what she wanted.

She heard a muffled, "I said cherry, Sweet Cheeks. Two of 'em," then he spoke into the phone. "Whose file you talking about?"

Delpha told him the alias she had, Rodney Harris, the year, 1969, and that there could have been a complaint for assault or worse. A man or men around sixty-five, seventy years old then. The other might be named Bell. Or Sparrow.

"Uh huh. I'm supposed to fire up my time machine, and root around for old files because some Miami reporter's pecking around for deep background?"

Deep background—that lost her. She sat until she

remembered Adelaide Powell would not be lost. "I'm not a reporter. I work for a firm of private investigators in Beaumont, Texas."

"Oh. Oh, excuse me then. Because some Texas P.I. is curious. Does that just about get it, you're curious?"

She could lie. Instead, she said slowly, "Yes."

"Some woman P.I., if there is such a thing." A laugh. A pause. A scraping sound, maybe of chair-legs against a floor. Delpha anticipated the clunk of the hang-up.

"Tell me what you look like first."

She had planned to redeploy Adelaide Powell but the initial laugh and the guy's jokey tone changed her strategy. Now she sat down, picked up a pencil, and bounced its eraser against the surface of her desk, the way Attorney Miles Blankenship had bounced his eraser against a legal pad.

"I'm six feet tall and I have black shiny hair in a French twist."

Silence on the line. Somebody yelled *Jones*! in the background.

"When you take it down how long is it?"

"First I need to know if you can get the files from four years ago."

"Sure. Down the hall growing mold. How long?"

"I said, four years."

"No, your hair. How long?"

"Oh." Delpha's mouth formed a straight line as she thought. "You know that hollow at a woman's back? Right at the waist, 'fore the spine starts up?"

Perch cleared his throat. "I do."

"That long."

Another silence. Faint ringing of a phone.

"My wife never had long hair, but she used to have that spot. Yes, she did."

"She still has it, Detective Perch."

A sigh. "Somewhere. What'd you say you wanted? And what was your name?"

Delpha repeated her name, request, and number.

"Files are a mess. It could take me a month of Sundays."

It didn't. Perch called back at noon, saying fifty-two citizens had been put to bed with a shovel in 1969. Most cases closed. One case still unsolved was that of a convenience store clerk, who'd disappeared in February of that year. Bones discovered some twenty months later in marshland, M.E. reported cut marks to base of skull, spine. As to the names she was interested in... He proposed a trade, without disclosing that, of course, and she played her part. She looked down at herself. Instead of describing the pale blue blouse whose buttons she had resewn tighter and the washed-and-rewashed navy blue skirt, she was wearing one of those straight Chinese dresses with the high collar and the slit skirt. Wine red silk. Tight. No stockings. High-heeled sandals, backless.

Now, those names she gave him. What did he find?

He breathed out, "Nothing, baby."

Delpha heard a soft crunch as her jaw hinges shifted. "You sure?"

Choppy breathing.

In the voice of the pitiless authority that was Adelaide Powell, she said, "Then what I got on, John, is your mama's house dress. Old sack that rides up when she sits down with her knees apart." She hung up.

That she'd played Perch's horny game rankled. And that he'd wasted her time. So much for her wise idea.

But nobody was hauling her off to solitary, were they?

XXXIV

PHELAN'S LIMP HAD receded, but he wasn't jogging. He wove his way through the small forest and up the grayed ramp to Jim Anderson's door. No one answered his knock, so he and his mildly sore knee walked the sandy, needled ground around the house to the back, where two people occupied a landscaped clearing in the pines. One sat in a chaise lounge chair reading a newspaper, his ankles crossed. He was wearing bifocals, a pajama shirt over khakis and no hat, thin gray hair uncombed. The other—the one Delpha said wasn't a teenager—was long-legged, wearing shorts and Keds tied with a double-knot. Light-colored bangs falling over his forehead, he leaned over the stone surround of a small homemade pond, planted with elephant ears and sedge grass, scooping a blue plastic pail in the green water. A pump hummed.

In the act of hauling out the full pail, the young-looking man by the pond turned his head, smiled, scattering water drips onto a stained white t-shirt. He waved and grinned at Phelan. Strange-looking guy, grayed-brown hair cut in lank bangs, chopped at the neck, fine wrinkles in the cheeks. He sloshed the pail and laughed, slow getting started then cracked himself up. "A-ha...a-ha...ah ah ah...huk huk kuk huk." The man-sized little boy glanced up brightly at Phelan, as if to see if Phelan understood, as the boy did, that the water and the pail were wonderful.

It *was* sort of a wonderful sight, Phelan thought, though sad. Or maybe not. He smiled back at the boy with the pail, then approached the man in the chair.

"Excuse me, sir. Like to have a word with you."

The older man in the chair turned a page and smoothed it down.

Phelan walked closer. "'Scuse me," he said louder, "Mr. Anderson. Could I have a word?"

"*Mannaggia!*" The old man flinched and rared back, crumpling the newspaper in his lap.

Phelan introduced himself, adding that he was a private investigator on a case commissioned by a man who, they had reason to believe, was Mr. Anderson's brother, though he wasn't using the name Anderson.

"Wait a minute. Don't know the name of your own client? What kind of an investigator are you?"

"Persistent. My best trait. Grant you it's an unusual case. The client paid us to find his brother. If that's you, well sir, I hope you've been dreaming of reconciliation."

The old man peered at Phelan over the bifocals. Slowly his wrinkled face hardened. He removed the glasses and rested his forehead on his hand. His chest rose and fell. A wind rustled through the circle of pines.

Phelan thought that here was an old man growing ancient, somebody who hoped he wouldn't meet the worst, and now he had. From the direction of the house came a dim chattering of birds. From the other direction, a rat-a-tat attack. He traced the loudmouth, a redheaded woodpecker high in an oak, just past the pines, then said, "Hope you'll help us get this straight, sir."

The old man spoke without raising his head. "Pal, you don't even know what you did."

The man with the bangs had dropped the blue pail in

the pond and was staring toward his friend and then toward Phelan, dismay mashed into his loose face.

"Then tell me what I did, pretty please."

"Bet he laid it on what an ingrate I am, what a dirty mooch. And he's Dudley Do-Right of the Mounties."

"Not exactly. Well, kinda."

"Boo hoo. Ten'll get you twenty he's got somebody on you, Slick. You'll track me, he'll track you and get to my brother first. Boom, you get fired. That'll be hunky dory with you because you already got paid upfront. Upshot is both of you jerks will go off patting your wallet and not know what really happened. It worked last time. When you find me, he'll find me." He jerked his head toward the pond. "And him," he said harshly.

"Your friend."

The old man pushed out his bottom lip.

Phelan let it go for a second while he thought of the dark sedan circling in the Bellas Hess parking lot. "Wait. So you're saying while I'm out looking for you, all this time, he's got a guy on me, so anywhere I went got reported back to him. Why?"

"Thinks he's a sharp cookie."

"What for?"

"He paid in cash, right? A lot. Promise you more?"

Phelan nodded.

"You got a office?"

"Yeah."

"Secretary? If you do, she may get a message for you."

"Yeah to both. What's the message?"

A huff from the old guy. "What name did he give you?"

"Xavier Bell."

"Bell. *Uffa*, Bell, what a joke. That's him. Lemme give you a prediction. Next coupla days, you're gonna get a phone call. He's gonna call off your job toot sweet. Finito, kaput. The other dick's working off some other name who knows what that is, he'll only know you. His job'll be over, too, and everbody goes on their merry way. Got it now, pal?"

He'd got it. The woodpecker was drilling away. Phelan cut his eyes up, telepathically wishing on it an attack by a flying tomcat. "OK. He tells us he wants to connect with his long-lost brother before he dies. He's old as hell, excuse me, we believe him. So why is he looking for you?"

"He's got a nail in his head."

Phelan noted the bitterness in the old guy's voice. "What?"

"Tryna tell you, that's the $64,000 dollar question. I gave up asking it years ago. I just don't wanna see his filthy snout."

"You two hate each other so much, why not go off different directions and never write letters?"

The old man glared. "'Cause he's lying, that's why. Not about hating me. Not exactly. I'd say he hates me 70 percent... maybe 80. Twenty percent, he thinks he loves me." He spun his index finger in circles by his hairy ear.

"Uh huh. Listen, how about we sit down inside and talk this over."

"Oh ho, no you don't!" A finger stabbed toward Phelan. "Think I'd fall for that. Not buying the Brooklyn Bridge and not paying you one red cent, either."

"And I'm not asking. This visit is on your brother's dime, Mr....Sparrow." Phelan waited to see if he'd be contradicted over "Sparrow." He wasn't.

"I'll only talk to you if you don't tell him where we are. But he's paying you, so you gonna tell him. I got nothing to say. Go chase yourself."

"He said something about a settlement coming to you here in Beaumont. How'd he find that out?"

"Goddamnit" started a vibrant verse of cursing. "Could only be Louis' office."

"Who's Louis?"

"Family lawyer. Also Ma's cousin. About a hundred and fifty years old. Croaked right after she did, not so long ago—"

Phelan's eyes widened. "Mother. Mind telling me how old she was?"

"Ninety-six. Nonna lasted to ninety. I'm ona break the chain."

"What, you have health problems?"

Anderson-Sparrow judged Phelan with a narrow look. "So, I was sayin'. Louis left his practice to his feeb son-in-law, Sebastian. I bought this house, told Sebastian where to send the money. He knows not to tell, he swore just like Louis swore. Nothin' to my brother about me, nothin', zip, zero, *niente*. Sebastian musta messed up and dropped a little blood in the water. Now here's Ugo and his fin."

"Ugo."

"That's your party, wanna know his real name. Ugo used to go by Hugh at the store, more American. But he's had other names."

"Like you're Jim Anderson?"

The old guy stared at him. "Now you're cookin'. It ain't so hard. By the way, what'd you say your name was?"

"Tom Phelan. Look, Mr. Sparrow. Like I said, he hired me to find his brother, give him the location. That's what the contract reads. It doesn't say shit about any contact with the brother. Maybe you have a good reason I should sit in on your meeting. Or that somebody should. Why would that be? Convince me."

"Reason. What's the matter with you? Reason doesn't enter into this." The old man folded the newspaper, reached out to set it on a stump. "C'mon, Raff—"

He launched himself out of the chaise lounge with enough force to tip it over, hurried and maneuvered to his knees beside the other man. The tall one had slipped down the stone onto the ground, lips twisted, his arms and shoulders shaking.

Both hands had cramped into fists, wrists straining at right angles. Sparrow pulled at his waist with both hands.

Phelan ran and helped him turn the convulsing younger man onto his side. A fist smacked his cheekbone. "Let's get his head off the ground." He peeled off his jacket and stuffed it under the guy's head—fists were clenched and flailing, a string of saliva oozing from his lips. His pupils had rolled up near his lids, showing wide white crescents below.

Phelan held onto him. "Lips are turning blue."

"Relax. They'll come back when it's over," Sparrow said in a soothing tone.

"This happen a lot?"

"Enough." Gently, "Raffie, it's OK. I'm here. I'm with you, pal." He started up a hoarse, short-winded chant. In a couple seconds, Phelan identified it as a song in some foreign language. Just enough tune to tell the song was in a minor key, and that its lines repeated. Automatically, the old man mopped snot from Raffie's nose with a handkerchief, dried his mouth. When his voice lifted on a single high note, his eyebrows also lifted, and the vertical wrinkles in his face grew longer.

Phelan waited it out.

He'd done this before, guys with epilepsy brought on by head injuries. Only one plain-vanilla epileptic, an FNG who'd kept his med history to himself because his dad, granddad on back to Pickett's Charge had been Army, and they'd let him enlist. Two noble buddies spilled his secret after finding him jolting facedown in his bunk.

Now Phelan scooped his right hand beneath his own jacket, keeping Raffie's head from pressing into the dirt, his left laid lightly against the gray hair. "He's breathing," he said. The shaking was falling off.

Raffie gasped and barked, then snorted, over and over. Sparrow rubbed his back, almost absently, hissing the song.

Phelan set his fingers to Raffie's wrist and counted the pulse. The older friend rumbled the same sounds twice, running out of steam. His tanned old face looked like it had been wadded up, let loose, and retained every wrinkle.

Phelan pressed his fingers against the throat this time, glanced over at Sparrow. "Heart's still way up." When he got no response, he hesitated, then spoke louder.

"Heart rate's high. Chance that might not be the seizure. You know that?"

Sparrow raised his face. His eyebrows were squeezed down, lids drooping over all but the inner corners of his eyes. He knew.

"It's a blessing," he muttered.

Phelan considered him for a while. "You get that side, I'll take this one." They helped the disoriented man upright. He swayed. Both of them took a step with him. Only the top half of his body went with them. He tilted forward, sagging.

"Lemme get his chair. Then we can push him to the back door there."

"I can handle him. Name's Raffie, right?" Phelan said, though that was the one name he was sure of.

"Yeah. For Rafael."

"Raffie, I'm gonna carry you a little ways. Don't be afraid, OK. Just to the screen porch over there. Won't drop you, I promise."

Phelan picked up the tall man, tough to balance. Got his bony length distributed, then plowed with him up to the screen porch, skidding once on a pinecone, which didn't help out his knee any. Sparrow held open the door for them. Phelan angled sideways then carried the man up two cement steps and over the spongy green Astro-turfed floor of the porch. A washing machine and a folding table piled with a jumble of towels and underwear stood to the right of the door. To the left, cardboard boxes of toys, a stack of plastic pails, and, farther left, bags of fertilizer and birdseed. Phelan inched and sidled over the green polyester grass in order not to knock Raffie's big Keds against the doorways, then against the walls of the hall. The older man led the way to the first bedroom, one with a rocking chair, a portable television, and a single bed. Together they draped and arranged Raffie onto it. Head to head, Raffie petted Phelan's face before he let go.

The stripes of the old guy's pajama shirt were heaving. He had to stand there and catch his breath. "Most people," he said, "less they know somebody with fits, they get embarrassed. Or scared. You know somebody with fits?"

"Army medic, once on a time."

"Well, thanks. I got him now." He dragged the rocking chair over thin, beige carpet, parallel to Raffie's bedside, and lowered himself into it.

Phelan gestured down the hall in the direction of the rest of the house, saying, "Could I trouble you to make a phone call?"

"I look like a sap? Hell, no."

"OK, can I get y'all anything? That filling station on the corner'd have cold drinks and Eskimo pies. Your brother says you made bad things happen. I'd like to hear your side before I notify him I found you."

The man in the bed drew the sheet up to his chin. His eyelids half-closed.

Sparrow slumped. "I made bad things happen. Yeah. Hadn't you? You wanna hear my side, well, there's a real switcheroo. You mean that, come back another time. I'm busy now."

XXXV

"IT'S HIM, ISN'T it?" Delpha leaned toward Phelan as he came into the office. "Jim Anderson's Rodney."

He hooked a hand at her, and she followed him, rolling a client chair to the other side of his desk. They confronted each other.

"Yeah," he said. "He is."

"Sparrow."

"Sparrow. Used it, and he didn't contradict me."

"I could call Bell, see if he answers his phone. Or we could both stay late and see if he calls us again."

Phelan said nothing.

The brightness faded from Delpha's eyes. "What's the deal?"

"We got interrupted. I got an invitation to finish up. Still—" Phelan told her, described his meeting with Sparrow, a.k.a. Jim Anderson, and Sparrow's low opinion of their client. Described Raffie.

"Raffie. Does sound like a little boy. But he's not. You saw him up close?" Her voice changed. "So. That black car at Bellas Hess was a P.I.'s."

"Good chance. If that's true then Bell's gonna know. If the guy was on me today. Didn't see him if he was. Thing is—"

"That maybe we're not on our client's side here."

Phelan met her eyes. "We said, in black and white, that we would find Bell's brother and tell him where he was. And the thing is, a contract is a goddamn contract. Like a promise is a promise."

"Yeah, Tom, but if your good friends Bonnie and Clyde asked you the address of your daddy's bank, you're not giving it to 'em. Listen, 'member me talking about Mr. Wally, the business teacher at Gatesville?"

"Yep,"—Phelan wadded up yesterday's sports section and swished the ball of newsprint into the wastebasket—"I do remember Mr. Wally."

She ignored the frustration and settled back against the client chair's high leather back. "OK. Mr. Wally used to read us a lot of rules and procedures. He also said not everthing's in the book. What I'm hearing is you like Mr. Anderson better than Mr. Bell."

"On the money," Phelan said quietly.

"So tell or not tell where Bell's brother is. When we been paid to tell." She didn't necessarily agree, but she liked Tom for saying a promise was a promise. Liked him for making this dilemma.

"If the other P.I.'s found Sparrow, then doesn't matter what we do." She shrugged. "If he hadn't, then hear the man out."

Phelan stared past her. "Wait a minute." He reminded her of the Elliott case, in which a fortune had hinged on one seemingly routine phrase in an annual company contract. "You got Bell's contract?"

Delpha went to the file cabinet and pulled a file, walked back to Phelan's desk reading it. She sat and read the whole first page, for the first time paying attention to paragraphs and not just the blanks to be filled in. "Where'd you get this form from?"

"P.I. agency in Houston. Said I had a thief in my body shop and couldn't figure which one he was. I took their contract and said I'd get back to them if my partner agreed. Got a bookkeeper to type it over with my business name and address."

Delpha said, "Joe Ford musta give you his advice one time or nuther. OK, read this part under 'Scope.'"

Phelan mumbled through the six or seven lines, ending with *The parties hereby agree that the following investigative services have been requested by CLIENT under this Agreement and will be provided by AGENCY, but that the actual time and manner in which the following investigative services are conducted shall be left to the sole discretion of the AGENCY.*

"'Time and manner of services'…," Phelan repeated, his voice cheering up, "'…sole discretion of the agency.' Can I get a witness?"

"Amen." Delpha returned the contract to its folder, and the folder to the files. They could handle Bell with their own discretion, their way.

She came back to tell him who she'd telephoned yesterday: the detective in Jacksonville, Florida, see if any Rodney Harris and/or Xavier Bell or Sparrow had disturbed the peace in that place during 1969. The cop had mistaken her for a reporter. "You know what deep background is?"

Phelan had flicked his lighter. Now he dragged on a cigarette, and courting danger, leaned back in his hazardous desk chair. "Newspaper thing. Reporter gets a story, but he can't quote the source by name. Still valuable to him because it's a lead." He looked up. "That's what you been doing?" He smiled. "Digging up deep background. Either that was quite a training course Mr. Wally gave y'all in Gatesville, or you got instinct."

"Didn't pay off. Told me a 7-11 clerk disappeared in '69. Turned up, finally, as a skeleton with cut marks on the bones. But information about a Harris or Bell or Sparrow, skunk didn't give me anything. Just thought if I could've found out stuff that went on between them before, we might know more about what's going on now."

"Delpha."

"What."

"Don't get set on one of 'em's wearing a white hat. Or a black, for that matter. This is family shit."

"I know that. Just gleanin' information."

"Cloudy all over, then. Don't suppose we had a call for another job?"

"We're open all day." She gave Phelan a modest smile so he'd get that she wasn't making fun. Though she was, a little.

Couple hours later, they did get a call, from a thin male voice that wanted them to investigate the accuracy of an obituary. As soon as Delpha honed in with specific questions, though, the voice waned further. It needed to think more, might call back, thanks, goodbye. She was reminded of a mouse she caught sight of one night when she was washing dishes. She took a step toward it, and it whisked away.

Phelan asked her about the call, hopeful, and she had to disappoint him. Around four-thirty, with strain between his brows, he came into her section of the office, told her he thought he'd attend Happy Hour over at Crockett Street. "Don't suppose you want a drink?"

She looked up at him.

"Right, parole, sorry. Well, any serious callers, including your deep background fellow, leave a note on my desk. I'll check in here before I go home. Tomorrow, I'll go finish up Anderson, and we'll use our discretion like crazy. But now, let's talk about your raise."

"I don't wanna bust the business for it. Need a job more than a raise."

"I understand that." He waited a minute then went ahead

with it. "That advertising mailing you did…anything ever come of that?" That was the task Delpha was working on the day Dennis Deeterman came through their door.

"Not yet. Might still."

"Send one to the D.A. Know they're more likely to hire a ex-cop investigator, but what the hell. And pay yourself another dollar an hour."

Her lips formed a straight line. "Appreciate it, I do, but—"

He contemplated her. "You don't trust me, do you, to carry that much? Couple hundred more a month."

She broke eye contact, rested her head on the palm of her hand. Spoke downward to her desk.

"I don't trust nobody, Tom. No offense."

Phelan's brow tightened further. In lieu of touching her, he tapped her desk, dislodging the little red dictionary on the edge of it. He caught it before it hit the floor, set it back. Murmured "No offense" and left for the bar.

XXXVI

COUPLE OF SALTY Dogs to the good, he ambled back to the office. Heat still rising from the concrete in this paved-over downtown, but a breeze played in a couple trees. Getting cool tonight, might dip to a few degrees under seventy. The ice had healed his knee as far as he could tell, and he was light-footed. A police detective in the bar with a girlfriend had recognized him, idled over to pull his coat about the bust at High Island. Mentioned that the Chief was happy as all get-out.

About to climb the stairs, Phelan startled at the sight of Elvis Presley's wife standing on the top stair, stepping carefully down. She stopped and chirped, "You're here!" Her colorful face lit up.

Mrs. Frank Sweeney?

Sure looked like Priscilla P.: glamorous eye makeup, that sweep of lofty dark hair, the minidress. Bare legs and high heels. A wave of earthy perfume swept him as she turned around and headed for his door. Phelan unlocked it for her, followed her in.

"Didn't want your secretary to send a bill," she said over her shoulder. "No need for any record of that, so I just came down here to settle up. Frank woulda blown through all that money, but I handle the checkbook. I got some left."

Phelan meant to go behind his desk to the drawer with the deposit slips, but she was holding out a handful of cash, so he had to come and get it.

"You don't keep it in the bank, Mrs. Sweeney?"

"Cheryl. Hell, no. I got coffee cans like everybody else."

Phelan smiled. "What you driving now, Cheryl?"

"Plymouth Belvedere. '66 push button. Looks like a ruler on wheels." One corner of her pink lips pulled up.

"You can go visit the Mustang down at the impound lot. Guess Frank's back working for his mother."

She nodded. "And bitching about it. Listen, Tom, I wanted to apologize to your face for that jackass kicking you like that. After you brought him home free and clear. Your secretary, she gone for the day?"

"Yeah. It's…" he checked his watch. "Six-ten. You almost missed me."

She flung back her long, straight hair, shook her head so it fanned out before splashing onto her shoulder. "Well, you know…" Her take-charge voice softened uncharacteristically. "I wouldn't wanna miss you."

A chime dinged above Phelan's left ear, softly audible, simultaneously visible in his mind's eye as a silver exclamation point. The signal to stop and look at what was going down. No XL work shirt hiding the curves—a long-sleeved paisley number with a ruffle falling over each wrist and a hem that would ride up to her crank case if she sat down. This must be a standing-up kind of dress. It came to Phelan that Cheryl looked…glittery. Not just her frosted pink lipstick. Glimmers twinkled from her pink cheeks too and her eyelids. Stardust.

He diverted the topic from himself. "How's your little man?"

"With his grandma tonight."

"And Frank Sr.?"

"Out."

Without turning away from him, Cheryl reached behind herself and closed the door of his office.

"So y'all didn't make up from your fight." Phelan slid his hands in his pockets.

"It's the kinda fight that keeps breaking out again, if you know what I mean." Her prettily-painted brows and mouth contracted. "It's not fair. It pisses me off. In the Bible it says 'A virtuous wife is the crown of her husband.' Tell me it isn't a goddamn virtue to keep your husband out of jail." She searched his gaze.

"What does the bible say about gratitude?"

"Says give thanks to the Lord. And I did that. But Frank'll eat dirt before he admits any thanks are due to me. He's most comfortable looking down on people." A sly intention formed in the black-outlined eyes. She stepped forward, took hold of Phelan's belt, and pulled his chest to hers. "You 'member we have an arrangement, me and Frank."

"I do, and it's none of my business." Phelan detached her hand from his belt.

She slipped her hand away from his, twined her arm around his neck, went up on her tiptoes and kissed him with great warm soft wet enthusiasm. It had been a while since Phelan had had any touch, and despite his opinion of her (*enterprising, married*) and her husband (*dog shit*), Cheryl's pliable mouth drew like a surge from him. Heart-shaped face. Cascade of dark hair down her back. But the chime had sounded. And the chime knew. What was in front of him was a clear and present treat followed by a comet's-tail of trouble. He pulled back. She tilted her head and kissed his neck, breathed in his mouth, and, at the same time, fit her left hand to him.

Aw, man.

His response was instant and solid. His hand slid under the short dress where it did not come into contact with nylon or cotton. Just Cheryl Sweeney. She moaned and dragged them both against the door. He muttered, "On the pill?"

"Close enough."

"Nah, huh uh." Phelan straightened.

"OK! IUD." She stepped to him and delicately licked the hollow beneath his Adam's apple. "One of those copper things that—"

"Got it. But you wanna be all carried away, listen…" he shook his head, "not gonna happen. Hold on." Phelan disengaged, went over to the desk and pulled out the generally unused middle drawer, reached to the back, returned, peeling open the foil.

Cheryl lifted her chin, stretching out a faultless jawline. "I don't have cooties."

He unzipped. "Frank has cooties."

He stepped out of one leg of pants and underwear, left the other puddling, and with one hand twined in her hair, kissed her lips, her neck. Murmured, "You don't even care if I mark you up, huh?"

"Not really."

She kissed him a while and then reached for him. Phelan bent his knees, hoisted her against the door.

"Stating for the record that you're using me, Cheryl," he said into her ear.

"Use me back, baby."

Her breasts rubbed him. Frank Jr. jumped to mind but then her legs clamped his waist, squeezing.

He got a better grip on her thighs and put his back into it. His knee wailed once, then shut up. Slow, hefting her, bringing her down on him. Lifting her again, pulling out. Bringing her down. Gradual as he could manage.

Until finally she groaned his name and his name again and they rattled the door. They rammed the door, they battered it. Cheryl's shrieky panting climbed the scale, accelerated until her face seized. She gripped the back of his shirt, wrenching it out till a button pinged off, while her thighs almost cracked his ribs. Cheryl's face crumpled tighter and then her lips popped open and then she was ticking regular *uhn…uhn…uhn* sounds like a hot engine once it shuts down.

Phelan took a little while more. When his vision returned, he quit mashing her against the door, lugged her a couple steps, and splayed her down into a client chair. Her eyes were closed.

His weren't. He jerked upright. Jesus Christ, his dick was shellacked red and his shirt tail streaked, smears on his thighs. He stepped back, warning, "Cheryl."

Her eyes opened. He pointed at her.

Her neck bent, and she caught sight of the thin line of blood, like a live thing, determinedly making a right angle to continue tracking down onto the chair seat.

"Oh shit. Oh shit." She jumped up and cupped her crotch. "Grab my purse, will you?"

Phelan stepped out of his other pantleg and disposed of the rubber in his office wastebasket. He skinned off his underwear, wiped himself with it, then whipped his pants back on. Went and snagged the leather-fringed bag lying beside the door and held it out to her. Still cupping herself, she clamped the bag under her right arm and rummaged with her left hand. Grabbed out a scrap of print cloth—*panties?*—and a white cylinder and let the purse fall onto the floor. Its contents scattered.

"Turn your back. Ow, now here they come. Now the cramps show up."

Phelan turned his back. After about twenty seconds of ripping, rustling, silence, and elastic snapping, she said, "OK." When he turned around, she was standing, the paisley mini pulled down to its maximum length, and her face no longer sparkled. It was raw and dragging.

He saw, sinkingly, that Cheryl Sweeney was crying.

"Oh God, I try," she said, a hand sheltering her brow. "I try so hard to do the smart thing, and it just never turns out smart, no matter what. Got this smart birth control and now when I have the curse, I bleed like Niagara Falls…" She swiped her wet face furiously.

"I made sure Frank didn't go to jail, and what do I get? He hates me for saving him. So I go get a little something for me because a human person can only go so long with no attention, you know? You know, with nothing? Then you got to put yourself in front of somebody, you need to. And I can't even do that right. I humiliate myself all to kingdom come."

Phelan set aside that he was a *little something*. He could forgive that thoughtless assessment because by his running lights *good golly miss molly* battering a door like they had was not short shrift. She wasn't wrong about the attention, either. Felt like his personal interior spanned a wider territory now.

"I've been around girls before, OK?" He found his handkerchief and squatted, steadied her chin and tamped the tear marks, scrubbed a smear of blood near her hairline. "All better," he said and gave her the handkerchief.

She crumpled it.

"Cheryl. That woman that came to my office a while back, wanting to keep her husband outa jail, she was smart. I'm telling you. And you wanna know who says so, besides me?"

Cheryl rolled damp, dour eyes toward him.

"My uncle, the police chief. And right this second, that woman is in my office again, and she is sitting in the very same chair you are. Listen up. You got a lot not to waste. Know what I'm sayin'?"

The eyes stayed on him, verifying. Her eyebrow, the corners of her lips quirked upward. "Oh," she whispered. "I 'preciate that."

She scooped up her purse and raked stuff into it, made a fist and grazed Phelan's belly with it. Then she turned toward the door and left, giving the V-sign. Victory, peace, he didn't know which, but she didn't check to see if he gave one back.

Phelan admired her exit. *Cool woman.* He hadn't lied about her smarts either.

He walked over by his wastebasket—he'd empty it now before he forgot—and bent down to pick up an object on the floor. Little bitty plastic change purse, the kind you squeezed to open. Inside, a folded ten and Cheryl Sweeney's driver's license.

Gazing down at her official photo, he thought about what she had said. *A person can only go so long without attention.*

And about Xavier Bell or Sparrow or whatever his name was.

Bell liked attention, and he didn't. He'd put himself in front of Phelan Investigations, seemed like he'd relished the interview, the idea of "allies." But then he'd dropped out of sight. Invisible, like Delpha had said. Hard to get attention when you're invisible. Must be a wingding of a conflict, when you love feast and famine just the same.

Had Bell ever been looked for? By a wife, a lover, a family member? Police, even? Or had nobody in his whole long life come looking for Xavier Bell?

And why would that be?

He should have been crawling but felt only twinges from the sore knee. Phelan was sobered up, loose as a goose, and twenty-five minutes late to a seven o'clock game. He knelt on the sidelines to double-knot his sneakers.

They played half-court because the north basket was already claimed by a gaggle of black kids playing ABA style, minus the fouls. They were maybe fourteen, fifteen years old, skinny boys made of rubber hanging loose at the line then snapping into choreography, no-shirt guard chesting the shoulder blades of a t-shirt forward, who'd launch into crossover dribbling, shoot an alley-oop to his t-shirt teammate. Tallest no-shirt kid spearing down shots to boos and aws, a t-shirt kid seizing the rebound, one bounce, super-stride, hello net, and he's dangling from the rim.

As the dangling boy landed, Phelan saw past him to a dark sedan parked on the corner. Mercury Montego. He took off runnin though he hadn't finished tying the shoes.

The sedan made a tight U-turn, blazed.

He wouldn't catch it on foot, laces flapping. He jogged to a stop, stomped the sidewalk. Mistake. Wrong knee to stomp with. But at last, another fucking thing verified. Course the Mercury coulda been a boy-lusting sightseer with his fist in his lap. But probably not.

Score one for the younger Mr. Sparrow. Likely the double P.I. story was true. And if the Mercury was still on Phelan, then he'd missed that day Phelan had found the Anderson-Sparrow house. He grinned. This info on a competitor went a ways toward making up for a couple of his own professional misjudgments: not taking a gun to catch the snack boys. Turning his back on Frank Sweeney.

Though Cheryl had graciously made up for that.

Phelan walked back to his game. He finished knotting his sneakers, then edged in, palming the ball from under Fred Kruikshank, shift manager out at Goodyear. Six-foot-five Joe Ford as usual dominating, talking trash from high school—but puffing some, hauling around a new pot belly. Joe might could still dunk 'em, but even with a wrapped knee, Tommy Phelan could outrun and out-dodge him.

At least until time got him, too.

XXXVII

DELPHA FANNED THE tiny pages of the plastic dictionary, uselessly stopping on *bell* and *sparrow*, then locked up. Didn't have the heart to stick around the office. She sat for a little while in one of the Rosemont's outside chairs and mulled over the conversation with her boss about her raise. Leaves blew past on the sidewalk. Finally she got up and went on into the lobby in time for the five o'clock news.

Elderly Mrs. Bibbo, fetching in a red-and-white checked shirtwaist accented with a red breast pocket in the shape of a heart, patted the couch beside herself. Delpha sat and was brought up to date on the Watergate affair.

President Nixon had refused to turn over the tapes to the Special Prosecutor—remember that?

Delpha remembered.

Well, a few weeks ago the liar had gone on TV and before the nation sworn he knew nothing about any break-in at the Watergate or any cover-up or any illegal activities. Mrs. Bibbo made a breathy noise indicating scorn. "And now we're hearing about the Vice-President. Both of them!" A federal grand jury had met recently to consider charges against Vice President Spiro Agnew, from back when he was a governor of Maryland.

"What they got him on?" Delpha asked.

"Bribes!" Mrs. Bibbo's face was fixed in incredulous folds. "A sitting Vice-President of the United States of America. Who has extorted bribes. How does such a person rise to the second highest office in our country?"

Simon Finn, former doughboy and high school teacher, sat next to Harry Nystrom at the game table, building a fence of checkers between them. "Agnew's a Greek, Roberta. It was a Greek that said 'We hang petty thieves and put big ones in office.'"

Mrs. Bibbo glowered at him.

"It's true," Mr. Finn said. "In baseball you're out if you get caught stealing. Not in politics."

Mr. Nystrom, retired from restaurant supply, frowned at Mr. Finn. "You don't know how to discuss, Simon. Jokes are the mark of a simpleton."

"For the first time ever I agree with The Big Mouth," Mrs. Bibbo said, meaning Mr. Nystrom, "because you know what's not funny?"

"Roberta"—Mr. Nystrom spun a checker—"I know so many un-funny things that it's not even funny."

"Ha ha, Harry. Listen, I'm making a point. I gotta point here. Where were you when FDR's funeral train was carrying him home? You probably don't even remember."

Mr. Nystrom slapped the table, toppling the checker fence. "Shreveport, Louisiana, in the kitchen of the Mayfair Hotel. Radio was broadcasting from Washington D.C., and Arthur Godfrey broke down on the air. Most of the kitchen broke down too. I didn't like the man, all right? But I stood there solemn with the rest of 'em. So that's how much you know."

"I was at the Orange shipyards," Mr. Finn said, his eyes on the window where a loose line of cars constituted the evening rush hour. "Boss yelled to stop. Told us the caisson was at the White House. Everybody stopped."

Mrs. Bibbo spread her hands. "This is my point. This is what I'm talking about. You did that from respect. Roosevelt didn't take bribes. He gave people some relief, he put people to work. Those crowds in the newsreels, we all saw them lining the tracks. Don't pretend you don't know why they were there. Respect."

Her voice roughened. "Now tell me, Simon. Who-all will stand along the railroad tracks when the coffin of Richard Nixon rolls by? You tell me, Harry, is this the way it is supposed to be in America?"

The intense face held for a moment, then like a strongman crumpling under barbells, Mrs. Bibbo's chin and cheeks quivered. Her parted lips quivered. She bowed from the waist, laid her forehead in her hands, and wept. The only sounds in the lobby were the muttering television and the old woman in the red-checked dress, sobbing.

Mr. Nystrom scowled and turned away. Delpha scooted over, slipped her arm around the narrow shoulders. After a minute, she sought out Mr. Finn's worried face. Delpha glared loudly at him.

"Point taken," Mr. Finn blurted. "Point taken, Roberta."

Mr. Nystrom turned back around and opened his mouth.

"Time to eat," Delpha said.

Supper was the spirit-raiser. Oscar served up ham with red eye gravy, biscuits and salad, pans of macaroni and cheese spiced with sautéed onion and peppers. Passing dishes, chewing, truce.

Delpha cleared and stacked, submerged the macaroni pans in hot water and soap flakes. Before she tackled the kitchen, she told Oscar, she wanted to run over to the library real quick. Ought to be back here by eight. Or so.

"Counting on it." Showily, Oscar consulted his watch. "I gave you that advance."

'Sides home and work, only other place you ever go, she said to herself, walking over to the library, and felt bad.

Then some other voice said, *So far*.

★

The wood floor creaked as she passed green-lamped tables, looking for Angela. Stained-glass windows spread the day's fading light into warm colors. Opal stood watch at the front desk, wearing a pink knit shirt a size too small for her.

"Hi, there," Delpha said.

The girl lifted some fingers.

Delpha tried conversation. "You interested in advancing in your new job, Opal?"

Opal's brown eyes pearled. Her lips turned down.

"My goodness. You don't like it?"

Slow rotation of her head, left then right.

"What is it you'd ruther do?"

A whisper. "Bakery."

"Well. Whyn't you go do that?"

"It's low-class to wear a hairnet to work."

"Says who?"

"Mother."

"Honey." Delpha laid her hand on Opal's pink shoulder. "Sometimes mamas make mistakes. But you know one thing that's never a mistake?"

Opal's head raised.

"Cinnamon rolls. Where's Angela this evening?"

The girl's eyes rolled to the left. Delpha turned that way. A pale, brown-haired woman in a navy-blue church dress with a lace collar had fanned several books on a table in front of a man who pushed his eyeglasses up on his head. Farther on sat a white high school girl gnawing a yellow pencil. That was it. At second glance, Delpha noted the church dress was vintage 1959 Butterick, except for the skirt grabbed the curve of the woman's butt like a roughneck fresh off a rig.

"Where?" she asked again, and again Opal shifted her gaze leftward. Then she brought up a chubby finger and pointed.

The woman with the lace collar turned toward the

desk. Brown hair held back with a black headband. Nice complexion except for a couple spots on her chin. Features so regular the oval face was like an outline in a coloring book, all ready for Crayolas.

The woman smiled with one side of her mouth.

Delpha said, "Angela?" The only dab of makeup she could see was the nude lipstick, which contributed to the blank-page look.

Angela skirted Delpha to install herself behind the desk, but then waved her over.

"So," she said, her gaze smoldering, "the regional director paid us a visit. In front of God and everybody he told me my makeup had to go, and if I wanted to keep my job, I better dress like a lady. Might just as well have said no buggy rides and keep out of pool halls." Her chin wobbled once, and she hiked it to the side to stop that nonsense. "Said this was my one warning."

"What a peckerwood. I like how you dress." Delpha could recall clearly the winter that the television set in Gatesville's common room was replaced with a color one. When the set was brought in—well, the raised eyebrows, the whoops, the amazed studying up-close of the rainbow-tailed NBC peacock. Angela had always provoked amazed studying up-close. "Where'd your dress come from?"

"Friend of my grandmother's passed on, and her son brought Meemaw all her clothes. Meemaw tightened 'em up for me." Angela tugged punitively at the lace collar. "You don't think I *paid* for this?"

Delpha was grave. "I didn't think that. You know, lotsa people wear uniforms. That's your work uniform."

Angela's chin raised. "But some good-looking guy comes in here, spies the old-lady clothes, tell me how that's gonna work for me, Delpha. Ha, you can't, can you. Didn't think so. Well, anyway. What can I help you with this evening?"

"Just an idea I had. Probably a waste of time, but I wanna know about sparrows."

"Oh, I do heaps of bird questions." Angela didn't seem to notice how she forgot the dress and perked up. "You know the Marbled Godwit's out at High Island this time of year? Had a call about them. Cross between a sandpiper and a sandwich-size turkey. Sparrows, though. Try outside, they're hopping all over the place."

"Yeah, but they all look the same to me."

"That's because that's how they look."

"So there's only one kind."

"Kind. You mean species? Animals come in species and families and other...categories."

Delpha thought brown bear, polar bear, grizzly bear. "OK, species."

A woman in a kerchief and blue jeans hefted a stack of hardbacks onto the desk. "Be right with you, ma'am," Angela said. She went over and spoke to Opal, the brown hair falling across her naked cheek. Opal skedaddled and rushed back with a book. After consulting the table of contents, Angela passed the book back to Opal, who peered at it and marked the page with her finger.

As her mentor had done, the girl read the first page of the book, thumbed, scanned a couple pages, and set the splayed book on Delpha's table. She stood waiting as if next she would be sent to fetch a heated brick to warm the patron's feet.

Delpha took her time. She followed the labeled pictures of fat little birds: black-chinned sparrow, black-throated, Botteri's sparrow, Cassin's, field sparrow. At Harris's Sparrow, she bounced her eraser against the tablet. Harris. That was the name, the alias, that Rodney Bell had used in his long flight from his brother Xavier. And maybe there were more. She used her finger on the page, tracing slowly.

The pictures continued, all types of sparrows. Species of sparrows. She ranged down and landed on a seaside sparrow and a swamp sparrow.

Opal loomed.

"What?"

"Starts on the page before," she whispered. "See where it says 'Genius'?"

Delpha flipped back to *Genus Passer: True Sparrows* and, sure enough, the very beginning of the sparrow pictures. A little red-headed pudge called an American tree sparrow. Then came…a gray-headed white-breast with brown wings.

Bell's sparrow.

A mumble from behind her shoulder. "…check out that book for you?"

"Thank you, Opal."

As her head lowered, the girl's lips puckered into a pleased knot.

Almost eight o'clock. The book hugged against her side, Delpha hurried to the office and took the stairs two at a time. She locked the door behind her and seized the *Brothers* list, the baby boys born in 1898 and 1900, which she had typed up in alphabetical order.

She paused, sniffed the air around her desk. Then her blouse. What was the perfume she was smelling? Sure wasn't Calvin's Aqua Velva.

Sweet Honesty? No, wasn't sugary. She leaned into Tom's office where the perfume smell was strong. Mossy, a whiff of dirt-after-rain, and some dank tang that jolted her nose—like the nest of a cat, in the deep humid woods. Delpha went back and sat down. In her own chair.

Who'd been here?

Only one answer. Tom had to have brought a woman back from the bar with him. She turned to the piles of papers

on her desk, but they no longer held mysterious potential—
they were scraps in her hands. The image was set: Tom and
a woman walking up the stairs, shoulders brushing. Arms—
where were their arms? Tom and some woman twined
together.

A minute ago, she'd been jogging over from the library,
anticipating. How could she feel cast down now? She knew
damn well why, and she didn't like it.

OK, she'd admitted to herself she found Tom good-
looking. He'd been kind to her. He'd hired Miles Blankenship,
and for that she was a thousand times more grateful than
she'd even told him. She had acknowledged all that to herself
but passed over it. Boxed it up. Believed she'd kept barrier
enough between her and her boss by sending away any
thoughts that didn't belong to Phelan Investigations. But the
wrong idea had seeped through anyway—that because they
spent every day together, her place with him was special.
Some women in Gatesville only came alive during visits from
boyfriends or husbands, forgetting their men were out in the
world seeing a hundred people every day. Delpha refused to
sucker herself like that.

But she already had. The evening she'd kissed Isaac's
postcard and put it away had been a restless one. She'd gone
down to the kitchen, took a beer from the icebox, and left
fifty cents for Oscar. Come back up, locked her door, sat on
her tangled bedspread, drinking. After a while, she set the
bottle down and pulled her t-shirt over her head. Stood
and pressed her whole naked body against the wall. Eyes
shut. Elbows bent and hands flat against the plaster, cheek
flattened, breasts, belly. Reliving Isaac's body. His white chest,
his concave belly beneath ribs she could count, the tender
skin on his hardness, the length of bone in his long legs. The
center of her was lit and wet, and she pressed the wall till she

shuddered, and she knew then, breath heaving, that Isaac's boyish form had thickened, the shoulders had broadened, and that the hands clutching her waist belonged to Tom Phelan.

Stop making a fool of yourself with this jealousy. You had Isaac. Tom probably has dates, maybe has girlfriends, maybe a steady one, and that ain't any more your business than the man in the moon.

Delpha had humiliated herself in front of herself. The thing she couldn't afford. Not if she wanted to keep going, keep her nerve. Not if she wanted to make headway, whatever that meant.

Breathing deep, she remembered, finally, that she had work—not only the dirty kitchen but the lists to turn to. The lists she had thought of as a net to catch Rodney. And they'd caught him, while the older brother had slipped through. She forced herself to sit down and pick up the list of *Brothers*. Touched her finger to the paper. Ran down names of baby brothers until...her hands leapt to her head.

She saw it. The bad feelings she'd been having retreated as she fixed on the name: Passeri. Not Passer. The word from the bird book—*Genus Passer*. The word that meant "sparrows."

Two brothers: Passeri, Ugo Filippo 1898. Rodolfo Antonio, 1900. Quickly, she shuffled the sheets of the list, looking for Sparrow baby brothers, though she was almost certain they were not there. She was right. No baby boy Sparrows at the turn of the century.

The family had not yet taken that American name.

She set down *Brothers* and jumped up. Pulled open the file cabinet and snatched out the folder that contained the original thick pile of babies mailed to them from Louisiana Archives. The pages she'd judged a waste of time.

Passeri. There would be parents' names. There would be a seventy-five-year-old address. There would be a profession.

She sat and tapped the pages on their edges and laid them

flat. Traced her finger down the first page, then set aside that page as she scanned the next one. She snapped on her desk lamp, brought it close, and hunted through a quarter of the original Archive stack before she found them. Her head throbbed. Jealousy had flown away. She read and reread the names.

The kitchen was still waiting. It would wait.

XXXVIII

THE LITTLE FINGERNAIL moon had got fatter and golder. Delpha called from a pay phone a couple blocks away from Kirk Properties, hoping Mrs. Kirk would answer, but she got her granddaughter.

"Hi. Aileen. This is Delpha Wade. I 'magine you'll remember me. I'm the one lied to your grandmother when I asked her for a list of sold houses."

"Oh yeah. One with the trouble. And that car. What do you want now?"

"Wanna talk to you, but I want to ask your grandmother's permission first."

"Why? I'm not a little kid."

"She's watchin' out for you, and I just think she'd ruther I do it that way."

"Too bad." Aileen gave a gloating laugh. "It's bridge night. They just left, and they won't be home until ten or ten thirty. C'mon anyway, and I'll talk to you if you give me something."

"Give you what?"

The laugh turned gleeful. "Lemme drive your car!"

"Not really my car, so that's not a good idea."

"I don't care. C'mon, just lemme drive it up and down the street, c'mon!"

Delpha felt stymied. Given her criminal record, and operating on the principle of CYA, she'd rather have a supervised conversation with Aileen. On the other hand,

Tom was going to see Sparrow tomorrow, so whatever she found out tonight might help Phelan Investigations. And, she reminded herself, Mrs. Kirk hadn't recognized Delpha's name the only time they'd met, so either she didn't remember or hadn't read the stories in the newspaper. Had to hope she wouldn't recognize it later.

"Ten minutes, Aileen."

"Yippee! Hurry then."

The remodeled garage that was the office of Kirk Properties was dark, glow of lights behind curtains in the house. Aileen wasn't in there, though. She leapt out of a porch swing and left it rocking.

Delpha had to show her how to move up the bucket seat. The girl proved she could drive the stick-shift by carefully making four right turns, stopping well in advance of each stop sign, braking for a squirrel.

"Why don't you get this car fixed, lady? The outside of it's a piece of shit."

"Owner had a lot of wrecks. Son-in-law doesn't want to give it back to him."

"Oh, got it. If you make it look nice, he'll want it back." She nodded in agreement, then snuck a look at Delpha as she turned gently left in the direction that led out of the neighborhood. She drove like she was tiptoeing the tires over the road.

"Just lemme go a little ways out 105, OK? 105's straight. Not all the way, I'll turn around. But Nana hadn't let me go anywhere yet. Please?"

Hour and a half before the Kirks finished their bridge game. The wind teasing at Delpha's hair felt good. Cool. Cicadas still in harmony, and she'd just read some information in the Archives that stood to unravel this case. Her heart eased up toward Aileen. Delpha didn't often dwell on her teenage years but tonight Aileen, pill though she was, made her remember learning to drive. Thirteen years old. In a 1939 Ford coupe, green and round-topped as a terrapin, three on the tree. Nineteen years later, and her right arm remembered pushing out and up into second then, like you were making a good decision, pulling straight down into third.

The Dart passed under the freeway heading west, past the grocery store and a gas station, past a lawnmower repair and a donut shop. Not a lot of traffic. Highway 105 rolled out.

Aileen upped the speed to fifty-five. Her chortling laugh cut through the rush of air.

Aw, let her, Delpha thought, glancing at the girl's excited profile. She sat back in the seat. They drove on, hair blowing now, tangling around their faces. A semi heading east into Beaumont laid on his air horn, and Aileen bounced in her seat and waved at the driver. Clouds sailing easy past the scratch of moon, failing to catch on its sharp ends.

Behind them, a pickup pulled out to pass. It held speed as it came even, and a boy hanging out the passenger side lobbed a can at their car. A hoot, and the pickup swerved into their lane ahead of them.

The can barely missed Aileen's open window and thumped against the door. She squealed at the spray of liquid. The boy by the window and a girl squeezed next to him in the middle of the seat scrutinized them through the truck's back window, crouching their heads down so the shotgun in the rack wouldn't cover their grinning view.

"Shitasses!" Aileen shrieked.

Delpha put her hand on the dash. "You know them?"

"Shelton Trotter from my homeroom. He threw a can at me!" She wiped the left side of her hairline and cheek and sniffed her fingers. "And it was a beer can!"

"Listen, want you to stop and turn around now."

"It coulda made me have a wreck. I wanna call the cops on 'em! Write down their license plate."

"Look up there ahead for a place to turn around."

"No way!"

Delpha raised her voice. "We're not messin' with these fools, Aileen. Turn it around."

"I got my learner's permit! I can drive legal with a licensed driver." The pickup was still pacing ahead of them, not taking off. Aileen leaned out the window and screamed at the kids in it.

"I ain't one, so turn it around."

Aileen slacked off on the gas only a little as she threw a glance at Delpha. "You mean…you don't got a driver's license?"

"I do not, and keep your eyes on the road."

Delpha couldn't see the green of Aileen's eyes, but she could feel herself getting bored into.

"Aw right. Sure."

Aileen tightened her hold on the wheel. Then she charged out into the left lane and stomped the gas. The Dart roared past the pickup like it was a flat raccoon on the center line, Aileen thrusting out her middle finger.

Delpha grabbed one hand on the console and the other on the door handle. The Dodge ate up Texas 105. Wind beat into the car like a hurricane. Her heart was beating the breath out of her as she scanned for cop cars, hair whipping her face when she twisted to search behind the Dart for the red flashing lights. Two miles, three, a feeble glimmer ahead marked a filling station.

Aileen braked, skidding the car through its oyster shell lot and onto the concrete pad next to the station's office. She quick-stopped it, throwing both of them forward and then back. There was one light on inside. A *Closed* sign hung crookedly on the door.

"Aw, man, I wanted a Coke." The girl peered at the pink watch on her wrist and slumped. She was still whining when Delpha slammed out of her side, stalked around, and yanked Aileen out of the driver's seat, out to the front of the car.

Delpha was crackling with anger—that a Texas highway patrolman and this smart-aleck kid might have got her busted back to prison set the crown of her head afire. God, was she sick of girls like this. The ones that shot their mouths off, flung around, showing off to power until power turned its blank gaze on them and instantly, on the spot—or day-by-day, hour-by-hour—reduced them. That at least once she'd been one of those girls—that made her sicker.

Aileen's green eyes were hateful little slits. "I'm on tell Nana you hurt me! She's gonna call your boss and get you fired! You—"

Delpha clamped her other hand onto Aileen's spindly wrist and slung the girl full force so that she careened across the concrete. Then Delpha jerked her hard enough to snap her teeth together, reeled her back in, and crowded the girl's shocked face.

"Your grandmother's a real nice woman, but she's so busy feeling sorry for you she hadn't taught you a lick of manners. That's already working against you. Old Shelton and his friends are out there in a pickup truck chunking beers at you. I'm betting you're not the most popular girl on the block, and I tell you what—before long somebody's gonna tie a big knot in your tail."

"Why'd I be nice to Shelton Trotter—he never ever once in his white trash life been nice to me!" A small smile perched itself below Aileen's narrowed eyes. "He peed his pants in our fifth grade class."

Delpha squeezed the girl by her shoulders, inserted both her thumbs into the soft spaces below Aileen's collarbone and dug. Aileen yelped and lost her mean squint.

"If a cop had caught us, you'd a got a speeding ticket and another ticket for driving without a real license. And you'd a got me in trouble. You never ever once thought about causing me trouble. Did you, Aileen? That thought didn't even enter your pea-brain. You reckon that boy gives a good goddamn about whatever shitty reason your mama dumped you? Hell no, and neither does anybody else. This is just the littlest baby knot I'm kinking in your tail tonight, you hear? Just to get your attention. Keep on like you are, and when the big knot comes, your head'll spin clear off. Get in the passenger seat."

Delpha released her, wrenched open the car door, and climbed behind the wheel. Aileen banged shut the passenger door, swollen with saying nothing. But when the dome light switched on, the girl cringed back.

"I let you drive. Now here's your part, Aileen. If you're up to it." Delpha held out the Louisiana Archive page.

Aileen's eyes tracked to Delpha and down to the paper, where they stayed. "I'm not holding that. You hold it."

Delpha stretched over until the teenager finally pinched hold and bent her head to read. Red-orange strands and stray hairs fanned out around her head in the yellow light. What hair was still gathered into pigtails swung forward. Her head bent farther as she read. Then she snatched back her hand and shook it off in the air. Delpha caught the page before it drifted onto the floorboard.

Had she stopped at the lines Delpha meant her to see?

Ugo Passeri, 1898, Rodolfo Passeri, 1900, Amalia Passeri, 1906.

"Why'd you bother me?" Aileen shrank back. "You coulda asked her. I told you. I told you this car was fast, and I told you about that little girl."

Delpha bit off the words, "I cain't see her, Aileen." She blew out an exasperated breath. "If you're so red hot at seeing stuff other folks can't, then prove it. Gimme some idea what happened with these children. Or maybe you're just a bunch of bullshit, like Shelton thinks."

Aileen scraped together a threatening glare. But her knob of a chin hiked up. The challenge had snared her vanity.

The girl stared into the paper and her lips curled back.

She made a digging motion. She scooped over and over and over, maybe ten or a dozen times before she opened her hand and patted. She was gazing past Delpha. The black beauty marks were prominent. Then she angled her head away, out her car window toward the single dim light in the gas station.

There was a lull in the car, stark after the tussle outside of it, after the rushing wind.

"She was a little thing," Aileen said finally, "and he... he buried her. In sand. Not a beach...a pile. One of those two boys did. Hard to tell which." The girl turned back. She touched her thumbnail to the page Delpha held and punched it through the paper between the brothers' names.

"See, they were both there."

XXXIX

JIM ANDERSON OPENED the door, but Raffie had him captured. The younger man was letting out hoots, tugging on the old guy's arm, trying to tow him somewhere. Walking backward, Anderson told Phelan to come back after ten thirty because the babysitter lady showed up around then. Otherwise—he cut his head toward Raffie—hullabaloo.

At eleven o'clock, Phelan said hello again and waited while the two men and a middle-aged woman in elastic pants and a nurse's white shoes shuffled down the hall, headed for the screen porch and the back yard. Phelan insinuated himself at the dinette table and took note.

Basically one big room. Galley-type kitchen to his right, and living room to his far left. Saggy floral couch that would take concentrated thigh-power to rise from. Two brown armchairs, an end table, a cabinet TV—all of which might have been purchased at Lester's Pre-Owned Furniture. No knickknacks. The grand features here were directly across from Phelan in the designated dining area: two cages, one big as a double wardrobe, full of green and blue and yellow parakeets and a few black finches that chirped, fluttered, whistled, and flitted to colorful toys. Next to the grand cage was another, smaller cage, about four feet by three feet with its own tenant. Its wire door stood open, a fringe of seed husks on the floor below.

Phelan laid his chin in his hand and wondered at the

constant commotion of the parakeet world. Chirping overlapped trilling and filled the air, though he couldn't tell which ones made the noise. A whole line of them were jerkily contorting to peck at their own feathers, a couple kicking themselves in the beak. A blue one, stealthy and deliberate amid all the singing, hopping, and flapping, crept across a perch toward a silent yellow.

When Anderson returned, he lowered himself into an armchair. A moderate-size gray bird with a bright red tail climbed out of the smaller cage and waddled across the wood floor.

Phelan rose from the dinette table and tailed it to the living room. Could you call a parrot pigeon-toed? This one was. It reached its owner, and gripping with its beak, swung its way up the upholstered back of the armchair. It claimed the man's shoulder, dipped its head, flicked its tail. Sheen on its slick feathers, Phelan observed, but *whoa monster-movie eyes*. The thing had white pupils. Its beak and scaly feet were a dark dead gray like a mummy left out in the yard.

"Perry here's doomed, too," the old man said, continuing a conversation that, as near as Phelan could figure, must have begun in his head.

"All three of us, we're all on the Titanic, ain't we, Perry boy? Got him when I was six. Had him since. Well, 'cept when Raffie was little. When he was…well, I let Perry go live with the kid for a little while. Raffie loves the old fart." Rudy turned from chucking the bird's head to give his visitor a lopsided smile. "Perry'll curl up like a baby and let Raffie hold him, won't ya, Perry?"

Phelan casually took a chair.

"Anyway, he's sixty-seven. I got him, Ugo got a puppy. Needless to say."

"Needless to say, what?"

"Unlucky dog. But brainy. One day, I took him with me on the streetcar to the end of the run. Shooed him off. He didn't come home. Name's Rudy, by the way."

"Not Jim? Or Rodney?"

The old guy brushed the bird away from his ear. "Rudy. From Rodolfo. OK, what you wanna know?"

"Your real surname. It's not Anderson, it's Sparrow, right?"

Rudy tipped his head.

"Well, Mr. Sparrow—"

"Rudy."

"Rudy, my client claims you're the hide and seek champion. Says he labored while you lived it up at the Ritz. So to speak. Tell me who to believe."

Rudy sighed. "Little early, but get us a couple beers, OK?"

Phelan obliged, popping the pull-tabs and tossing them into the sink. Hot-footed it back to the living room and handed Rudy his Schlitz.

"OK. You wanna know, he's nuts. Always has been. Our parents wouldn't admit it, but ever once in a while I'd catch Ma or Papa givin' him the eye. The happiest I ever seen them was when he came back from the war with a medal."

"A medal? How'd he win it?"

"Didn't mention the medal? Hunh. Argonne Forest. 1918. He and a guy named Antoine Richard from the Quarter snuck around and took out a German machine gun nest camouflaged under some trees. Silver Star."

"Big stuff. Musta made your parents proud."

"Not so much proud as relieved. Like, maybe Ugo was all right."

"But you didn't think so."

Rudy gave a coughing laugh. Phelan's eyebrows hiked when the gray parrot mimicked him. Exactly.

"Mr....what's your name again?"

"Tom Phelan."

"Right, Phelan. Mick name. Hell, no, I didn't think Ugo was all right. You kiddin'? I'm his brother, grew up black and blue. Anyway, he got this gleam when I asked him about his medal. Seen that look before, believe you me. That poor dog, and…well, seven, eight years after the victory parade, musta been '26, '27, I run into this Antoine, same one was his Army buddy. Bottle of busthead, drunk as a monkey. Told me when they crawled up behind 'em, he'd had his '03 leveled on those three German boys, ready to take 'em prisoner. Ugo had his, too, bayonet fixed, but he had a trench knife in his right hand. Ever seen one of those? You have? Then you know it's double-edged, hilt shaped like brass knuckles. Ugo rushed in and cut their throats. Too late to surprise the last one, he ran. Said Ugo jumped at his back with the bayonet, man died standin' up. Got the idea Antoine saw the gleam."

"Kinda shit goes on in every war."

"I wouldn't know. Too young for the first one, too old for the second. But…listen, you ever wonder why it goes on?"

"Depends. Maybe you gotta be quiet. Maybe you're out of bullets." Phelan made a *huh* sound in his throat. His squad had never been out of ammo. "Maybe these gunners mowed down your buddies and you couldn't hold back. Or could be colder. Straight-up psy-ops, let the other side know how bad you are."

"Yeah…yeah, you say so. But there's…well, you're missing one. Maybe you always hankered to slit somebody's throat. Here's your chance."

Phelan frowned at the old man, sitting there fingers laced, parrot hooked onto his shoulder, a buccaneer on Social Security. "Really. You're saying that a personal desire accounted for that Silver."

"Not for everybody, believe me. Just Ugo. The hero." He

lifted his hands. "My take. And he didn't like it that I didn't look up to him. Ohhh no. He always expected that from his little brother. Had to look up to him." Rudy shot out an index finger, lowered his chin, saying in a deep voice, 'Don't you dispute me now. Don't dispute me.' That's what Ugo used to say, like nobody else in the world got to have an opinion. Come on. But then…you know, then I stop thinking and put him far out of my mind." Rudy posed his index finger and thumb around four inches apart and squeezed away the distance. "I make Ugo fade away. See him get littler and littler till he's nothin'."

"Yeah? How do you not think about something?"

"Practice."

Phelan nodded. He had some practice himself in this field. "What's wrong with Raffie?"

The parrot dipped its head, stretched its feathery neck toward the old man.

"Raffie's Raffie."

"Never went to a doctor…say about the fits, even?"

"Nothin' they could do. Any of 'em."

"He's your…friend?"

The old man sputtered. "What I'd be doing with a friend like Raffie? C'mon."

"So he's a relative. Your son?"

Perry's dead-gray beak pried open, displaying a dead-gray tongue. The bird nipped the old man's ear lobe.

Wincing, Rudy clapped his ear. "*Stronzo*! Perry, you asshole!" He seized the parrot between both hands and, wings squeezed to his sides, delivered him to the cage and tossed him in. The bird hopped onto a perch and rocked from claw to claw.

Rudy latched the cage door and thumped it. "Put a cork in it!" He came back to the brown chair. "Ugo's."

Phelan sat forward. "Raffie's Ugo's son? How do you come to have him?"

"Took him."

"You kidnapped your brother's son, and that's not why he's chasing you?"

"No and yes. He'd say that if he needed to. Some kinda pinch. Truth is, he dumped the little guy."

"Little? Gotta be close to six foot. One eighty."

"Wasn't always. Shoulda seen him, for crying out loud. It was pitiful. He'd cling onto me, arms and legs, hide his face in my belly, wouldn't let go. Made these sounds, godamighty, like a puppy gettin' beat. Oh, Ugo didn't like it I took Raffie out of St. Vincent's. Don't get me wrong, there was a real *botta da orbi*." Sparrow held up two bony fists, punched at the air.

"St. Vincent's. Why was he in an orphanage?"

"Kinda special ward of the orphanage. They couldn't handle him."

"But you taking him, how was that legal? Nuns, right? Nuns just handing him over."

"I'm his uncle. Ugo signed."

"Why was that if he was mad—"

"Leverage. There were magic words."

"What magic words?"

"He just signed, OK."

"OK. Where was Raffie's mother?"

Rudy flapped the back of his hand, dismissing the mother. "Elsa. Hotsy-totsy flapper from Brooklyn, New Yawk. All I can say, Elsa and Ugo didn't act so happy. Then, Raffie. Didn't sleep, didn't talk, fits. The drop that made the vase run over." His facial expression kaleidoscoped into patterns of love and grief, fixed finally on exhaustion.

"Raffie, he's a lotta drops. Ugo said the wife scrammed back to Brooklyn. Nobody in the family ever saw her again."

"How long has Raffie lived with you?"

"Oh, less see. Since he was seven, that was...'34."

Phelan stared, then was startled by Raffie's laugh. "A-ha…
a-ha…ah ah ah huk kuk huk."

Expecting Raffie, Phelan glanced around, bypassing the
multi-colored confetti of the parakeet cage to zero in on the
monster-eyed parrot, sashaying on his perch. "A-ha…a-ha…
ah ah ah huk kuk huk."

There was a faint call from the back yard. *Oodee.*

"Wait, I gotta make a star appearance. Just a minute."
Rudy set his hands on his knees and hoisted himself to his
feet, and walked away down the hall. After a few minutes he
returned, saying, "That enough of my side?"

Phelan chugged a swallow of beer, stood and slipped
his hands in his pockets. "I'll be going. Just a couple more
questions. You'd a been a young buck then. Why take on
Raffie? And why buy a house now, at this stage of the
game?"

Rudy Sparrow gave him a straight-on stare. "You know
it's funny. When I was young, I'd a run a hundred miles not
to say this. Now I don't care anymore. I never had romantic
inclinations, Phelan. Not Jack, not Jill. With Raffie around,
I never had to play like I did. And lemme just say we been
invited to vacate our rental dwellings a time or two. Raffie
rubs some people the wrong way. Decided nobody's gonna
run us off anymore. Especially at this stage of the game. But
now, Ugo." Rudy shook his head. "'Bout all I got to say. Nice a
you to help me with Raffie and all, but your shadow's gonna
tell him where you went, and you're gonna second that we're
here, so pardon me I don't shake your dirty hand."

The old guy tilted his head, as though considering another
angle. "Less you wanna switch sides. Don't suppose you could
go away and forget you ever saw us? Like Ma used to say, *Il
diavolo fa le pentole ma non i coperchi.*" He crossed himself.

Phelan said, "What?"

"The devil makes the pots but not the lids. Wanna put a lid on Ugo?"

While Phelan was processing pots and lids, Rudy sighed and headed toward the kitchen area. "Why wouldja, he's payin' you. And your fellow gumshoe's probably got the address anyway." He opened a cabinet and took down a red and white can, plunked it on the counter, yanked at a drawer that at first stuck, then rushed open, clattering and clinking.

"I'm tired, kid. Got this house now and the budgies. Me and Raffie like to watch 'em while we eat." He jabbed backward over his shoulder with his thumb, either toward the cages or to the dinette directly across from them. "We still get out, but not every day anymore. Babysitter comes a few times a week, lets me get some rest. We're fixed up. Me and my boy, we can just cruise on into the sunset."

Rudy reached into the drawer, took out a can opener. Lumbering footsteps sounded from the hall. Raffie stumbled out into the kitchen, making a distressed sign at his uncle. The babysitter padded in asking what on earth it was Raffie wanted. "Juice," Rudy said, "you want some, too?" He opened the fridge, poured out two glasses from a carton. Raffie downed his and pulled on Rudy's arm.

They ended up by the parrot cage, where Rudy fetched out the gray bird and helped it into Raffie's arms. A grin lit up the younger man's face. He gurgled happily as he cuddled the parrot and petted his gray head. Perry surrendered his monster dignity. He lay on his back, red tail jutting up at forty-five degrees, claws spread helplessly on either side of its feathered breast.

XL

DIM UNDER THE front yard's bewitched pine forest. Phelan walked out into a yellow day, not a woodpecker in range, just the sound of tires spinning by on the avenue a block away. If there'd been a black Mercury parked around here, it was gone now. Plenty of time to go off and call Bell or rather, Ugo, and report on this location. Had the car been there the day he found the two men in the back by the pond? Who knew, but the trees would have blocked them. Maybe. Unless his competitor got out of the black car and prowled around the side of the house. If the other P.I. had caught any of that scene, Bell knew now.

Phelan drove to the corner, turned into a filling station, pondered, kept an eye on the street. Then he hit the outside pay phone and called Delpha. Told her where he was and what Rodney had divulged about Ugo and Raffie: the tall old boy was Ugo's abandoned son. "Last name Sparrow like you said. Real first name's Rudy. Not Rodney."

"Yeah. I found that," Delpha said. Reported how, beginning with the book on sparrows in the library, its heading *Passer*, she'd found the Passeri family in the Louisiana Archives. Three Passeri children. Not two, three. A little sister born 1906 that Xavier Bell had denied he had. Amalia.

Phelan slid down the block wall to a squat, a hand shading his eyes from noon sun as he heard every detail. "Sister?"

"What the record said."

"Rudy didn't say anything about her."

"Well..." Delpha hesitated to tell him the Aileen story.

"Well, what?"

She warned him about grains of salt, then she told him. The sister, a tiny girl buried in a pile of sand. Both brothers had been there.

They held their receivers a while.

Phelan told her that Rudy had said Ugo's wife beat it back up to Brooklyn. Said the family never laid eyes on her again. He added Rudy's story about Ugo and his medal. The trench knife and the bayonet.

"What's a trench knife?"

Phelan described the double-sided blade, brass knuckles on the handle.

Delpha's stomach fluttered. "You sayin' it's Bell. And that he mighta killed his wife too?"

"Gotta admit it comes to mind. Could even toss in the missing clerk from '69 your nice friend in Florida gave you. I mean, if you were constructing a theory here."

Delpha assembled that picture. All right, not a hunter like Deeterman. A man who committed murders years, even decades apart? She frowned. That picture was hard to reconcile with old Mr. Bell's bright-eyed enthusiasms: *The Thirty-Nine Steps. Profile of Madeleine Carroll. Not the hair of course, hers was wavy...I'd call him when I could still find him...*

She said, "Maybe Rudy's lying. Look, he took Bell's...I mean, Ugo's kid. Ugo could have a whole different story."

"Ugo *did* have a whole different story. But who's in the black car?"

Phelan wouldn't be back to the office. He was going to hang out, keep an eye on the house. Maybe even knock on the door, if Ugo showed up. A neutral person might be handy at the brothers' meeting. And now, he needed to say something: he'd really like it if she'd go on home to the Rosemont.

"But I could wait outside the house. In the Dart. If Ugo shows up, I could follow him back to where he's living. Then…we'd know." She stopped there. Phelan Investigations might or might not be the only party interested in his whereabouts.

"Yeah, well, if you do that, absolutely do not get outa the car. Lock the doors. Just write down the address and go back to the Rosemont. Please."

XLI

DURING THE AFTERNOON, Phelan cruised by the house
every half hour. He passed Delpha in the Dart around ten
after four, parked down the street. They exchanged glances.
An hour later at five o'clock, a gold Galaxie 500 was parked
at the curb in front of Rudy's pine forest, blocking out the
stenciled street numbers. Phelan'd had time to sift through
the ways this easy case had turned weird on him. He couldn't
see that he had a choice.

Through the trees, up the ramp to peer in the window.
Bars of the budgie cage, hopping and flitting parakeets, a blue
one clinging upside down like he might kamikaze his cheerier
roommates. Past the parakeets Phelan saw two old men in
the brown armchairs, facing each other. Rudy nearest the
door, half-glasses, short-sleeved shirt, gripping the armrests,
feet planted on the wood floor. The other, in the navy blazer
Phelan had first met him in, sat with legs crossed. He had
a bald crown wreathed by thin, whitish hair. No hat, no
shades, no briefcase-brown mustache. Phelan would not
have recognized the plain white face. The hooded eyes and
thickened, pinkish nose, its tip grayed from cigarette smoke,
yeah. Xavier Bell, unveiled. Ugo Sparrow. Must have brought
his own—a liquor bottle sat on the end table next to the
armchair, and he was holding a glass.

So. Rudy and Ugo Passeri. In America, you could change
names. New name, new life. You could change names after
a child had died under unfortunate circumstances, so the

connection to that death became more distant. Change names to start a business. Old man Passeri chose the translation Sparrow. Simple.

Phelan knocked, his story, thin as it was, already concocted.

Rudy's hand flailed toward the far armchair, where his older brother sipped from a glass. "Come back to see your handiwork? I told you. Godamnit, I told you."

"Don't want to intrude," Phelan started.

"Intrude yourself into one of those dinette chairs while my brother finishes his visit." Rudy's voice aimed for tough but was falling more than a couple decibels short. Phelan took a second look at him. A muscle pulsed above his jaw.

"Why on earth would you barge in here, Phelan? I terminated you yesterday. No one answered your phone, unfortunately, so I dropped a note in the mail. Done."

"Just being thorough, Mr. Bell. That's my contractual obligation to you. Verifying that Mr....Anderson is the party you asked us to find." Phelan had tried out Delpha's peaches-and-cream voice and failed. He sounded like a politician.

But look-a-there, Bell's grimace relaxed halfway. "Oh. Yes, Mr. Anderson. You found the right man. If there's a balance on my bill for expenses, just have your secretary with the Madeleine Carroll profile send it out. You can be on your way now. Shoo."

"You'll never see another nickel, pal. Sit your ass down. Case my brother here gets rowdy."

"Leave, Phelan," Bell ordered. "This is a private matter, and you know it."

Yes, he did. But Phelan had heard the plea in Rudy's growl. He pulled out a chair and sat down on it straight so he could get out of it quick. "Not planning on horning in, sir. Your brother Rudy has a point, though."

Ugo studied him, then Rudy. His upper lip twitched. "All right, you said you were my ally. You should know that he— he wasn't." In a falsetto voice, pierced with pent-up intensity, the older Sparrow mocked the younger, "Save me, Mama. Get back, big bad Ugo, little Rudy's going to run away and hide."

Rudy barely let him finish. "Oh, c'mon, don't play like you forgot the hitting, cutting, locking me up in stuff, shoving me out in front of that car. Thighbone's never been the same since. I couldn't lindy-hop with the rest of 'em."

The puzzlement in Ugo's face said he *had* forgotten. He waved it off. "Rough-housing. Far in the past."

Rudy thrust out his palms like he meant to catch a child tumbling from a third-story window. "That's what you're talking about! The goddamn past! Only for you some of it's over, and some of it's not. All the shit *you* did, you call that over. You forgot about it. *I'm* supposed to forget about it, like it never happened. But whatever—God help me what*ever* it was you wanted out of me—you decided that's *not* over. Screw that, here's a scoop. The rest of the sane world doesn't do it that way. Your belfry was *always* fulla bats."

"Me?" Ugo punched a finger at his own chest. "*I* was the workhorse. I was the donkey. I worked all those years in that pen of a shop so you could get an allowance and go off somewhere else. So Ma could send you an allowance. And buy her houses. The one on Prytania with the balcony. The duplex in Marigny. Day after day. Years and years and years. While the leech, the freeloader went bird-watching. You . . ." Ugo lowered his tone to a growl. "I paid for your entire life."

Rudy's lips twisted. "Aw, take it somewhere else. No sale here." But there was a sale, Phelan could tell. Rudy was banking on his talking game, but he was scared.

"You paid for Ma's life, Ugo. *She* wanted those houses. Liked playing the property owner. She sent us rent money, that she did, and I took in bookkeeping and worked it at night. We got by living in dumps. It's like…like you got this stupid rosy-ass view-finder you see our dear old parents through."

The older Sparrow lifted his chin. "Papa was stern, I don't deny that."

"Stern?" Rudy rubbed his forehead like there was gum stuck on it. "It was stern to break your arm and lock you in a closet all night? And don't bring up my share."

Ugo picked up his glass, tilting it to let the liquor pitch back and forth. "Turn him over to me and I'll leave."

Rudy's head fell forward. "You…conscienceless bastard. When hogs fly."

"I'm his next-of-kin. He's *my* son, and I've got his birth certificate. With my name on it."

"And I've got your name signed on a custody agreement from St. Vincent's."

"Birth certificate trumps that. I'm prepared to tack on kidnapping. All these years, I've missed my son—"

"I'll tell 'em about you leaving him on the bayou at night. Like a tow sack of kittens."

"He got lost."

"Didn't believe it in '33, and I don't believe it now."

"Your lifelong lack of intelligence is not my affair."

"It's Raffie's lack we're talking about, that was always the problem. He can't help it. You know what he did when the search party found him? Musta had a hundred mosquito bites on his arms and legs. I picked him up and he laughed. Didn't look any different than any other kid in the world. Get this straight"—Rudy's voice quavered—"you're not takin' him anywhere. I got the paper."

"Where is my son, anyway?"

Rudy gestured toward the bedrooms. "Nap. Before supper. He's never slept right at night, maybe you remember that. And keep it down. If he heard your voice, he'd run out the back door."

Ugo's chest swelled, his mouth popped open.

Phelan rose from the dinette chair and carefully approached the brothers. "Gentlemen," he said. But the two were hooked into each other.

"Well, she's finally dead!" Ugo snarled. "You'd better believe I'm contesting the will. You're not bleeding me one more minute—and don't you dispute me about that!"

"Dispute…Holy Mother, dispute…" Rudy gave a short version of his wheezing laugh. "Seventy years of your shit, Ugo, *che cazzo vuoi*? Lemme alone. You know where I am, and I'm not running anymore. Beat it! Don't come back, or I'm calling the cops. Getting a restraining order. Which I shoulda done the first time your crazy mug showed up."

Ugo Sparrow stood up so straight his heels rose off the floor. Liquor sloshed from his glass. He banged it onto the side table and fumbled in his jacket, withdrew a silver cigarette case, lit a cigarette, a ready-made. He began to pace, dragging deep. The blue and green parakeets were chirping and swinging on their triangles, ruffling their wings.

Phelan could see it was costing Rudy not to track Ugo. His hands were more clenched than folded, and their tremor wasn't age, it was fear.

"I can't help it Ma left it to him. I never asked her to! Ask Louis. I mean Sebastian, ask the son-in-law. The will was a goddamned surprise. I expected her to leave him something, yeah, for upkeep. We gotta eat. But not everything. I didn't expect that, and I never asked her for it. Think Raffie cares about a duplex in Marigny? Sell her houses, take half the money. You'll outlive me and Raffie both."

Rudy stood up, one of his knees jolting in a St. Vitus dance.

"You don't have to worry about me telling. Who'd I tell? Who'd care? Sixty-five years ago. *Dio mio*," he groaned, "that little baby. Amalia, *piccola*."

Ugo flicked away the cigarette butt. His facial expression said he was about to scream, but he spoke softly, relentlessly, "But you did tell, Rudy. I always knew you would eventually. You told Ma. And she changed the will. But first…first, she called me to her house. Said she was dying of shame that she gave birth to me."

Ugo walked heavily over to his brother and waggled his hand, two middle fingers folded, index and little finger straight out like horns. "She made the sign, Ma made the *mal'occhio* against evil. Against m-me, Rudy. Because you told."

Flecks of sweat on Rudy's upper lip. His jaws moved, wordlessly.

Phelan stepped in between them, speaking to Ugo. "Enough. Time for you to head back to New Orleans. We found your brother, you said your piece. Your brother's offered you half of everything. Talk to that family lawyer and let him take it from here."

Ugo slithered a hand toward the inside breast pocket of his jacket, and Phelan was instantly beside him, gripping his right elbow so that his hand came away empty. Ugo threw him a savage look and attempted to shake him off. With an effort— the old man was strong—Phelan prevented that. Ugo's eyes darted to Rudy, then his head turned as he apparently scanned the birdcages, the kitchen, the hall that led to the bedrooms. He stood, rigid. Phelan could feel the man's tension in the arm he was grasping.

"All right," Ugo said hoarsely, "all right. Let the law decide. Take your hand off me, Phelan. See to my brother. He looks…indisposed." This time Phelan let Ugo Sparrow shake him off. The man smoothed his suit jacket and left the house, closing the front door, allowing the screen door to slam.

Rudy half-fell into an armchair, clammy and panting. "Thanks for running him outa here. Earlier woulda been better, though."

Phelan took the other chair. Feeling like a guard, or a nurse, he sat with Rudy while the old man tried to calm himself. The goddamn parrot chose this moment to blurt a high-pitched scream that quavered like a kid being shaken. Rudy lurched up from the chair.

"Take it easy." Phelan had mashed a hand over his ear, then he rose and settled Rudy down again. "Man, you got one rude pet there." Thumps came from the back room, probably Raffie getting up from the nap. Phelan glanced at his watch: 5:24. He was more than ready to leave but couldn't go without asking. Delpha would want to know.

"Hey," he said, as soon as Rudy wasn't breathing open-mouthed like a fish on a dock, "you saw it…when he killed your sister? What happened?"

"Didn't know I did. Till later. Ma and Papa, the whole neighborhood, they were downtown Mardi Gras night. Comus' night—you know Comus? High-falutin' krewe—the float, the costumes. We had these pointed hats Ma had made, and we were jumping around. Papa tripped over me, hurt his knee or something, ordered us to stay home. They went off without us. Ugo, he lived for those parades. Loved Comus best of all."

Rudy's gaze shifted inward. "Like Papa loved Amalia best. Who wouldn't? We all did. You shoulda seen her—this baby cherub." He clawed his chest suddenly, crumpling the cloth of his shirt. "God have mercy, Father of mercies, forgive me, I been sick for sixty-five years, thinking about it. I was looking for her, went over to the courtyard next to ours. Looked through the arch and saw my brother brushing himself off. Under the stairs, there was a sandpile by a pallet of bricks. That's what I saw."

"Sandpile. That's it?"

"Till we couldn't find her. Till the whole neighborhood was turned upside down, and Ma and Papa were crazy. And all a sudden the picture's just there in my mind. I see Ugo in his pointed hat, standing back from this sandpile. Brushing himself off. That's where they found her. Two days later."

"He see you?"

"Didn't seem like it. One night, though, Papa beat us bloody for letting Amalia out of our sight. Ugo caught me looking at him. He saw I knew."

"Why didn't you tell them then?"

"Never had the nerve." Rudy dragged his fingers down his cheeks, fingertips scoring his weatherworn skin. "Everything woulda been different, God help me—"

He rambled on a while, but the screech of a car's tires reminded Phelan that his Chevelle was parked on the street, and he truly wanted out of this house. Case closed. If Rudy Sparrow decided to go after Ugo Sparrow for a sixty-five-year-old killing, well, the New Orleans lawyer could handle that, too. Phelan was damn sure Louisiana rode with Texas on this one: no statute of limitations on murder.

XLII

DELPHA HAD BEEN touched by Phelan's urgent request
that she go home to the Rosemont, but she was too wound up
to go. She parked the Dart at a distance from Rudy Sparrow's
house. A little before five o'clock, a gold Galaxie rolled to a
stop at the curb, Louisiana plate 59R498 Sportsman's Paradise,
and a thickset, pale man, white hair beneath a bald dome,
walked up the ramp. If he was Xavier Bell, he'd got rid of the
brown hair and the mustache, the sunglasses and the panama.
The whole costume. She couldn't swear the man was Xavier
Bell, but he must be. Phelan turned down the street seven
minutes later. He parked and got out of the Chevelle, pointed
toward the house for Delpha's benefit, and went that way, up
the ramp.

Would Tom witness some overdue peacemaking or referee
a ring-tailed fight? She wouldn't lay a bet either way. Good
thing she had a full tank. Delpha started up the Dart and let it
idle, *whew*, made the car even hotter. Occasionally, other cars
passed. Not much traffic down this side street. She could have
been lounging in the Rosemont's medium-cool AC, watching
Watergate hearings. Instead, she'd sat here since four o'clock with
the car windows rolled down. Delpha's armpits were soaked, her
blouse damp to the waist. Sweat had her glued to the seat.

At twenty minutes till six, the man with the stark white
face stalked out of the trees, to the left of the wooden ramp.
He heaved himself into the gold car and burned rubber.

She threw the Dart into gear. She'd never tailed anybody

but supposed it would mean not losing the car and not having the driver catch her following him. The first was the important one so she kept no more than a car length away from him. Followed him downtown on I-10E, like she was going to the office. The Louisiana car peeled off the freeway onto Willow Street, then drove through downtown and took a left on Fannin into a parking lot next to the Jefferson Theatre. Delpha drove past, a car behind her honking and then charging around her.

No one got out of the Galaxie. Smoke drifted from the driver's window.

Trying to keep her eye on the car in the lot, she waited till traffic let up and U-turned, coasted over to the side of Pearl where she could park, and twisted around in her seat. She waited, cursing when a bus came by, worrying that maybe after it passed, the man who'd hurried out of the trees would have fled the car.

But close to six-thirty, the car door opened and he got out. Definitely the right age. Once he'd stepped onto the sidewalk and headed toward the theatre, Delpha slipped out of the Dart and ran on her toes across the street. He paused at the ticket window under a marquee that advertised *Opening Night High Plains Drifter Clint Eastwood*. Delpha walked, head mostly down, toward the Jefferson's flashy vertical sign.

She stopped at the posters displayed behind glass, pretending to take in the beach-strolling lovers in this evening's Sneak Peek late show: *The Way We Were*. Then she gave up being cagey and peered hard at the ticket-buyer. The man took his change, flicked a glance both ways down the street. As he turned in Delpha's direction, she caught his face straight-on and raised a hand in front of her own, fingers spread, fluffing her hair. Angled away and exaggeratedly checked herself out in the glass reflection of the poster, registering: *Xavier Bell*.

Hugh Sparrow.

Ugo Passeri.

Tom.

Tom Phelan was back in that house. Tom and Rudy and Rudy's laughing friend, Ugo's son. The meeting could have been upsetting for the brothers—Ugo had gunned away from the house—but surely nothing worse, she told herself. Here he was now at the movies.

Still, she thought of Tom's theory, everything Ugo might have done in his life. A toddler buried in sand, soldiers butchered, a wife disappeared, the cut bones of a store clerk. It was the end of September, hot as a plate left on the stove, and a chill began to slink along her ribs.

For a few moments after he'd entered the glass doors of the theatre, she stood on the sidewalk with its sparkling mica chips, fake-primping. Then she stepped over and leaned in to the ticket-seller, a brunette with salt-and-pepper roots.

"'Scuse me, I just caught sight of my uncle that's been promising my aunt he's going to A.A. meetings every night. He just bought a ticket." Delpha showed an unhappy face to the woman behind the window. "Don't tell me he comes here a lot."

The woman lifted only her eyes to look up at Delpha. "All the time. Watches 'em twice. Says he goes to the Gaylynn Twin too. Listen, hon, no A.A. meetings here, and no liquor allowed either. I hope your uncle hadn't been toting a flask inside."

A line of people was forming behind Delpha. She made her face look even more unhappy. "What time's this movie get out?"

"Eight fifty-five. Then there's the Sneak Peek. Oh, sugar, it's a tearjerker. You wanna see this Clint Eastwood? Kinda a cowboy movie, but it's real mean."

No, even if nothing had happened at Rudy's house,

she didn't want to go into the theatre and loiter around watching a man who'd maybe smothered his baby sister. She still carried the bulk of Dennis Deeterman. Carried him so that Aileen—however the girl did it—had spotted or sensed or smelled or been brushed by the grasp of his presence. Deeterman barging into the office, thick arms swelled out from his trunk. Head swiveling to make sure Delpha was by herself. Vacant eyes two minutes away from igniting.

Her backward steps.

The heavy man looming, heft and knife.

This time she was not trapped. But the spreading numbness returned, even as the sidewalk's heat radiated through the soles of her black flats. This time help was reachable. Wasn't it?

"Customers behind you, hon. You want a ticket or not?"

Delpha shook her head no.

XLIII

SHE PARKED THE Dart in Visitor Parking under a live oak
and hated every step up to the Beaumont Police Department's
front desk.

The desk man was a middle-aged cop whose starched
shirt could have worked the shift without him. No, Sergeant
Fontenot was not on duty. And no, Chief Guidry was not here,
either. It was...his crewcut head cut to his wrist... almost
quarter till seven in the evening, and the chief worked regular
business hours unless there was an emergency. Delpha was about
to give this desk officer her information when he narrowed
already-narrow eyes and shot her a thought bubble. *How stupid
was she not to know that? Whyn't she get outa his range of vision?*

Delpha shoved back at him with a level stare, something
she'd known better than to do in prison.

The cop's jaw hardened.

The door from the squad room opened, and two young
cops burst out. A shaggy-haired white one ranging backwards,
hands sawing back and forth in a Kung Fu fakeout maneuver.
Next, a black one had to be the same age, with a stealthy crouch
in progress. The white one angled around. His eyes bulged.

"Hey, I know who you are. Saw you in the squad room
that day in your bloody shirt." He settled his cap and hit his
full height. "Officer Wilson. And this is my partner Officer
Johnson. Can me and him assist you?"

Bypassing the desk man, Delpha spoke fast. She needed a

house checked out, if they would do that, and gave them the address, a house where there might or might not be a need for the police. She told them there'd been some suspicious happenings connected to a visitor to that house. The desk cop looked back and forth between her and his juniors, partially doffed his attitude, and picked up the phone. After muttering into it, he asked her, "You know where this visitor is?"

"I don't know for sure he's done anything. But I followed him outa there to the Jefferson Theatre."

The black cop's nose scrunched up. "Went to the picture show?"

The white one hooked his chin at a car out past the glass doors. "Whyn't you wait for us at the cruiser, Miss Wade. Turns out anything's wrong, we'll need you to I.D him. Be right there."

She paced by their police car under the live oak while the two did whatever they did. The light latticed between the sinuous black branches blazed copper and copper-red and then red at the horizon before the two young cops came loping out. The white one skidded up beside her. "We already got a unit out there."

Delpha swallowed bile. "Somebody hurt?"

"Yes, ma'am, ambulance called to the scene." He didn't make eye contact before jogging around to the driver's seat and jumping in.

The cold pooled in her stomach rose up and branched through her veins. She subtracted Tom Phelan from the world and felt her mind go blank. Delpha leaned into the passenger window and demanded of the driver, "Tell me if it's Tom Phelan."

"Ma'am," the other cop said from behind her, "b'lieve the ambulance departed. We got cars there, that's all we know. Whatever it is, the B.P.D.'s on it." He held open the door to the back seat.

Cars, more than one. Delpha murmured, "Don't do that thing with my head, OK?" She raked back her hair, slid onto the seat, and rode with both arms hugging her midriff.

XLIV

PHELAN WAS LOOKING back over his shoulder before
driving away from the house when he heard shouting.
A flash of movement then Rudy scuttled down the ramp
semaphoring, hollering at Phelan for help. They ran up the
ramp to the house together, Rudy wild-eyed, babbling about
CPR. Yeah, he knew he'd said it'd be a blessing if Raffie's heart
gave out, but he couldn't let him go without even trying, you
had to try, you had—

Phelan said *Yeah, you had to.*

A pillow lay on the carpet in Raffie's room. The black and
white portable TV was low-volume yammering on a dresser,
a rocking chair in the corner. Raffie's head was flat against the
sheet, bangs fallen back, mouth gaping. One of his eyes was
open, the other closed. Phelan's nose wrinkled at the smell.

"Heart, right?" Rudy begged. "Right?"

"Call 9-1-1, hurry."

Rudy rushed out of the room. Quickly Phelan checked
Raffie's warm neck for a pulse, got none.

He tried anyway. Did mouth to mouth and chest
compressions, three minutes, nothing. Rudy hovered behind
him, muttering. Six minutes, Phelan mentally pleading
with the ambulance to get here. Almost ten minutes when
they heard the siren, and Rudy ran out to flag it down so the
ambulance wouldn't pass by the house with all the trees.

Phelan knelt, took in the abraded corners of Raffie's
bluish lips, the open eye that was dilated and fixed, bloodshot.

He pulled down the lower lid, saw the red specks that meant bleeds in the capillaries. Specks on the upper lid and its inner surface, too. Indicators of strain. Phelan's face twisted. Poor Raffie—he'd suffered. Heart faltering, stopping, he'd strained mightily to breathe.

Thundering of boots on the ramp and a three-man rescue crew took over the room, the lead guy squatting to check a pulse, to study Raffie, the fingertips of one hand. He cut his eyes to Phelan, "You did CPR?"

"For about ten minutes," Phelan said. He stared back. The same look was on both their faces. Then they looked over to Rudy, braced against the wall so as to be out of their way, his face molded into one of those Tragedy masks theatres use for decoration.

The crewman fit on a pocket mask over Raffie's nose and mouth. He repositioned the still man's head upward and began resuscitation efforts. After five minutes, he paused and spoke to a guy in back of him, who flung at Rudy, "Use your phone, sir?" and dashed off in the direction Rudy pointed. The crewman started in again, kept it up until his partner entered the room and spoke in his ear. He listened, head bent. Then he stood up, angled toward Rudy there against the wall.

"Sir, we can transport him to the hospital, if that's what you want. But we talked to the doctor, and given the signs we have here, I'm afraid—"

"OK. I can see." Rudy stepped forward, toward the bed. "You tried," he said. He tipped his head toward Phelan, "He tried. I get it. He's not coming back."

The rescue crewman reached out as if to offer him something, but Rudy didn't notice. He'd already begun to fumble down onto his knees beside the bed. The men glanced at each other and moved out. Phelan lingered long enough to make sure Rudy was stable here, not in any danger himself.

The old man was hugging his body to Raffie's, cheek to chest. "My boy," he said. "Always my boy." His eyes were crushed shut.

Phelan joined the ambulance crew in the kitchen area, told them he'd stay with Rudy, see that whatever needed to be done got done. The lead man handed him a button. "Give him this," he said. "It was in the bed. Couple mortuary guys have sticky fingers." The parrot cackled one of its canned lines, turning them all around. The men nodded at Phelan and filed out.

Phelan looked down into his hand. Not a button.

A coin. A gold coin with two faces on it.

He felt a blow in his chest, like a blunt ax that hooked then ripped into his stomach. He ran down the hall, stopped at the doorway to scan the Astro-turfed porch. Its single door, a screen door, wafted slightly, open to the back yard's trees and pond. Open. The ax sensation penetrated into his navel. Burned. What had happened would have happened with Phelan and Rudy right in the other room. Him making sure the old guy relaxed because he truly hadn't looked well after his bout with Ugo. Then talking. They were talking while Ugo was clamping the air out of this…child.

Phelan called the station, asked for a squad car, sat down at the dinette table near the phone.

After a while he went back into the bedroom where Rudy still lay against Raffie. When finally Rudy struggled to stand, Phelan helped and then got out of Rudy's way as he hefted the rocking chair over and positioned it parallel to the bed. Phelan snapped off the television and waited, his insides roiling. Rudy sat forward and laid his hand on Raffie's head, smoothing his hair tenderly. Calmly, as if Raffie could feel it. Phelan would not be the one to break that calm. Rudy rumbled that song Phelan had heard him sing before, quit. Then the runners of the chair rocked silently against the carpet. Phelan gave him a handkerchief, and Rudy swiped his cheeks. "Guess I should call…a funeral home?"

Anticipating the police, Phelan told him there was no hurry.

Rudy nodded like that was what he wanted to hear and took hold of his nephew's hand.

The skin of Raffie's face looked tight, blanched. Bruise-like discolorations might be forming even after death, around any area on the face or body that had been pressed on before Raffie's heart stopped beating. Phelan didn't know much about that. Not the regular kind of damage he'd seen in the Army.

It had been the smile, the laughing, the manner of an excited child that had made Raffie young. The man on the bed didn't look like a boy anymore.

XLV

AT THE JEFFERSON, the cops flashed badges at the ticket-taker in the booth. Delpha pulled up her posture till her breastbone popped away from some other bone. Both times she had faced a man yearning to hurt her, she'd been alone. Both times, and the fight had got to a place where she was wild as he was, and it had had to go there because she was still alive.

A teenager in a maroon usher uniform led the lady and the two cops into the auditorium of the Jefferson, a grand old theatre fallen on the end times, and then he scooted back toward the yellow-lit popcorn lobby. Delpha, confronted by a twenty-foot cowboy whose teeth clenched a stogie, let her vision become used to the dark. She surveyed the seats. Roughly about thirty customers. Three sitting alone, one at the end of a row next to the aisle. Two of those were balding, light-haired men, one a girl or a boy with long hair. The cops strode forward, but she held up her hand. Her fingertips quivered.

They followed down the aisle a few paces behind her. She walked to the one she considered most likely, bent, kept space between her and the man in the aisle seat. Reek of sweat. Cigarette smoke, whiskey.

"Well, hello," she whispered to the rapt profile.

His head angled around. Ugo stared without focus, no recognition at all. Delpha kept from bolting by concentrating on which name she should use. Not wanting to rile him, she strained to conjure up the vocal powers of Zulma Barker.

"Ugo. How nice to run into you here."

His features stuttered, upper lip and nostrils contracting, a flare of blood hate in the eyes. In his lap, his hands sprang open. The pale old face awakened.

"My word, my…I don't mind telling you, Miss Carroll, that I am moved by your courtesy. How kind. That *you* should say that to *me*." Water gathered in the dark eyes peering from their curtains of skin.

His face collapsed—lips dragged downward, brow painfully squeezed, eyes shut tight, toppling tears onto his furrowed cheeks. Shoulders curved in, chin tucked into his neck—he shriveled. His fingers flexed outward, as though to ward off dread, and in that posture he froze.

A girl-baby in a blue smock, a pile of sand. How she'd have kicked and cried. Maybe he climbed up and sat on her, bearing down until she stopped struggling and he could begin to scoop and dig and bury her. Delpha straightened and inched back from Ugo Sparrow.

Ugo huddled still. His open palm had stayed up, too late to ward off ruin.

Then, by degrees, Ugo Passeri's movements reversed themselves. His hands folded into his lap, his upper body eased. No longer weeping, he turned his head to the screen and gazed up at it. Ugo's features became bland and open and absorbed as the colossal cowboy taunted his enemies. As the outlaws blustered. Behind the swinging saloon door, a line of black mountains. The music playing sounded like violins and sirens.

Delpha lifted her hand. It was steady now. Officers tramped down the aisle.

After giving all the information she had, and getting nothing specific in return, Delpha walked through the warm night and climbed the stairs to Phelan Investigations. No one there. She taped a note on the door that she hoped, very much, would be read soon and headed to the Rosemont.

She stood in the kitchen dark, rubbed her eyelids with her index fingers. Felt like grains of sand in her eyes.

Nine forty, Delpha saw by the clock, when she snapped on one of the yellow overhead lights, not both, opened the back door to the insects' song. Made sure the screen was tight-latched. Slowly, she scraped crusted dishes and silverware, loaded the tubs, started the first one through the Hobart. She switched on the radio and the pull-chain for the fluorescent light over the sink where the pots were soaking. Some man on the radio hollered, growled and hollered, bully bass line, flirty piano. Once the pots had been scrubbed, dried, and clanged back on their shelf, she did the cast-iron skillet, using salt to scour away the ring of hardened drippings. Then she wiped the skillet dry. She dried the stack of plates. Al Green was crooning *Call me.*

What time was it now?

11:17.

Delpha chipped a speck off a hot fork, then she put up the plates and silverware, the serving pieces. Laid the big serving utensils in their drawer. Piled up the damn ramekins in their haphazard towers. Got a clean rag and washed the counters. Fetched the broom. Swept. She emptied the dustpan in the large kitchen garbage can and pushed it over by the door for Oscar to take out tomorrow.

Almost midnight. Bob Dylan was singing about knocking and heaven. The song put her in mind of Serafin—maybe he'd show up back here soon, his mama up in heaven like one of the stars.

She rolled out the mop bucket. Squeezed out the mop and stroked it across the greasy green and black linoleum. Under the kick spaces, in front of the stove. Contorted herself to get the mop beneath the chopping table. When she reached the doors to the lobby, she propped them open so she could wash right up to the threshold.

She stuck the mop in the bucket. Brought up the skirt of her apron, tamped her face and neck, dropped it.

Gladness splashed through her.

Tom Phelan was crossing the Rosemont lobby. One lone viewer turned from the TV to track him. Delpha watched him all the way to the kitchen door. The burdensome way he carried himself, the weight in his eyes—by the time he reached her, she knew one thing he was going to tell her.

"Rudy or Raffie?"

"Raffie." Phelan's head moved infinitesimally sideways and back. "Cops think Ugo put a pillow over his face."

Delpha's hand flew to her mouth. "Why? And how did he—?"

"Let's take a load off." They sat down in a couple of the blue velour chairs, Phelan stretching out his legs with a groan, his head falling back. "Why," he said.

He described the old secret spilled, the mother's will, the mother's words to Ugo, the whole scene. Him and Rudy talking, believing the feud was settled, or getting there. Talking, while Ugo had slipped around the house through the trees, across the porch and into Raffie's room. Phelan'd heard some noise, but put that down to Raffie stirring around after his nap. So he shook hands with Rudy, relieved to be done with the Sparrow brothers. Then, Rudy, running through the trees, yelling that Raffie'd had a heart attack.

But he hadn't. Not a natural one.

Delpha's eyes hadn't left him.

"Why," Phelan said, and counted on his fingers. With Raffie dead, Ugo, as next-of-kin, would inherit everything, leaving Rudy high and dry. Revenge on Rudy—that motive was up there. Ugo was furious with how his reunion had turned out.

"Wanted Rudy to tell him everthing was all right," Delpha said, "even the old murder. Even that, that's what I think. How's Rudy doing?"

"In the hospital. Couldn't hold it together after…after he understood what'd happened."

Phelan wrenched himself upright in the blue chair and leaned forward elbows on his knees, staring down on his laced hands. "Shoulda broke it up sooner, Delpha. Thrown Ugo out, made Rudy lock the house and call the cops."

"And tell the cops what? Two brothers had a fight? You didn't know Ugo'd do what he did."

"No. Shoulda known he was capable of it, though. Did know that, didn't I?"

"This ain't your fault, Tom."

"Hard not to see it that way."

"Was it my fault Deeterman came in the office to get that book?"

"Course not."

"Well then." Roughly she broke apart his laced hands so she could squeeze one of them. "Rudy didn't think of calling the cops either, and he knew his brother a lot better than you—than we did. You wasn't there at all, he coulda killed 'em both."

"Never know, will we."

"Never will." Delpha released his hand and assumed a brisker tone. "What about all the birds?"

Phelan wished she still had hold of his hand, wished they could sit that way for a day or two. He turned his head finally, looked at her. "Humane Society. They were sending out two ladies with a bunch of cages, but I didn't stay for it. Went and milled around the hospital. And the station."

"Humane Society take the big bird?"

"Perry."

"Perry?"

"That's his name. Sixty-seven years old. Rudy's long-time companion. Lawyer'll pick him up."

Delpha's eyebrows rose. "Whose lawyer?"

"They located the family lawyer in New Orleans. Guy named Sebastian Rush. You don't know about him, but... guy's not a feeb. He'll handle the funeral. Also arrange a lawyer for Ugo, but bail—man, I wouldn't count on bail."

He took in a deep breath, let it out, glanced at his watch. "It's Saturday."

Phelan told her to take Monday off. Rest up. He knew Delpha'd worked extra hours that hadn't appeared on her timecard. He smiled. Damn if Mr. Hank Aaron wasn't playing tonight. Going for Number 713.

Delpha saw that it wasn't his pretty smile.

XLVI

"GOT ONE OF these for you." Phelan came in Tuesday with a white bakery bag from Rao's in one hand and the last bite of his breakfast in the other. Noticed that Delpha was occupied. He tossed the bite in his mouth, murmured *ummm*, and used the napkin in the bag to wipe the icing from his fingers. After which he studied why Delpha might have her desk chair situated by the secretary window and its blinds pulled up.

On the wide back of an aquamarine puffy-chair was balanced the office first-aid kit, its lid lifted. Phelan peered closer. Plastic bottle of alcohol sitting on the windowsill. Two teeny silver balls and a needle on a paper towel in her lap, and she was holding a compact, its small mirror angled at her face.

Phelan walked over and took a gander downward, finally identified the silver items as really plain ball and post earrings. Next, he considered the mirror and the first-aid kit.

"Stickin' holes in your ears, right?"

"My room faces the alley. Light's better here."

"Need some help?"

The compact lowered, she glanced his way, raised it again. "Believe I can get it."

"*Pfft*. With that set-up? Can't stick and hold the mirror at the same time. Wait a sec."

In his office, he rummaged in the desk drawer. Stashed a pen between his teeth and rolled his wonky office chair into the outer office, sat in the chair, and butted its wheels against hers.

He set down the felt-tip pen and a plastic lighter. Unspooled a length of gauze from the first-aid kit and cut it with the doll-size scissors. After uncapping the plastic bottle of isopropyl, Phelan poured the alcohol over the gauze strip and swabbed his hands. He discarded the gauze onto the floor, spooled out and cut off some more strips, draping them over the aquamarine chair-back. Looked practiced at it.

He guided her forward, ever so gently, by her ear lobes until his face was close to hers. If he'd prodded her shoulder or an arm, she'd have stiffened. Ears—that was unexpected, she let him do it. There were uncustomary things going on behind his eyes. He lightly stroked alcohol-soaked gauze over one ear, then the other, then a crescent portion of her neck beneath. Her skin chilled and tingled.

Sitting back, he looked down at his hands in his lap. "You sure you got this covered, I'll bug off."

She didn't answer.

"I can see your ears better, but…seems to me like you might have to trust me to do this."

The muscles around Delpha's eyes contracted.

"Can you?" He kept his head down, scrubbed his knuckle creases with the wet gauze.

She became still. Gazing at the top of his head, at the dark parted hair falling forward, the cleaned hands—nine fingers—the way he sat square, elbows on his knees, shirt sleeves rolled. An old, silvery gouge behind the hair on one forearm, and the edge of some kind of tattoo on the other. Pictures seen through a fever-haze surfaced: Phelan in a chair by the hospital windows, head down like this; slouched back dead to the world; leaning forward, lips on his laced knuckles, staring doubtfully toward her in the bed. Clear pictures: him wrestling an office key off his key chain on the day he hired her, fresh off his first case and missing a shoe. Miles Blankenship striding into the police station bright as a valley sunrise. Phelan handing her a white blouse with the tags on it, not entirely turning away as she put it on in the car.

Far off a siren whined, almost unbearably shrieked by on Orleans Street, shrank into the distance.

She mouthed *Yeah*, found her voice. "Yeah."

He still didn't look up. "Could you say it?"

"Yeah, I guess I could…trust you to do this," Delpha whispered.

Phelan raised his head, looked into her eyes, and there it was again, more than she could take in: some kind of driving mainline, bursts, pain, illuminations. Then he blinked, picked up the felt-tip and uncapped it. He steadied her chin with a knuckle, eyeballed, dotted.

"OK," he said hoarsely. Cleared his throat. "Check it out. Even?"

Delpha lifted the compact, studied one ear, turned her head, studied the other, touching its lobe, nodded.

He recapped the pen, dropped it on the floor. Took a big breath and settled into his body. "Now. Once upon a time there was two people, a man and a woman, and they were snared in a briar patch…"

"Oh, huh uh."

"What."

"Distractin' me so I won't notice when you stick the needle. I'mon notice, Tom."

"Aw, no. Not that wily. Come a little bit forward. Tuck your hair back. There. Be *still*, Delpha. And listen here…" His jaw was almost touching hers.

And she was listening, she was. To Phelan say her given name. He smelled like cigarettes and cinnamon powder.

"…I mean, in this briar patch, there was green briars

and scarlet briars, privet hedges and holly, there was stinging nettles. Ever get stung by those? Boy, that sting lasts a long time, I guarantee."

He plucked the needle off the paper towel in her lap. Scooped up the purple lighter, flicked it, and passed the needle through the flame. "Anyway, there were these two people, in the middle of thorns and thistles. Go one way, scratch, go the other, sting. Couldn't see any way out." His hands doing something she couldn't see with the isopropyl. Then a couple fingertips tilting her jaw a little. She felt more alcohol wet, sharp-smelling, cold on the back of one ear. Prickles raised on her arms.

Knuckles gentle against her neck. Quick pinch, tickle of blood, then a gauze-covered finger and thumb clamping the spot, numbing out the sting.

Alcohol on the pinch. Moving hands.

"One day, a bear came into the thicket, bit the man's finger, and tried to run off. The man grabbed its neck and ripped a strip of fur off its back." Fingertips warm on her other ear, another stick. Tamping of dry gauze this time, the chill of alcohol, cold metal against her skin.

"His finger was gone, but the man laid down the fur and walked over it, got out of the briar patch."

"Where was the woman?"

"She stayed in the thorns."

"She wouldn't do that."

"Powerful bunch of thorns."

Metal chill against the other ear…back, front, cinched. Swabbing more alcohol.

"Then one day a kudzu vine showed up. It snaked and looped over the briars, covered them layer on layer 'til not a nettle saw daylight. Kudzu grew up under her feet like a green quilt, and the woman walked out." More gauze tossed.

"Thank you. Then what?"

"Then what? More briar patches, more bears, more kudzu. You didn't think this was a fairy tale?"

Her lips curved. "Ain't there any surprises?"

He'd moved back only a little, face still near hers. "Yeah, Delpha. I think there will be surprises."

He held up the compact. She took it. Angling her head, Delpha maneuvered the compact mirror, beheld the silver ball in her smarting right ear, the silver ball in her left. Blood cleaned off. Neat. Even. Stainless steel.

Her blue-gray eyes flicked up to meet his brown ones. Him and her were knee to knee. A shot of heat scalded upward through her, then a shot of scared: tiny drops that scattered out.

The telephone rang. Over on her desk.

She pressed her lips together, tipped her head as she threw a glance toward the phone. Tom rolled his chair back to give her room. Delpha got up and answered it, holding the receiver almost horizontally, to keep it off her earring.

"Phelan Investigations. How may we help you?"

Tom bent over and scooped up the used gauze strips, the pen, and the lighter that lay on the floor. Slipped the lighter in his pocket, balled up the gauze and rolled it between his palms. Drilled it into the wastebasket by the side of her desk. Before disappearing into his office, he brought over the white Rao's sack and set it by her elbow.

The End

Notes and Acknowledgements

A FEW OF the 1973 dates of actual events have been slightly adjusted to fit the chronology of "The Bird Boys." Other irregularities readers may find are inadvertent and are all my fault.

I'm enormously grateful to the good people who read drafts or chapters of the book and gave invaluable comments: David Baker, Eddie Elfers, Lynda Madison, Shelly Clark Geisler, Susanne Kehm, Greg Kosmicki, Laura Hays, Celia Ludi, Ruth Berger, Sheryl Cotleur, and Thomas Wörtche. I appreciate very much that Gerald Richardson; Steve Wiggins, Beaumont D.A., ret.; and Beaumont Police Chief Jimmy Singletary took time to speak with me about local background. Former Nebraska police officer and current Humane Society enforcer Mark Langan, author of "Busting Bad Guys," shared his expertise on interrogation. Lifeguard and swim teacher/writer Katie Gallardo and her employer Ben Slovek kindly offered specific information on lifesaving, which I've stashed for the future. For encouragement and hospitality, I thank Sterling Municipal Library in Baytown, TX, (especially Jenna Harte), and its loyal and charming association, Friends of the Library. I am proud and happy to be able to use the cover photo, "Nevermore," by renowned photographer Keith Carter. Finally, I owe a big debt to editor Lee Byrd and to Bobby and John Byrd of Cinco Puntos, the hardest-working press this side of the river.

LISA SANDLIN WAS born in Beaumont, Texas, where she grew up in oil-refinery air, sixty miles from the Gulf of Mexico. After raising a son in Santa Fe, New Mexico, she taught writing for over twenty years at Wayne State College and at the University of Nebraska Omaha. She has since returned to Santa Fe.

The Bird Boys, a sequel to *The Do-Right*, which won the Shamus Award and the Hammett Prize, is her sixth book. She likes writing about brand-new detective Tom Phelan and his ex-con secretary Delpha Wade, who's fighting for a place in the free world. They've set up business in downtown Beaumont, Texas, where the architecture runs to Art Deco and Gothic Revival, and the population to homegrown evil. It's 1973, "Killing Me Softly" is playing on the radio, and they just might make a living.